❧ THE ❧
ALBION INITIATIVE

Newbury AND Hobbes
Investigation

Also by George Mann and available from Titan Books

THE
ALBION INITIATIVE

GEORGE MANN

TITAN BOOKS

THE ALBION INITIATIVE: A NEWBURY & HOBBES INVESTIGATION
Print edition ISBN: 9781781160077
E-book edition ISBN: 9781781166468

Published by
Titan Books
A division of Titan Publishing Group Ltd
144 Southwark Street
London
SE1 0UP

First edition: July 2022
10 9 8 7 6 5 4 3 2 1

This is a work of fiction. All of the characters, organizations, and events portrayed in this novel are either products of the author's imagination or are used fictitiously. Any resemblance to actual persons, living or dead (except for satirical purposes), is entirely coincidental.

A CIP catalogue record for this title is available from the British Library.

Printed and bound by CPI Group (UK) Ltd, Croydon, CR0 4YY.

To all the readers of Newbury & Hobbes who've joined us on this adventure over the years—my heartfelt thanks

♚

CHAPTER 1

Bedlam.

If the dominion of Hell had ever found a footing on Earth, it was here, confined within the towering walls of this palatial edifice. Here, where the warren-like corridors and treatment rooms echoed with the screams of the lost. This, Bainbridge knew, was a repository of nightmares, a storehouse of all the worst horrors that afflicted the Empire. This was where the very worst criminals were sent to live out their days, to become objects of scientific study; observed, restrained, and experimented upon. Here, people went to become less than human, to disappear.

And they had the gall to call it a hospital.

Bainbridge stood in the courtyard, peering up at the foreboding building, while the carriage driver and the attendant nurse unloaded their passenger into a wheelchair behind him. Huge Tesla coils, affixed to the roof either side of the central dome, sparked in the mizzling rain, crackling with arcing light, like a false dawn rising over the surrounding grounds. Light glowed in the serried rows of windows, and the distant echo of a wailing creature—man, woman, animal, Bainbridge could not tell—caused the hairs to prickle at the nape of his neck.

"Come on, hurry it along," he said, turning to the nurse, who fussed over the slack-mouthed man in the wheelchair as she tucked a blanket across his lap. The patient was wearing a vacant expression, a bowler hat pulled low on his brow, obscuring much of his appearance from view.

"Yes, sir," said the woman. "We'll be with you momentarily."

Bainbridge nodded, then turned his attention to the porticoed entrance. There were two porters loitering beside one of the columns, watching them with interest. Bainbridge raised the head of his cane in a gesture of greeting. The man on the left flashed a toothy grin by way of reply.

"We're ready, sir," said the nurse from behind him.

"Very good," said Bainbridge. He glanced at the driver, who was clambering up the slick side of the carriage to his dickey box. His hair was plastered to his face. "Driver—wait for us around the back. I don't anticipate this is going to take very long."

"Aye, sir," acknowledged the driver, cranking a lever. The vehicle's engine sputtered, and a spume of black smoke erupted from the spout of the exhaust vent. A few seconds later the carriage rolled into motion, its engine chugging noisily as it trundled away into the night.

"Come on, let's get out of this rain." He headed for the entrance, the nurse pushing her charge alongside him, wheels stirring the wet gravel.

The porters—two men dressed in black suits and white shirts with open collars—eyed them curiously as they neared. "Evening, guv'nor," called the one on the left, the one who had smiled at him. "Got another one for us, have you?"

"Something like that," muttered Bainbridge. He'd visited the hospital on numerous occasions over the years—never by choice—and knew it was likely he'd be recognised. In fact, he was counting on it. "I'm here to speak with Dr. Warrender."

The other porter was a swarthy-looking man with a scraggly black beard, who shifted from one foot to the other. "Do you have an appointment, sir?"

Bainbridge bristled. His moustache twitched in annoyance. "I don't *need* an appointment," he said, his voice stern. "You know who I am. And if you don't, you *should.*" He paused, looking from one porter to the other. "This is Her Majesty's business. If Warrender knows what's good for him, he'll see me."

The swarthy-looking porter swallowed. "Of course, Sir Charles. Let's start by getting you out of this rain." He took a step forward, flinching as one of the Tesla coils above emitted a violent discharge, splitting the sky with a thunderous clap. The man seemed to judder for a moment as the light flickered brightly and then died back, leaving him once more engulfed in the shadow of the building behind him. He reached the wheelchair and took the handles from the nurse, angling the chair towards the doorway. The other porter beckoned for them to follow him inside.

"Seems quiet, this one," said the man pushing the chair, as they walked along the marble-floored passageway inside the door. The wheelchair's wooden rims creaked with every revolution.

"Drugged," said Bainbridge. "To keep him that way." He removed his hat, brushing the raindrops onto the floor beside him as he walked.

"So, he's a lively one, is he?"

"You could say that," said Bainbridge. "But as I said, this is Her Majesty's business."

They lapsed into silence as they continued down the passage. Now, Bainbridge could hear the wailing for what it was–the pitiful screams of a confined prisoner, or patient, elsewhere in the building. Not for the first time, he wondered whether this whole endeavour was folly. Could they possibly hope that the man was still capable of being saved? Was it not already too late?

He supposed they didn't really have much of a choice. The Queen had made her move, declaring the Secret Service a renegade organisation, marking all those associated with it as traitors. Assassins had been despatched to exterminate the agents, many of them Bainbridge's personal friends. Everything he had helped to build was at risk.

So no, they had no choice. Their hand had been forced.

They rounded a corner, passing another knot of porters engaged in what appeared to be a deep conversation. They passed a series of closed white doors, behind which Bainbridge could discern muffled moaning and the crackle of applied electricity, presumably drawn from the Tesla coils above. At the end of the passageway they turned left, deeper into the bowels of the building. He tried to keep track of the way they had come, memorising the layout as they went. His cane clacked against the tiled floor to mark his passing.

Nothing about the place felt clinical, despite the rich tang of carbolic and the trailing cables looping along the architrave humming with barely contained power. It was closer, Bainbridge considered, to the lair of some madman—the habitat in which he'd expect to find someone such as Aubrey Knox, his former colleague who had spent years conducting secret, horrific experiments upon wastrels plucked from the slums. He'd seen places such as this too many times in the course of his investigations: the terrible workshops at the Grayling Institute, the caverns beneath Fairfax House, Knox's laboratory in the sewers. The only difference here was that Bedlam, or Bethlehem Hospital as it was more properly known, had been sanctioned by the Queen. All of the procedures and experiments carried out here were done so at her pleasure. To what end, Bainbridge could only imagine.

Although in truth, he didn't *want* to imagine. He knew now what she was capable of: experimenting on foundlings and medical patients in the vain hope of gleaning the means to preserve her ailing existence, ordering the murder of good men and women to protect her secrets, manipulating world powers to further her private agendas, and so much more besides. The thought made him nauseous. And now he had to look himself in the mirror every morning and know that he'd devoted decades of his life to upholding her nightmarish regime.

Well, no longer. Now, his sole purpose was to help to tear it down.

Presently, they came to a passageway where the corridor terminated abruptly in a set of polished mahogany doors. The man in the wheelchair was lolling forward, drool pooling on the lapel of his jacket. The porter didn't seem to have noticed. He drew the chair to an abrupt halt and the patient slumped forward, almost toppling out upon the tiles.

"Careful!" snapped the nurse, coming around to straighten her semi-conscious patient, pushing him back into his seat.

The porter sighed and looked away, muttering something beneath his breath. Bainbridge wondered how someone could become so desensitised to the suffering of others that they ceased affording them even common courtesy. Perhaps, he considered, it was a prerequisite for a job like this.

"Carry on, carry on."

The other porter flashed his toothy grin once again and turned to rap loudly on the door.

A voice sounded from within; hoarse, weary. "Come."

The hinges creaked as the porter shoved the door open and ushered them to step inside. The nurse, her expression sour, bustled the swarthy porter away from the wheelchair and took hold of the handles, her knuckles whitening as he issued another mumbled curse.

"Thank you, gentlemen," said Bainbridge, his voice low and even. "That'll be all."

"But—" started the talkative one. Bainbridge silenced him with a raised finger.

"We'll send for you, should we be in need of any assistance."

The man nodded, clearly put out, but then turned and punched his colleague lightly on the shoulder before starting back the way they had come. "Come on. It's almost time for our tea break."

Bainbridge watched them go. Then, drawing a deep breath, he indicated for the nurse to carry on. Tight-lipped, she rolled the wheelchair ahead of her into the room. He followed behind, allowing the door to swing shut in his wake.

Here, the light of the Tesla-coils spat and sparked overhead, visible through the greasy panes of a long skylight that ran most of the length of the room. They appeared to be the only source of light, causing the entire room to strobe in and out of existence like it was trying to drag itself free of some inky, half-remembered dream. It was a cavernous space, given over to an office-cum-workshop. A large wooden desk had been placed at the far end, facing the door, with several dull portraits of austere-looking men peering down at them from the walls. To the left stood a marble-topped table that reminded Bainbridge, disturbingly, of a mortuary slab, and behind it, a wall lined with bookcases and shelves. Medical equipment, vials and stills littered a wooden workbench closer to the door. On the right, two mismatched sofas and an armchair sat before a small hearth, and upon one of these sat Dr. Warrender, the man responsible for this grotesque establishment, and the man whom Bainbridge had come here to see.

"Warrender."

The doctor looked up at the sound of his name, his quizzical expression turning to anger as his eyes narrowed in recognition. The crackle of the electrical discharge overhead cast his lined face in a sinister aspect, half absorbed in shadow. He was smoking a cigarette.

"Bainbridge." Warrender almost spat the word. He pushed himself up from the sofa, tossing aside a sheaf of papers he'd been studying. The tip of his cigarette glowed like embers in the gloom. "To what do I owe this unexpected pleasure, *Chief Inspector*?"

Bainbridge cleared his throat. "I've brought you another of her rejects."

Warrender approached, frowning. "I've had no such communication from the palace."

Bainbridge shrugged. "Just following orders."

"Yes, you're good at that," sneered Warrender. "Or so I hear. What was it she called you? 'A useful little tool, once, but blunted now by overuse.' I'd always thought there was never much point to you." He smiled at his own joke. "No wonder she's got you playing errand boy."

"Better that than being knee deep in the Royal shit," said Bainbridge. "I don't envy you that, or whatever else it is you're forced to do to keep her breathing."

Warrender scowled, then turned to regard the patient, still lolling in the wheelchair. "Who is he, anyway?" he snapped.

Bainbridge shrugged. "Like I said, just following orders. Presumably some minor noble who can't just disappear like the rest of them. Or an agent who's rubbed her up the wrong way. Someone who'll no doubt find himself sedated in one of your cells and left to go slowly insane."

"Then he'll fit right in," said Warrender. He took a long draw on his cigarette; let it out. He studied Bainbridge for a moment. "All right. Leave him with me. I'll keep him sedated overnight and seek word from the palace in the morning." He shrugged. "Worst case is I end up with another subject for my latest project."

"Then we'll be on our way. Nurse?"

"Yes, Sir Charles."

Warrender laughed as Bainbridge turned his back. "I must say, Bainbridge, you've really brightened my evening." The Tesla coils crackled loudly overhead. "I always had you marked for a pompous fool, and to see you reduced to this . . . well, it warms my heart."

Bainbridge's shoulders dropped. He levelled his breathing but didn't turn around. "Warrender?"

"Yes?"

"I just want you to know that I'm going to enjoy this."

"Wha—"

Bainbridge's cane hit the floor as he pivoted, throwing his weight behind the movement. His fist came up and around, bunched hard, and struck Warrender beneath the chin, slamming the man's head back so that his teeth clattered loudly as he went down. The doctor didn't have time to register the shock—he was unconscious before he hit the ground. He flopped onto his back and was still, save for the steady rise and fall of his chest.

Bainbridge shook his hand, flexing his fingers. "Ow," he said.

"Well, he went down easier than I expected," said the nurse.

"Glass jaw," murmured the patient in the wheelchair.

"Glass jaw my eye," muttered Bainbridge. "It was the quality of the uppercut that did it."

"If you say so, Charles."

The nurse laughed.

Shaking his head, Bainbridge pointed at the unconscious doctor. "Well, come on then, Miss Hobbes. We haven't got all night. Search out his ruddy keys!"

Sighing, Veronica Hobbes turned to her patient. "And don't you think you can sit there laughing, either," she said. "Get out of that contrivance and give me a hand."

With a chuckle, the patient shook off his shawl and tossed his hat across the room, before pushing himself up out of the chair. He smoothed the front of his jacket, brushing the last vestiges of drool from his lapel. "A terribly undignified means of gaining entry, that," he said.

"Getting in was the easy bit, Newbury," said Bainbridge. "It's getting out that's going to be the real challenge."

Newbury grinned, crossing to Warrender's desk to begin searching the drawers. "Nonsense, Charles. With an uppercut like that, you'll have us out in no time."

CHAPTER 2

"Constance? Constance, where *are* you?"

Amelia Hobbes rolled her eyes in exasperation. She stepped down from the footstool she'd been using to reach the airing cupboard in the servants' quarters, a bundle of recently laundered towels still clutched in her hands.

"I'm here, Mr. Trimbey," she called, injecting just enough singsong into her voice to sound enthusiastic at the idea of dealing with the man. Her shift had technically finished half an hour ago, and it was growing late. She could have dropped to the floor where she stood and been asleep without another thought.

"Ah, there you are," he said, marching into the room as if he'd caught her with her hand in the petty cash. He blinked at her expectantly, acting as if she hadn't deigned to answer his call and he was now waiting for her to apologise for making him search the house for her whereabouts. He had a fondness for taking credit for every tiny thing in life, she'd noted. Some might even call it a compulsion. It seemed against his nature to allow anyone else the slightest glimmer of satisfaction. Not when he could so easily steal it from under their nose.

He stood for a moment, regarding her from just inside the doorway, as stiff as a board, hands clasped behind his back. He was a stern, serious man—too serious, as far as Amelia was concerned—and although he had the outward appearance of a man in his forties, she was convinced he was actually far younger and it was only his sour, obsessive outlook on life that had aged him so prematurely. Or perhaps he really was just a bitter old toad of a man.

Amelia—who was currently masquerading under the assumed name of Constance Markham, a moniker Newbury had assigned to her during their eventful trip to St. Petersburg a few months earlier—returned the man's stare. "Yes, sir?" she said.

He seemed momentarily flummoxed. "Well, don't let me stop you. Carry on, carry on." He waved at the bundle of towels and indicated the cupboard. "The towels won't put away themselves."

"Indeed, they won't," said Amelia, forcing a smile. She stepped back up onto the stool and began placing the towels, one by one, into the warm cupboard. When she'd finished, she closed the door, stepped down from the stool, and turned back to the man, feigning surprise to find that he was still waiting. "Oh, I'm sorry, sir. Can I do something for you? Only, it's getting rather late and I'm anxious to retire."

Trimbey gave a carefully measured cough into his gloved fist. "You may retire when I give you leave to retire, Miss Markham. You do understand that?"

Amelia bit her tongue. "Yes, sir. Of course, sir."

"You are a member of Her Majesty's royal household now, lest you forget. A great honour. A *privilege*. But such a lofty position comes with certain responsibilities."

Amelia nodded her understanding. It was a speech he had given several times in the weeks since she'd taken the position at the palace, working undercover at the behest of Sir Maurice to glean what information she could from the Queen's household. "Of course, sir."

"Very well then. There is a task that requires your attention. The curtains must be closed in Her Majesty's dressing room." He smiles smugly. "I decided you should be the one to see to it."

Inwardly, Amelia groaned. This was Trimbey's idea of teaching her a lesson for being less than reverential. She knew the Queen hadn't even visited her dressing chamber for several years—let alone her bedchamber, but, as she had learned, the entire household had been deployed to maintaining the charade of the Queen's health. Fires would be lit in unused rooms. Lamps would glow in windows. Curtains would be opened and closed at the requisite times. Even bedsheets were stripped and washed daily, despite the fact they had remained clean and unused. It was as if everyone at the palace was trying to convince themselves, as much as the outside world, that everything going on there at the seat of the Empire was perfectly normal. But, Amelia knew, it was as far from normal as could conceivably be.

"Yes, sir," she said, forcing a grateful smile. "I shall see to it immediately."

Trimbey nodded in appreciation. "Excellent. You know, Constance, we might make a half-decent maid out of you yet." He turned towards the door.

"I wouldn't count on it," she muttered beneath her breath.

As sharp as an owl, Trimbey's head swung around to regard her. He cocked it to one side. "I beg your pardon?" There was a note of warning in his tone.

Amelia maintained her smile. "I merely asked if I might retire after the task is complete, sir, or whether you wish me to report back to you here?"

The man's eyes narrowed for a moment, and then he gave a curt nod. "That will be the end of your duties for the day, Constance. I shall see you again at breakfast."

"Very good, sir."

He left the room. Amelia waited until his footsteps had receded down the hall, and then scooped up the footstool to return it to its place in the corner of the room. Then, smoothing the front of her apron, she made for the upper floor.

The Queen's dressing room had a musty, disused air, despite the best efforts of the ladies-in-waiting. Freshly cut blooms sat in vases on the sideboard, a riot of yellows, reds, and blues. Little netted bundles of *pot pourri* hung from violet-coloured ribbons on the back of the door. The fire had been lit earlier that evening but had now reduced to a handful of warm embers, coal dust, and ash scattered upon the tiled hearth. None of these measures could dispel the underlying odour of dust and decay, however; the sense that the room was no longer lived in.

Indeed, Amelia hadn't caught a single glimpse of the monarch in the weeks she'd been at the palace, and she'd now managed to explore most of the numerous wings, chambers, hallways, offices, bedchambers, libraries, and various other nooks and crannies that comprised the gargantuan estate. All save for the audience chamber and its attendant complex of side rooms, to which she'd so far been unable to gain admission. There were also rumours of several secret passages and an underground tunnel system opening out into the sewers, but she was certain such talk was mere hokum. Silly stories told by the maids to pass the time, or to give credence to rumours of suitors sneaking in for secret liaisons with other members of the household staff.

She'd been at pains to listen to such tales, to befriend the other women below stairs, to gently tease information from them about the Queen and the goings-on here at the palace. Frustratingly, she'd managed to discern little of use to their cause. A cause that still caused a frisson of excitement and fear in Amelia every time she considered it—to supplant the Queen and put an end to her murderous schemes.

However, either the women of the palace were ignorant of Victoria's scheming, or they hadn't yet learned to trust the newcomer with the really juicy stories. She was beginning to believe it was the former, though. No one seemed to know anything bearing even the faintest whiff of scandal or wrongdoing. Most even believed that the reason they hadn't caught sight of the Queen around the palace was simply because they weren't of worthy enough rank to warrant being in her presence.

Amelia had to admit, such a mixture of loyalty and indifference was making her task somewhat challenging. She'd been ensconced here—with fake references and a carefully crafted backstory—by Newbury and the others to dig for anything that might prove useful to their cause. Evidence of conspiracy or wrongdoing. Scandal. Political leverage. But all she'd been able to discover so far was that the Queen didn't sleep in her bedchamber and that most of the male staff were chauvinistic fools. Nothing exactly revolutionary in that.

She crossed to the window, where the rain was pattering gently upon the pane. Beyond, the city glittered in the storm light; bright and bold and beautifully ugly. Her pale reflection stared back at her from the glass like a wintery ghost. Her lips were too thin and her nose too button-like, but her shape was beginning to return, and her eyes no longer looked sunken and hollow. She felt like a new woman—to go with the new name—and yet she still had difficulty accepting the fact she was healed, healthy. That Petunia Wren's strange fungus was crawling around inside her head, repairing the fault lines that nature had wrought in her brain. She had no reason to believe that the alteration wasn't a permanent one. It had been three months since that fateful train journey to St. Petersburg with Newbury, and the visions that had once plagued her waking hours showed no sign of returning. She was finally starting to believe that she actually had a future ahead of her now. It was all so much to take in.

Lately, though, she'd found her mind lingering over the most disquieting thought: that she actually missed the strange visions that had accompanied her illness. The thing was, she'd grown used to the idea of dying, but perhaps more than that, she'd become accustomed to the insight that the clairvoyant episodes had granted her. The sense of foreknowledge. The notion, however misplaced, that she understood the world and knew what it had in store for her. At first it had seemed freeing to wake each morning with no thought for what the day might bring, to know that her days were not dictated by the things she'd seen in her dreams. But now, after several months, she missed the comfort of it, the anticipation, the familiarity.

Of course, she could never go back. Would never even consider it. The seizures, the fevers—when Newbury had freed her of such horrors, he had done what no doctor had been able to do. In taking that burden upon himself, he had proved himself to be a man of extraordinary compassion. Was it all because of his love of her sister? Had he only helped her to prove himself to Veronica? Amelia liked to think he would have chosen to do so regardless. It was a disservice to him to think otherwise. She had cherished the time they'd spent together, the intimacy of the rituals he'd performed—but it was incumbent upon her to look upon the man as a friend, or perhaps a brother, and nothing more. Perhaps, in the fullness of time, she would meet her own dashing hero. She supposed, now, that anything was possible.

A noise down in the courtyard snagged her attention away from her reverie, and she glanced through the beaded glass and streaming rain to try to discern what was going on down there.

A wagon was pulling up below, churning the slick gravel with its iron-banded wheels. Steam rose from the horses' flanks, and froth bubbled from their lips. They stamped their feet anxiously as the driver hauled on the reins to bring them to a dead stop. She watched as the man climbed down, calling to someone out of sight. His voice was lost in the drumming rain.

Amelia watched with interest as the rear of the vehicle opened and two further men climbed out. It occurred to her that it wasn't, in fact, a carriage at all, but some kind of covered wagon, made up to resemble the sort of carriage one might expect to be used by a noble visiting the palace. She'd heard tell that ground trains and mechanised carriages were discouraged from entering the palace grounds–the Master of Household was a stickler for tradition–but she'd seen a whole variety of service wagons coming and going in an almost constant stream from the kitchens. Never before had she seen one disguised in such a fashion.

The men disappeared from view, but a few moments later the two from the back reappeared, this time carrying a thin, wrapped bundle, not unlike a rolled carpet or rug. This they tossed unceremoniously into the rear of their vehicle, before once again disappearing from view. After a few seconds they appeared again with a second bundle and repeated the process, before disappearing once more.

So, this wasn't a delivery. It was a removal. Perhaps there were plans to redecorate one of the downstairs rooms, and the men had come to take the existing items away for storage or disposal. But why do so in the middle of a rainstorm? And why this late at night? It was past ten o'clock. Most of the house would have already retired. Herself included, if it hadn't been for Trimbey's tyrannical regime. Perhaps, she considered, that was entirely the point. Why else would they be doing whatever it was they were doing at this hour?

Amelia jerked the curtains shut and turned away from the window. She racked her brains for a moment, trying to decide on her next move. She could head to her room, scratch out a brief missive to send to her sister. Or she could try to find out a little more about what they were doing down there.

Decision made, she approached the hearth, grabbed the empty coal scuttle and made for the door.

CHAPTER 3

As Bainbridge and Veronica bound the still-unconscious Dr. Warrender with a rope they'd smuggled in via the wheelchair— it really *had* been a most uncomfortable experience—Newbury located the man's rather ungainly set of keys, which were kept in a small, unlocked briefcase beneath his desk. They looked like something rescued from the Tower of London, a relic of a bygone era: huge, cast iron things dangling on a heavy ring the circumference of Newbury's upper arm. He jangled them triumphantly at the others. "Only a man of supreme arrogance would operate with such lackadaisical security," he said, grinning.

"I rather think it's the other way around," said Veronica, offering him a sardonic smile. "In that we're the only ones foolish enough to try to break *into* an asylum."

"Good point," said Newbury, pocketing the keys. He circled around the desk.

Bainbridge was tying off the final knot, binding Warrender's hands behind his back. He straightened, winced at his creaking spine, and then, for good measure, retrieved a white handkerchief from his breast pocket and stuffed it into Warrender's mouth. "There," he said. "That should keep him quiet for a while. Pompous oaf."

Overhead, lightning crackled and spat from the fizzing Tesla coils. The rain was coming down in driven sheets, drumming loudly on the glass ceiling.

Veronica glanced to the door. "Now we have to work out where they're keeping him."

"Before the porters discover his lordship here and call the alarm," added Bainbridge.

"All in hand," said Newbury, heading to the door. He pushed it open a few inches and peered out, before swinging it wide and beckoning the others to follow.

"In hand?" said Veronica, hurrying to keep up.

"Yes. I . . . well, I paid him a visit recently." Newbury set off down the corridor, his voice low. Veronica fell into step behind him, with Bainbridge bringing up the rear, one hand inside the fold of his jacket. Newbury hoped his friend wouldn't have cause to make use of the revolver he was clutching there.

"You did? To make peace?"

"Not exactly. To make sure he knew that he'd failed. That we were *all* still alive." He glanced back at Veronica, cocked a half smile. She shook her head, exasperated.

"You came to gloat," said Bainbridge, the disapproval evident in his tone.

"I suppose I did," said Newbury. "I needed him to know. To draw a line under it all."

"Hmmm," muttered Bainbridge. "So, we can't count on a warm welcome. He'll probably assume we're here to assassinate him!"

Newbury approached a turn in the corridor, signalled for them to wait while he peered around the bend, and then waved them on with the all-clear. "A bridge we'll cross when we get to it," he said.

Meandering corridors led them deeper into the complex. Here, the walls were lined in tiles that had been fired in a sickly brown glaze and the air reeked of carbolic and other unidentifiable chemicals that stung his nostrils. Doors were bolted from the outside, and the wards were drenched in shadow and eerily quiet. He presumed many of the inmates had been sedated for the night. Discarded trolleys and wheelchairs were pushed into every available corner.

At this time in the evening, the place was near deserted. Only the distant, disconcerting cries of the lost were to be heard, punctuated by the ever-present rumble of the lightning storm visible in strobing flashes through the barred windows. Newbury wondered what Warrender was doing with all of that raging power. He'd read of theories from the Continent that posited the use of electricity in the treatment of patients suffering severe mental distress, but he remained dubious of the efficacy of such things—he'd seen the effects of Bainbridge's cane, after all, and what it did to the body of anyone who came into contact with the wrong end of it, leaving them a burnt, smouldering ruin. But then Warrender had a license from the Queen to experiment on those unfortunate enough to find themselves placed under his so-called care. To what ends, Newbury could only imagine. He hoped they weren't already too late to see their plan successfully deployed; that Warrender hadn't already broken the man they'd come here to see.

Voices sounded from around the next bend. He reached back, his fingers brushing Veronica's arm as he waved the others still. Two women, and the trundle of wheels. Coming their way.

Newbury glanced from side to side, seeking somewhere to hide. There were several recessed doorways in the passageway behind them. He crossed to the nearest and tried the door, gently sliding the bolt free. It remained resolutely locked. He didn't have time to start trying all of Warrender's keys, and forcing it would make too much noise—even assuming it wasn't reinforced. He turned to Veronica and Bainbridge. "Try the others!"

The voices were growing nearer, chatting inanely.

"No good," hissed Bainbridge. "Locked."

Newbury could hear the roaring of blood in his ears; the thudding of his heart as it beat an anxious tattoo. If they were discovered now, it would ruin everything.

"Over here," said Veronica, urgently. He glanced around.

One of the doors yawned open behind her, revealing a darkened room beyond.

The voices were nearing the corner.

"No, I've never enjoyed a mushroom," said one of the women. "I mean, just think about it for a moment—they grow on shit."

The other woman laughed. "So does everything else!"

"Well, you may have a point there," said the first woman. "But you're still not persuading me to put one of the ghastly things into my mouth."

Newbury swallowed. Across the corridor, Bainbridge was bustling into the room. Veronica had her hand on the door, beckoning urgently. Would he be better lurking in the doorway, hoping they wouldn't notice him? He glanced at the turn in the passage, saw the foot of a gurney emerge, swinging wide at the behest of one of the women, making ready to swing around the corner.

He had no choice. He stepped out, took two hurried steps, and then he was at the door, being pushed into the room by Veronica as she hurriedly swung it shut behind them.

Outside, the voices of the two women—presumably nurses—grew louder as they continued on their way, evidently oblivious to the interlopers in their midst.

"I'll tell you what, though. You could try them in a beef and ale stew. I promise, you'll hardly even notice they're there."

"Then why bother, Jean? What's the point?"

Newbury stood facing the door, breath held, until their voices had receded into the distance.

"Too damn close," muttered Bainbridge, when it was clear they were safe.

Newbury nodded, and then realised Bainbridge might have missed the gesture in the gloom. His eyes were only now adjusting to the dim light. The shadows seemed to cloak him, reaching out in chill embrace from the corners of the room, banished only by a paltry shaft of moonlight slanting in from a tiny window in the ceiling.

The room was sparsely furnished, with only a small wooden cabinet bolted to the wall and a single, wood-framed bed. Newbury was appalled to see a man lying upon the mattress, his wrists and ankles bound in padded leather braces. He was unconscious, yet his lips were moving, mouthing some unheard curse or scream. He was perhaps in his late thirties or early forties, clean shaven, balding, and dressed in the same plain pyjamas as the other inmates Newbury had glimpsed. Disturbingly, he had three iron bolts affixed to his head, one at each temple and another at the centre of his forehead. Around them the flesh was livid and puckered, and as Newbury leaned closer, it became apparent that the bolts had been punched right through to the skull, or perhaps— he considered, with a mien of distaste—into the brain itself.

"What have they done to him?" whispered Veronica, from the other side of the bed. He could hear the gentle ticking of her new heart, measuring out the seconds in the gloaming. He still found it difficult to believe that the delicate clockwork organ he had balanced in his palm back in St. Petersberg, so small and fragile, was now embedded inside her chest, sustaining her. He had quite literally held Veronica's life in his hands, and the profundity of that thought terrified him. He had brought the device back to her across half the world, from Fabergé's workshop, to save her life after her own heart had been damaged by a murderess in the employ of the Prince of Wales. All things considered; it was a miracle she was standing there before him at all.

"What kind of treatment is this?" asked Veronica.

"The dubious kind," muttered Newbury. Overhead, the Tesla coils sparked loudly and the man on the bed gave a sudden, alarming jerk, eyes flickering open as he strained at his bonds with grunted frustration. Newbury and Veronica fell back in unison, shocked by the primal ferocity of the man's abrupt transformation. He thrashed for a moment, unable to wrench himself free of the restraints, and then, just as suddenly as it had arrived, the fugue passed, and he fell back into a deep and immediate slumber.

Bainbridge gave a low whistle. "I want you to promise me now, Newbury, that you'll put a bullet in my skull before you ever allow them to reduce me to something like this poor sod."

Newbury hesitated for a moment. And then: "You have my word."

"Very well. Good," said Bainbridge.

Veronica sighed, shaking her head. "You men." She crossed to the door, opened it and peered out. "Come along. Let's get this over with. I don't want to spend any more time in this dreadful place than I have to."

CHAPTER 4

"Constance? Shouldn't you be in bed? You've got an early start in the morning, remember."

Amelia sighed, and turned to regard the concerned face of Tom Chappell, the junior footman, who was lurking in the doorway of the pantry. He'd obviously heard her coming along the passageway and waited to see who it was. She'd probably scared the life out of him. She knew he had a tendency to sneak down here late at night to help himself to Cook's sausage rolls. He was credulous enough to believe that no one knew, but Cook had long since fathomed out the culprit and, instead of referring the matter to Trimbey, had instead started adding extra to her weekly batch to compensate. It seemed like everyone *but* Trimbey knew.

Despite such petty thievery, though, Chappell was well-liked among the staff, and seemed kind-hearted enough–although Amelia had been around enough men to know that there was a reason for his apparent interest in her well-being. His shy smile and the way he refused to make eye contact were enough to confirm her suspicions. He was young, too, and ill-experienced; always putting his foot in it or saying something awkward.

She shrugged. "Trimbey has got me running errands. First it was putting away the laundered towels, then it was closing the curtains in Her Majesty's dressing room, and now it's fetching a fresh bucket of coal so it's ready for the morning." She held up the empty coal scuttle in her hand. "I think he must have taken a dislike to me for some reason."

Chappell shook his head. He brushed an errant pastry flake from his chin. "But it's pouring down out there." He lifted his eyes to the ceiling, as if he could see the storm roiling far overhead.

"So be it," said Amelia. "You know what the man's like."

Chappell stepped forward, extending his arm. "Give it here. I'll do it. We can't have you getting soaked through to the skin, can we?"

Amelia smiled. "Very gallant of you, Tom, but think of your suit. Besides, Trimbey will probably be waiting for me to make sure I've done as he asked. It'll only make matters worse for both of us if he thinks I've been enlisting you to help with my work."

Chappell lowered his hand. "Very well. But I think it's pretty despicable, making you go out there on a night like this."

"He's a pretty despicable man," said Amelia.

"You're not wrong. He must be doing something right though, eh?"

"What makes you say that?"

Chappell shrugged. "Well, he's got the Queen's favour, hasn't he? Always coming back and forth from her private chambers."

Amelia frowned. "Her bedchambers?"

Tom laughed. "Not *that* sort of favour. Although that's quite the rumour. No, I mean the off-limits area. Her Majesty's audience chamber. Always sneaking about up there with a smug grin on his face."

"I hadn't noticed," said Amelia, silently cursing herself for the oversight. So Trimbey was part of whatever was going on in there. She'd have to pay him closer attention in future. She glanced at the coal scuttle. "Look, I'd better be getting on. This isn't going to fill itself." More importantly, she didn't want the mysterious carriage to disappear before she'd had a chance to take a closer look.

"All right," said Chappell. "But if you need anything, you only have to ask."

"Thank you, Tom." She started off down the passageway again, towards the servant's entrance. From there, she could circle around to where she knew the carriage was parked, and still maintain her cover story if anyone else intercepted her.

Behind her, Chappell melted back into the shadows of the pantry.

Outside, the storm had yet to abate. The rain lashed the building beneath bruised and swollen clouds. In the distance, lightning crackled over the rooftops of the city. The skies, she saw, were empty. Even the usually ever-present flotilla of airships had been grounded to avoid calamity. No one was taking any chances. Stranger still, then, that three men should have called at the palace in their unusual carriage to collect *something* under the cover of darkness.

For a moment she paused in the open doorway, breathing in the heady scent of the rain. Then, laughing despite herself, she stepped out into the torrid downpour and splashed across the paved courtyard.

There was a time, not so long ago, that she could not have imagined ever feeling the touch of raindrops upon her upturned face again. Locked in her rooms and fussed over by nurses and doctors, or else trapped in horrifying facilities and subjected to terrifying experiments and induced seizures—her life had been one of confinement and fear. Even after Veronica and Newbury had rescued her from the Grayling Institute, she'd been so desperately unwell that the thought of running outside in a rainstorm seemed like utter madness, an impossibility. And yet here she was. To many, the stinging rain, the chill water running down their backs and soaking their dresses, the ominous rumble of the thunder would have been a minor disaster; to Amelia they seemed like nothing short of freedom.

Within moments her hair was plastered to the side of her face and her dress was stuck to her wet skin. Her stockinged toes squelched in her shoes. She thought to hold the coal scuttle above her head to ward off at least some of the downpour, but it was blowing in sideways, and besides, the water mingled with the coal dust to form a river of black ink that ran up her sleeves and dripped onto her cheeks. She blew droplets off her top lip as she ran around the side of the building, feet sploshing in the dancing puddles. She could hear nothing but the constant torrent, thrashing the building, gurgling in the drains.

She slowed as she approached the corner, around which she knew the carriage to be waiting. Carefully, she pressed herself against the wall and peered around. It was still there, rear doors sitting open, raindrops drumming on its roof. The three men were nowhere to be found. She presumed they must have finally seen sense and taken shelter inside. Which gave her the perfect opportunity to poke around.

Staying close to the wall, she crept nearer, keeping her eyes peeled for any sign of the driver and his two colleagues. Light spilled from an open doorway further along the wall; warm, yellow, and enticing. Despite her momentary burst of joy at being out in the storm, she was now beginning to reconsider the wisdom of her actions. Even if she didn't get caught, or managed to maintain her—admittedly flimsy—cover story, how was she going to make it back to her room without leaving a small river in her wake? And how was she going to launder her clothes without having to explain herself? She supposed she'd have to handle that when the time came.

She was approaching the open door. She could hear laughing from within; several men making banter. A shadow crossed the opening and her breath caught in her throat . . . but no one came out. The rain was pinging loudly off the brass coal scuttle in her hand and she considered discarding it, but that would bring questions too, and besides, without it she didn't even have that poor excuse for being out here.

She glanced at the door again, counted to three, and then hurried past, circling round the side of the carriage so as to be out of the eyeline of anyone inside. The poor horses were shivering, heads lowered, manes dripping. A tawny stallion with a brutish, muscular chest, peered at her nervously, shaking its head and baring its teeth around its bit. She edged away, approaching the carriage.

She could see now that the side doors—the ones that would be used by passengers—were, in fact, simple black lacquered panels with gilded decoration designed to mimic the appearance of a normal door. Likewise, the windows, which, despite their glossy sheen, were nothing but highly polished wood. Perfectly impenetrable. The whole thing was as clever a piece of deception as Amelia had ever seen. It was enough to convince even the most astute of casual viewers, particularly racing past at speed. The real question was why. Why bother with the whole charade in the first instance? What were these people trying to hide?

Amelia shivered, hugging herself against the cold. Her breath fogged before her face. She wouldn't be able to stay out here much longer, not without risking a chill. She crept around to the rear of the vehicle, trying her best to stay out of sight. She couldn't see anyone moving around inside the building. This, she realised, was the closest she'd ever got to the area of the palace that was supposedly off-limits—although, as far as she could discern, the side entrance here opened up onto a whitewashed passage, much the same as the one leading to the servant's quarters.

The back of the carriage had been cleverly arranged so that the whole rear of the vehicle opened along a seam in the centre, swinging open as two doors to reveal a large wagon bed within. Here, there were several of the wrapped bundles laying in a heap. Each identical, their contents were unclear. The inside of the vehicle was unfurnished and there was a thick aroma, even in the rain, of something putrescent, like unwanted food left to go off in the heat. Amelia wrinkled her nose. She counted the bundles: seven. They definitely weren't rolled carpet, but more like canvas sacks, tied at the top with twine. She wondered for one horrible moment if they were bodies, but quickly discounted the idea. They were the wrong shape. Too thin. But then, that smell . . .

She glanced back over her shoulder. The coast was still clear. Gently, she placed the coal scuttle on the gravel by her feet and reached for the nearest bundle. She grabbed a fistful of canvas and dragged it towards her. It was lighter than she'd expected, and she almost exclaimed and fell back as the thing slid easily over the others, almost falling out into the rain. She pushed it back into place, and leaned over it, attempting to untie the twine.

Her fingers were slick and cold, and she fumbled, unable to gain enough purchase. The twine bit into her fingertips and she cursed softly under her breath.

A voice sounded from the open door. A man, laughing.

Panicked, Amelia shoved the bundle back into place and turned, stooping to fetch up the coal scuttle in one smooth motion, just as the man came around the back of the carriage, his head bowed against the inclement weather. He was smoking a cigarette, the tip glowing like a tiny star in the gloom. He looked up, and his grey eyes settled on Amelia. Rainwater ran down his lined face. His jaw was set firm, but there was a slight hint of amusement on his lips.

"Oh, you scared me," she said, putting a hand to her chest, feigning relief. In truth, her heart was hammering so hard it threatened to drown out her every thought. She'd be surprised if this man couldn't hear it.

He nodded towards the bundles in the back of the carriage. "Having a good poke around, were we?"

Amelia looked scandalised. "What? No, of course not." She held up the coal scuttle; gave her best vacant smile. "I was just fetching some coal for Her Majesty's dressing chamber."

The man's lip curled. He took a long draw from his cigarette; blew it out through his nostrils. "And you thought you'd just stick your nose in where it wasn't wanted while you were at it?"

Amelia shook her head. "I was taking cover from the rain, that's all. I saw the doors were open and rushed over. I'm drenched." She pulled at the front of her sodden apron as if to underline the point.

The man looked unconvinced. "Why didn't you just come inside like the rest of us?"

"Because if Mr. Trimbey catches me, he'll have my guts for garters," said Amelia, adopting a conspiratorial tone.

"Oh, now I have to see this," said the man, laughing. "Trimbey? You there? Got a little surprise for you out here."

Amelia bit back a scathing retort. If she said the wrong thing now she could ruin everything.

Footsteps on gravel. And then Trimbey's snide face, beneath the arch of a black umbrella, appeared around the side of the carriage door. He looked her up and down, his expression sour. He looked embarrassed.

"Constance? What the devil is the meaning of this?"

"I didn't mean anything by it, Mr. Trimbey." She waved the empty coal scuttle. "I'm terribly sorry if I've caused you any embarrassment or alarm. It's just, when you sent me upstairs to close the curtains in Her Majesty's dressing room, I noticed that the fire was low and the coal scuttle was empty, and thought I'd see to one last errand before bed."

"Whyever would you do that?"

Amelia almost choked on the lie. "Because I wanted to impress you, Mr. Trimbey."

His eyes narrowed. Amelia shivered. His lips cracked into a sly smile. "Well, while I do appreciate the . . . um . . . ingenuity you have shown, Constance, the execution leaves something to be desired. And what are you doing hanging about this carriage."

"She claims she was trying to shelter from the rain," said the man with the cigarette.

"Is this correct?" said Trimbey.

Amelia nodded.

"And what about the . . . merchandise?"

"These sacks?" said Amelia. "I presume Her Majesty is having her rooms redecorated?"

"Redecorated?" echoed Trimbey.

"Yes. The carpets," replied Amelia. "All rolled up like that."

Trimbey glanced at the cigarette-smoking man. His shoulders dropped in evident relief. The man crushed the butt of his cigarette between his fingertips and flicked it away into the downpour. "Yes. Most perceptive of you, Constance."

Amelia wiped her hand across her face. "Might I go inside now, Mr. Trimbey? It's awfully cold here in the rain."

"Of course. Of course, Constance." He stepped aside to allow her to pass.

Heart still thrumming, clutching the coal scuttle to her chest, Amelia pushed herself away from the carriage and slowly walked between the two men. They both watched her go.

As she neared the open door, breathless, she heard Trimbey clear his throat. She stopped on the threshold, half in and half out of the rain. "Ah, Constance?" he called. "Aren't you forgetting something?"

She turned to look back over her shoulder, half expecting one of the men to grab her from behind and try to bundle her into the carriage. But there was only Trimbey, standing beneath his umbrella, watching her. "I am?"

"Why of course," said Trimbey, with a wicked smile. "The coal scuttle. We couldn't have Her Majesty's chambers getting cold, now could we?"

Amelia forced herself to give a strained laugh. "How silly of me," she said. "I'll see to it right away."

"See that you do. And Constance?"

"Yes?"

"In future, if I find that you've been poking around where you're not wanted, I shall not be so lenient. As generous as I am, even I have my limits. Do you understand?"

"Yes. I understand perfectly."

"Very good. Now, the coal."

Amelia turned and hurried off into the rain.

CHAPTER 5

"This is it," said Newbury, as they approached another set of double doors at the end of an echoing passage. "The only way through to the ward we're looking for."

Beyond the doors, the tortured moaning of an inmate went apparently unanswered by the staff. Elsewhere, someone was screaming, barely audible beneath the rumble of electrical discharge from above. Others were shouting, peering out through the small barred windows in their cells, but Newbury had trouble discerning their words with any clarity. It was a sheer cacophony, a choir of madness and torment. He wondered what terrors racked their minds—whether they were physical or imagined, perpetrated by man or demon.

He repressed a shudder. If he'd wanted further proof of the Queen's complicity in outrageous horrors, he'd need only have come here to see them laid bare. How could they force people to live like this? Tortured, devalued as human beings, granted no compassion or respect. Even the worst of criminals deserved better than this living hell.

Moreover, how could he have missed it all for so long? Or perhaps worse, wilfully ignored it? Was he then complicit, too, for turning a blind eye and allowing the monarch to carry on perpetuating such crimes unimpeded? These were questions he had yet to answer. Questions that he knew he would someday have to face.

But not today. Now, he was here to do something about it. To help Bainbridge to enact the Albion Initiative.

He glanced over to see Veronica was at his side. He'd stopped a few feet from the door, as if arrested by the sheer horror of the sounds originating on the other side. She put her hand on his shoulder.

"Shall we?"

He gave a curt nod. Together, they marched for the doors and pushed their way in, Bainbridge bringing up the rear.

Beyond, the ward was in chaotic uproar. Two male porters—thankfully not the two they'd encountered upon their arrival—were attempting to subdue a scrawny young man in filthy woollen pyjamas. This patient—wild eyed, jerking frantically, gnashing and scratching—was the source of the sounds Newbury had heard earlier. Bizarrely, he looked to be trying to fight his way back to his cell. The porters, both burly men—and both bleeding from scratches and bites on their forearms—were trying to force the patient into a wheelchair.

A severe-looking woman, wearing the uniform of a nurse or matron, stood watching this battle unfold, hands on her hips, lip curled in disgust. Around this scene, cells lined the walls to either side, and other inmates had their faces pressed up to the barred windows in their doors, screeching in laughter or bellowing their encouragement to the young patient as he continued his bid to escape the clutches of the porters.

"Come on, lad! Do 'im!"

"That's it. Go for the nose!"

Newbury caught Bainbridge's eye. There was no other way around to where they needed to be.

Bainbridge gave a nod in the direction of the exit, a matching set of doors at the far end of the ward. He was going to try brazening it out. Nodding his agreement, Newbury strode directly for the doors, walking straight past the tussling porters without another glance. He'd almost reached the doors when the matron's voice sounded from behind him.

"Wait!"

He considered ignoring her but decided it would only cause more trouble if she raised the alarm. He turned to face her. "Yes?" he asked, imperiously.

"Who are you, and where do you think you're going?" She glowered at him expectantly. The lines around her eyes tightened. She looked from Newbury to the others, as if their mere appearance might help to explain everything, but then, evidently none the wiser, fixed her glare upon Newbury once again. She was a tired-looking woman, probably in her fifties. Someone well-versed in enduring the very worst that humanity could throw at her. A woman who'd fashioned her own armour against the world, and who wasn't likely to be taken in by Bainbridge's bluster.

Nevertheless, he stepped forward, puffing out his chest. "He's with *me*."

The nurse narrowed her eyes. "And *you* are?"

Bainbridge looked down his nose at the woman. "Why, I, madam, am Sir Charles Bainbridge, Chief Inspector of Scotland Yard and servant of Her Majesty the Queen."

The woman eyed him suspiciously. Behind her, the two men were still grappling with their agitated patient, who had now started mumbling something—a phrase—over and over, each iteration growing louder in volume.

"It's all going to end," muttered the patient. He gnashed his teeth a few inches from the end of a porter's nose. "Soon. *Soon!*" He laughed maniacally. "It's *all* going to end." A cheer went up from the other inmates. Newbury could feel their eyes on him. There must have been a dozen of them in here, many of them pressed up against the bars in their cell doors, deriving what enjoyment they could from the unfolding spectacle.

"Whatever you say, matey," ground out the porter, before

grabbing the man's legs and tackling him down to the floor, whereupon his colleague seized the wriggling inmate by his shoulders and pinned him in place. The man, eyes wide, stared up at Newbury, as if searching Newbury's face for an answer he couldn't find. "It's all going to end," he repeated, as the porters began to drag him towards the waiting wheelchair. "All of it. But you know that already, don't you?"

Newbury looked away.

The matron was giving Bainbridge what amounted to a dressing down. ". . . Who you are, or what your business is—without Doctor Warrender's express permission, I cannot allow you in here. You're upsetting the patients."

"*We're* the ones upsetting the patients?" said Veronica, glancing pointedly at the two porters, who were bundling their now-placid charge into the wheelchair. "Right. I see."

The nurse turned to look her up and down. "And who do you think *you* are? You're not one of my nursing staff. Whoever you are, don't think for a minute you can go getting all hoity-toity with me," she said, smartly. "You can just turn your pretty self around and head back the way you came. Go on, back through those doors. We've got plenty of lords and ladies in here, and you can see where all their airs and graces landed *them.*" She waved at the doors dismissively. "You can wait through there until I've spoken to Dr. Warrender."

Newbury watched Veronica's hand slowly curl into a fist. He could feel the situation running away from them. He turned to the inmate in the wheelchair. "It's all going to end," he said. "You're right. All of it."

The man issued a raucous giggle, before launching himself out of the chair with surprising speed, brimming once again with sudden energy. "It's all going to end!"

Before the two exasperated porters could stop him, the wiry little man had thrown himself at the nurse, wrapping his arms around her hips and trying to drag her down to the floor, mirroring what the porter had done to him just a few moments before. Yelping, she twisted, trying to bat him off with the flats of her hands.

"Get off! Get off!"

"It's all going to end!"

Newbury made for the door; the others close behind him.

"We haven't got long," said Bainbridge, as they hurried across the small treatment room on the other side of the door. "That harridan will be after us before we know it."

"Worse," said Newbury, "she'll likely find Warrender and set the entire place on us." He skirted around a polished wooden operating table, making for another door. Above the table, a nest of wires dangled from the ceiling like the proboscis of some gargantuan beast, oily and black. A silver trolley beside the table was piled high with bone saws and drills, and a small kidney dish contained more of the iron bolts that they'd seen protruding from the head of the troubled man in the side ward. Bloody rags were heaped in one corner. On a workbench by the barred window were laid out fragments of what appeared to be bone, arranged beside an enormous microscope. The whole room reeked of death and spilled blood.

Evidently, this was where Warrender carried out his experiments with the electrical discharge of the Tesla coils.

"Through here," said Newbury, as he reached the door. He turned the handle. Locked. Grimacing, he yanked the ring of keys from his pocket and began testing them in the lock.

"Hurry up," urged Bainbridge, drawing the revolver from inside his jacket.

"You're not going to *shoot* them?" said Veronica.

"I'm going to do whatever is necessary to ensure the success of this mission," Bainbridge replied. "You know what's at stake here, Miss Hobbes."

"Nevertheless . . ."

"Let's hope the gun will be enough to warn them off," said Newbury, silencing any further debate. The last thing he wanted was for any innocents to get hurt. Yet Bainbridge was right, the fate of the entire Empire rested on their shoulders, and upon the man behind this door. Their entire plot to depose the Queen was at stake. They might be left with no choice.

He tested another key. Then another. "It's got to be on here. . . ."

Back in the ward, the inmates were cheering loudly. Newbury tried not to imagine at what. It had been unfair of him to use the inmate the way he had, to create a distraction, but they were running out of options. Fail here, and everything they'd fought for would be lost. Including their lives.

He pushed another key into the lock, and this time it snagged with a satisfying click. He yanked on the door; heard someone call in alarm from the other side. Newbury fell back as Bainbridge edged forward; revolver held at the ready.

"Don't shoot. Please." It was a man's voice, tremulous and dry, like the creaking of old wood.

"I'm not going to shoot you," called Bainbridge, his voice level. "But you need to do as I say. Come forward, with your hands up."

"All right. I'm coming out now."

Slowly, in a shuffling, awkward gait, a figure emerged from the gloomy passage, hands raised by his sides. He was dressed in the formal attire of a footman—smart black suit and tie—but was stoop-backed and elderly with a bald pate and creased, liver-spotted skin. Newbury recognised the man instantly, although time had clouded his memory and he couldn't quite remember the fellow's name. He'd been a footman at the palace some years ago, running about after the Queen and her household, but he should have been long retired by now.

The man looked up at Bainbridge with rheumy eyes. Newbury could see that one of them was misted by a thick cataract.

"*Percy?*" said Bainbridge, lowering the gun. "What the devil are you doing here?"

"Sir Charles. I might ask the same of you."

The two men looked at one another for a moment. "Well?" Bainbridge pressed.

"I've been seeing to his needs," said Percy, sniffing. "It's not right, a man like that being in a place like this. Someone had to keep an eye on things, make sure everything was done proper. So, I petitioned Dr. Warrender and, after a time, he allowed it. I've been coming here every day since." He folded his arms across his chest. "And I'm not about to stand aside and let you go in there with that gun, either. So best you turn around now and walk away. I don't care what she's told you to do."

Newbury might have laughed at the man's gall, but there was something deeply affecting about his heartfelt demonstration of loyalty.

Bainbridge sighed. "We're here to get him out, Percy."

"*Out?*"

"Yes, and we're in a damn hurry!"

"Out as in away, somewhere safe?"

"Yes!"

"Well why didn't you say so?" The old man shook his head. "I suppose I'd better get out of your way, then."

"The sooner the better."

Things in the adjoining ward had grown unexpectedly quiet. Newbury didn't dwell on what that might mean for their escape.

Slowly, the old man shuffled out of the doorway. Huffing, Bainbridge led the way into the room beyond.

Here, a small antechamber was sparsely furnished with a wooden table, a chair, and a pile of reading matter—mostly yellowing children's story papers and a few novels with faded red covers. The walls were bare, peeling plaster and the only light originated from a gas lamp mounted behind the door. Another door appeared to lead to an adjoining cell.

"In there," said Newbury. "That's it."

Veronica crossed to the door and tried the handle. "Locked."

"Hold on, I'll find the keys," said Newbury, fishing the ring back out of his pocket.

"No time," said Bainbridge. "We need to move." He motioned to Veronica with a wave of his arm. "Stand aside."

"What are you going to—"

Her question was cut short by the ringing boom of the revolver—six deafening shots echoing in the confined space as Bainbridge unloaded the weapon into the lock. The sharp stink of cordite and singed wood filled the air. Newbury plucked a splinter of the doorframe out of the back of his hand.

With a grunt, Bainbridge shouldered the door open, tossing the empty gun to the ground, where it clattered upon the flagstones. "Your Highness? Are you there?"

The cell beyond the ruined door was well appointed, with a wooden bed complete with downy mattress and pillows, a small mahogany wardrobe, a sink and toilet, and several well-stocked bookcases, along with a small Davenport writing desk and chair. Even the walls had been papered to resemble a drawing room or study.

Sitting in the chair was a portly man in a tailored black suit, with a receding hairline and neatly manicured grey beard: Albert Edward, the Prince of Wales.

His eyes widened at the sight of the three agents as they swept into the cell. "You!" he roared, standing so violently that he sent the chair crashing to the floor in his wake. He rounded on Newbury, spittle flecking his lips, cheeks flushed with indignant rage. Before Newbury even had a chance to raise his hands in defence, the Prince's fist struck him hard across the chin, and Newbury went spinning groggily to the cold floor.

CHAPTER 6

"Your Highness! We're here to help you *escape*!"

Veronica's urgent plea seemed to cut through the red mist threatening to overwhelm the Prince, and he stepped away from the prone Newbury, upon whose chest he had been about to unceremoniously stomp.

"Please, calm yourself."

"I assure you, Miss Hobbes, one is quite calm," said the Prince, still glowering at Newbury, who was now pulling himself up into a sitting position, rubbing at the livid bruise that was already manifesting along the line of his jaw.

"I suppose I deserved that," he said, sheepishly.

"Your Highness, we have to move quickly," said Bainbridge, indicating the door with the tip of his cane. "We have a carriage waiting around the back, but we're anticipating some resistance."

"Indubitably," said the Prince. "But what I'm failing to understand is why I should even consider placing myself into the custody of the people who committed me to this cell in the first instance. One might question your motivation in breaking me out, and my subsequent safety."

"We didn't put you in this cell," snarled Newbury, getting to his feet. "Your mother did. Not to mention your own moral turpitude. You only have yourself to blame for what happened."

"*Newbury,*" said Bainbridge, through clenched teeth, "you're not helping."

Newbury gave an exasperated grunt. "Look, despite everything, it has become abundantly clear that you—and believe me, it pains me to say this—that *you,* Your Highness, represent the best chance the Empire has of surviving its current crisis."

"And what crisis would that be, *Sir Maurice*?"

"The continued survival of your mother, the Queen."

For a moment, Newbury thought that the Prince was about to strike him again. But then the Prince threw his head back and issued a barking guffaw. "So, you wish to install me on the throne of England?"

"Yes."

"And you're rescuing me from an *insane asylum* to do it?"

"Yes."

"After I tried to have you assassinated for exactly the same end."

"Yes."

"It's the most ridiculous thing I've ever heard."

"Nevertheless, it is the truth of the matter," said Newbury. "The Queen's interests have diverged from those of the people."

"The Queen's interests have never aligned with those of the people, Newbury. That's what I've been trying to say," the Prince eyed him warily. "But we can continue this discussion at a later juncture." He turned to Bainbridge. "Sir Charles—your plan?"

"To get out of this hell hole as swiftly as possible," said Bainbridge. "We have a place in mind. Somewhere you'll be safe."

"Then I am at your command, Chief Inspector."

"Very good. Lead on, Newbury."

Newbury gave a curt nod, and then turned for the door.

The first thing he noticed upon entering the antechamber was the incongruous stench of burning meat—the sort of smell one would hope never to encounter inside a hospital. It stuck in the back of his throat; thick and sweet and oily. He hacked into his fist, immediately alert, and waved for the others to stay back. They'd caught the stink of it, too, now, and were wrinkling their noses, only too happy to linger for a moment longer in the doorway.

Carefully, Newbury crept forward, crossing the antechamber to the door, which still hung open in its frame. Out in the laboratory the stink was even more cloying, but he could sense no movement, no presence. None of the furnishings or equipment appeared to have been disturbed. So, what was the source of the alarming odour?

Steeling himself, he crept out into the room. He turned on the spot, searching the darkened corners of the room. He cursed under his breath as his eyes fixed upon the slumped figure in the corner, propped against a row of low cupboards.

He crept closer, keeping his breathing shallow and covering his mouth with the crook of his arm.

It was Percy, the old man who'd been standing guard over the Prince. He hadn't even made it out of the laboratory. Something had burned him to a crisp. His flesh was blackened and peeling in long strips, revealing the charred bones beneath. His clothes still steamed with the heat of his horrific wounds, and there were singed patches on the front of his jacket, one on either side of his chest. His eyes had burst in their sockets, their fluid boiling down his burning cheeks. His jaw was clenched so tight that several of his teeth had shattered.

The man had been killed by an electrical blast of extreme discharge, as if struck by lightning. Newbury had seen it before, many times, only far less powerful; Bainbridge's electrified cane induced a similar effect in its victims.

Newbury glanced up at the nest of electrical cables hanging down from the ceiling. Had they somehow transmitted the voltage from the Tesla coils on the roof? Was this all a terrible accident? It didn't seem likely.

He straightened, turning to call for the others, when something shifted in the gloom to his left. Before he'd finished turning his head towards it, a creature—for it was barely a man—collided with him heavily, sending him sprawling across the tiled floor. He struck the back of his head against the wooden base of the operating slab and must have called out, because he heard a commotion from the door.

Groggily, he moved, throwing himself across the floor just as his attacker came in for a second try. Their fist struck the wooden panel so hard that he heard something splinter. He wasn't sure if it was the wood or the bones in the thing's hand.

He scrabbled to his feet, backing away from the hulking mass of the creature. If the animalistic snarl on its face was anything to go by, it was a man in body alone. It resembled the patient they'd seen in the side room earlier–three large metal rods jutting from his skull, but unlike that poor patient, this creature was a hulking brute, a slab of muscle and anger. A blue halo of sparking electricity crackled and spat between the metal conductors in its head, and a large battery pack was strapped to its back. Wound knots of copper wire looped into implanted sockets in its chest and neck.

It stalked forward, reaching for Newbury, electric light dancing along its arm, travelling towards the tips of its fingers. This, then, was precisely what had become of the unfortunate Percy–the creature meant to kill him with its touch.

"Get back!"

Over its shoulder, Newbury saw Bainbridge rushing to join the melee, his lightning cane charged and ready, the air humming and sparking as its central pillar rotated.

"Charles, *no!*"

Bainbridge slid forward, wielding the cane like a rapier, so that its sharp tip pierced the creature's lower back, burying itself several inches in the pallid flesh.

It howled, arching its spine and lurching away from Newbury, as the discharged electricity from the cane flooded its body.

Sparks fizzed and popped from its lips. Its eyes widened in abject pain. A web of lightning crawled across its skin, causing the flesh to smoulder and blacken in searing patches. And yet the thing kept moving.

Bainbridge fell back, dragging his cane with him. He stared at the creature, appalled. "What . . . ?"

A flashing bolt shot from the creature's head, striking a nearby metal trolley and sending it spinning across the lab, divesting itself of dishes, knives and surgical implements in the process.

A quick glance told Newbury that Veronica was edging the Prince towards the exit. He'd have to try to buy her time.

The creature—enraged, and still writhing in flickering tongues of current—had turned its attention to the source of its pain and looked to be readying itself to spring at Bainbridge. To his credit, Bainbridge was holding his ground, clutching his now-discharged cane like a club—but Newbury knew a single touch from the creature might be enough to stop his friend's heart. He wasn't prepared to see that happen.

As the thing launched itself at Bainbridge, Newbury dived, shouldering him out of the way, sending him crashing hard to the floor just as the creature lashed out.

Its hand brushed Newbury's arm, and he felt the world light up.

It was like every nerve in his body came alive at once. Blue fire crawled across his flesh. His jaw clenched involuntarily, so hard that he thought his teeth might shatter. He toppled to the floor, shuddering and shaking, every major muscle in spasm.

The creature loomed over him, its eyes bloodshot and malevolent. He couldn't move, couldn't think. It was going to finish him, burn his flesh from his bones until he peeled, just like the old valet.

It opened its mouth, revealing bleeding, broken gums. It jutted its head forward, its neck muscles bulging. It looked as if it were trying to say something.

And then it was falling, out of his field of vision, and in its place stood Veronica, clutching an enormous—and now bloody—microscope.

She dropped it to the floor with a clang, and then dropped to her knees, checking his racing pulse, slapping his cheeks to bring him around.

"Maurice?"

"Yes, yes, I'm all right," he said, his voice a dry croak. "I think."

"You're a damned fool," said Bainbridge from close by, his voice booming.

"It might have killed you," mumbled Newbury, getting up unsteadily to his feet. He lurched sideways, took an unsteady step, and then righted himself. His head was swimming, fuzzy.

"It might have killed either one of you," said the Prince. "Or both. What the devil was it?"

"One of Warrender's experiments," said Bainbridge. "You're lucky you've been spared the knife."

"Hmmm," said the Prince. He looked distractedly at the door. Raised voices were sounding from the other side.

"We need to move, *now,*" said Veronica. "Sir Charles—help him, would you?" Bainbridge obligingly slid an arm under Newbury's shoulder, propping him up. "Now, forgive me, Your Highness," she added, "but I assure you this is entirely for your own good." She grabbed a clean white sheet from one of the cupboards and promptly draped it over the Prince's head, obscuring his face and torso from view.

"What in the name—" he started, but Veronica cut him off.

"A disguise. Of sorts. We can't very well have you being identified as we make our escape, can we?" She took his hand in her own. "Now hold on and follow me." She marched him towards the door. "And Sir Charles—try to keep up."

The escape from the hospital passed in a haze for Newbury—a series of half-glimpsed images as he swooned in and out, circling unconsciousness.

The world seemed to exist only as a series of stuttering stills. A corridor. The leering face of an inmate pressed to the bars. A gloomy side-room. A porter on the floor, clutching a bleeding lip. There were the sounds: shrill screaming, a barked command, the snap and thunder of the Tesla coils, the thwack of a well-timed punch.

And then they were outside and the chill air seemed to sweep away the swampy, dream-like fuzz, making everything seem hyper-real. Raindrops bursting on his face. The crunch of the gravel. The bite of the cold.

The last thing Newbury remembered before sweet blackness claimed him was the sensation of being bundled into a carriage, and the clomping of the horses' hooves as they rattled off into the night.

CHAPTER 7

Detective Sergeant Quint of Scotland Yard was already having a terrible day, and it wasn't yet lunchtime. First, he'd overslept when his miserable excuse for a landlady had failed to wake him, taking the opportunity to put her feet up for half an hour instead of seeing to his breakfast. Given the eye-watering amount she charged for such lackadaisical service, he was seriously considering a move.

Then, as he'd dashed along the roadside, stomach growling, ignored by several passing hansoms, his fresh suit had been spattered with a generous spray of god-knows-what as he was caught in the wake of a rumbling ground train. He'd tried to dab it out with a towel when he'd finally arrived at the Yard, but he'd succeeded only in smearing the foul-smelling substance further into his trousers. And now, ruffled, hassled, and generally feeling as if the world was aligned against him, he was seated in a small gallery beside a brooding Inspector Foulkes to witness the execution by hanging of one Matthew Parker Esq., notorious feaster upon human hearts. Hardly how he'd envisioned spending his day.

Not that the man didn't deserve his fate. Quint had been among the arresting officers at the scene and had witnessed everything first-hand: Parker with his hand buried deep in the open chest of his victim, their heart a pulpy mess in his fist. Blood had been slathered over his face, dripping from his open lips, and he was muttering the same strange word over and over: MATHERAT. MATHERAT. MATHERAT.

The word had turned out to be the name of Parker's personal god. The subject of his sick worship. A fantasy he'd concocted in his own head; an angry deity he'd invented to justify his grotesque impulses.

And there'd been more. Other bodies that followed a similar pattern. They'd been looking for Parker for months when they found him. He'd killed seven others before the man with the red hair, the one whom Quint had found him mumbling over. Seven other poor souls who'd died with his fist in their chests and their flesh in his mouth. People, men and women both, whose last breath had been taken as he'd burst their hearts. And that was just the ones they knew of. Parker claimed to have sacrificed more, although the remains of any such rituals were long gone.

So yes, in the eyes of the law—in the eyes of Quint himself—the man deserved everything that was coming to him. Yet Quint still couldn't stomach the thought of watching the man die. The very thought of it made him queasy, set his teeth on edge. His head was buzzing like a fly. He wanted to be anywhere but in that room, anticipating the horror to come.

He shifted uncomfortably on the hard wooden seat. Beside him, Inspector Foulkes glanced over, wrinkling his nose in disgust. "Damn, there's a foul smell in here today. Bastard's probably shat himself." Foulkes shook his head, cast his eyes over to where Parker had been led in by his guards and was standing before the wooden platform that denoted his last few steps in this world. "What a way to go."

Quint tried to sound his agreement, but the noise that came out was more of a high-pitched mumble. He felt his cheeks flush hot and red. He tried to conceal the stain on his trousers, turning his body slightly away from the inspector and folding his hands on his lap.

Undeterred, Foulkes leaned closer and slapped him heartily on the back. "You smelled it too, eh?" He grimaced. "Let's hope it's over quickly. Damnable business. If I'd wanted to watch men die, I'd have taken up as a medical man." His bulky shoulders heaved as he laughed at his own joke.

"Yes, sir," said Quint, attentively studying the back of his hand.

"Still, I can't say I won't be glad when this one's six feet under," said Foulkes. "You were there, weren't you, when they caught him at the end?"

"I was," replied Quint.

Foulkes leaned closer, lowering his voice conspiratorially. "Was it as bad as they say?"

"Worse thing I've ever seen," said Quint. He tried not to picture it again in his mind and failed. The man had seemed . . . bestial, inhuman. Possessed.

"And that's saying something in this job," said Foulkes.

They both looked around at the sound of the door swinging open. A man had entered. He glanced with apparent disinterest at the condemned man, who was clearly doing his best to remain dignified despite his dire circumstances. He then crossed to the rear of the room, where he stood with his back to the wall. His face– partially hidden beneath the brim of a hat–looked old and lined, and despite being mostly clean shaven, a few errant white whiskers sprouted rudely from his chin. His eyes were lost in shadow.

Quint glanced at Foulkes, seeking any sign of recognition, but the inspector simply shrugged and looked away.

Probably just some other official, come to preside over the dead. It was a paltry turnout, really. Two policemen and a bookkeeper. A doctor, a hangman, and two police constables whom Quint vaguely knew, Travers and Molesworthy, serving as guards. No one who'd miss Parker when he'd gone.

Quint hoped that when *he* finally went, he'd be surrounded by his loved ones and not choked by fear the way Parker appeared to be. Which he supposed was understandable. As

Foulkes had implied, it was a terrible way to go, even if Parker had brought it upon himself.

The man was screwing up his face now, red and sweating, his eyes flicking nervously from side to side. For a moment he seemed to be looking directly at Quint, but then he mouthed something under his breath and turned away, and Quint realised that whatever the man was seeing was not in the room. Touched by madness, that one.

Quint sighed. He ran his finger under his collar. He felt hemmed in. The room was small and functional, with two exits—one leading to the cells, the other the upper levels of the Yard. There were no windows, no air. The only furniture was the small gallery upon which he was sitting and the gallows themselves: stark and functional, and worn with use.

Quint had only witnessed a single hanging before, and if he was truthful, it wasn't something he was anxious to see again. The contorted face, the purple lips—he felt his queasiness returning.

"Are you quite well, Quint?" said Foulkes.

"It's been a long day."

Foulkes scoffed. "It's only half past eleven!"

"Precisely," said Quint.

The other men were speaking amongst themselves now in the low drone of formality. The measured, sombre tones of those about to commit a man to his death. And then the prisoner was being led up to the platform, the noose hooked over his neck. . . .

Quint watched in a kind of dislocated horror as the sentence was recapped, the prisoner provided the opportunity for any final words—perhaps unsurprisingly resulting in a bellowed plea to "MATHERAT"—and then the platform hinged open and the rope snapped taut. Quint averted his eyes. The wooden beam groaned as it took the weight of the dying man. His legs kicked twice, and then there was nothing but Quint's laboured breathing and the sound of the old man in the back clearing his throat phlegmatically.

Quint peered over, but the man seemed fixated on the gallows and didn't turn to meet Quint's eye.

The sergeant turned back to regard the swinging corpse. All life appeared to have fled the man. His lips were already turning purple, eyes bulging.

Beside him, Foulkes shifted uneasily, studying his boots. As imposing as the man was, both literally and figuratively, there was a human quality to Inspector Foulkes that Quint found appealing. He'd worked with the inspector on several cases over the years and always found him a reasonable sort, as concerned for the victims of crime as he was with catching the perpetrators. Which was far from typical in the Yard. As Quint understood it, Foulkes was quickly rising through the ranks under the direct patronage of Chief Inspector Sir Charles Bainbridge. The Yard could definitely do worse.

The executioner grunted as he stepped up to sever the rope, sawing for a moment with a serrated knife. The two guards came forward to catch the body as it was released, lowering it to the platform with surprising reverence. The doctor—a portly, bespectacled man with a sweep of grey hair and a neatly trimmed beard—waved them aside as he knelt beside the body. He took Parker's wrist, counted under his breath for a few moments, and then gave a curt nod, resting the dead man's hand upon his chest.

The guards moved back in, hoisted the body onto a trolley, and wheeled it out of the door. The other men filed out behind them, without even a glance towards the gallery. And then it was over. It had all been so . . . perfunctory.

Quint sat for a moment longer, unsure what to do with himself. He heard footsteps and turned to see the old man making his way towards the door. He thought to engage him, out of curiosity if nothing else, and started to rise from his seat, but then Foulkes was beside him, clearing his throat.

"I don't know about you, Quint, but I could use a drink after that. Join me for an early lunch at the Taverner's?"

Quint felt his stomach rumble at the prospect. "Umm, yes, sir. I'd like that. I'd just like to"—he turned, but the old man had already gone—"ah, wash up first."

Foulkes nodded. "Aye. Seeing something like this—it can leave you feeling dirty, can't it. You run along and do what you have to. I'll have a stiff one waiting for you."

"Thank you, sir."

Quint turned at a commotion from the door. Two men appeared, red-faced and flustered. Quint recognised them as Inspector Burroughs and his wiry little sergeant, Jones. He'd never had much to do with Burroughs, but Quint knew Jones to be a sadistic bastard, who was well known around the Yard for his tendency to employ excessive force during his arrests. Given the sort of men he was usually arresting, most in the Force were given to turning a blind eye. Today, he was positively beaming. Something had clearly brightened his day.

Whatever it was, it had had the opposite effect on Burroughs. The man looked positively dismayed as he bustled into the room, making a beeline for Foulkes.

"Foulkes. Thank God. Have you heard the news?"

Foulkes glanced from one man to the other, making no effort to hide his consternation. "I've heard nothing that would warrant you charging down here while they're still carrying out the corpse of a dead prisoner. So whatever it is, you'd better spit it out."

Burroughs took a deep breath, tugged on one end of his bushy moustache. "It's the chief."

Foulkes's brow creased. "As in Bainbridge, the chief inspector?"

Burroughs nodded. "Word's come down from on high. We're to bring him in."

"Hold on a moment, Frank. What are you talking about?"

Burroughs sighed. "He's a wanted man. To be arrested on sight."

Foulkes gaped. The sadistic Jones was grinning like the Cheshire Cat.

"I . . . I . . . ," stuttered Foulkes. "Why?"

Burroughs glanced at Quint, then back to Foulkes. He looked as if he could barely believe what he was saying. "Last night, the chief inspector broke into Bedlam and kidnapped the Prince of Wales."

"He *what?*"

"There are multiple witnesses. There's no doubt."

"No doubt, my arse!" bellowed Foulkes. "Now get out of my way!" He shoved a surprised Burroughs to one side and stormed hurriedly from the room. Jones watched him go, smirking in satisfaction.

Quint sat on the nearest bench, and expelled a long, weary sigh. He supposed that lunch was probably off again, then.

CHAPTER 8

SEVERAL DAYS LATER

"Tell me again how you found this detestable place." Albert Edward, Prince of Wales, son and heir to Her Majesty Queen Victoria, lowered himself into a small, rodent-bitten armchair, causing a plume of dust to puff into the air around him. He coughed, waving a hand before his face in abject disgust.

They were sitting in the living room of a house in Tottenham, abandoned now for some months, and somewhat poorly kept before that. A thick patina of dust covered every surface—the carpet, the mantelpiece, the windowsills and sideboard—and there were mouse droppings behind the sofa where the horrid little creatures had chewed their way in through the fabric. Veronica was loathed to sit on it, partly because she feared disturbing a nest of the creatures and partly because the place held uncomfortable memories for her.

The future king, it seemed, had no such compunction, despite his obvious distaste.

"It belonged to a doctor named Julian Wren," said Veronica, "along with his wife, Petunia."

"And where are they now?"

"Dead," said Bainbridge from the doorway. "And good riddance to them, too. Despicable people." He entered the room bearing a tray upon which sat a teapot, cups, and saucers.

"So, you're in the habit of squatting in the homes of dead people now, Chief Inspector?" said the Prince.

"Not if I can help it," replied Bainbridge, a little tartly, "but I knew the place was empty. I . . . oversaw the case in which the doctor perished."

"And his wife?"

"She died on a long-distance train journey," said Veronica.

"Hmmm," murmured the Prince, apparently unconvinced. "Well, I must say, the accommodation was of a much higher standard in Bedlam," he added. He took a cigar from a box on the side table, snipped the end, and lit it with a vesta.

Veronica bit her tongue. She'd had nothing but constant sniping from the man for days now, ever since smuggling him here from the hospital. He hadn't even said thank you. Although, given that he still held them somewhat responsible for his incarceration in the first place, she supposed she could see why he was a little prickly.

He looked at Bainbridge, who was pouring the tea. "Things have really got that bad? Tell me now, I want the unadorned truth of it."

"Your Highness, she committed her own son to a lunatic asylum," replied Bainbridge, his voice level.

"Yes, yes. But that was personal."

Veronica stared at him for a moment. "You're not saying you're willing to *forgive* her?"

"Oh, God, no!" said the Prince. "She might have once been my mother, but whatever she is now, the woman who once cared for me is long dead. I want her gone as much as you, Miss Hobbes. More, probably." He accepted a cup of tea from Bainbridge and looked at it with outright suspicion. "No, the thing is, she's always cared more about the sanctity of her Empire than anything else in this world. What I'm struggling to believe is that she'd risk it all on some petty revenge."

Bainbridge took a sharp intake of breath. "Whatever reason she has for doing what she's doing, there's nothing petty about it. She's now sanctioned the murder of more than a dozen good men and women. People who once supported her. People who care about everything she built." He looked away, unwilling to show the sheer anger in his eyes before the Prince. "She's systematically dismantling the Secret Service, one body at a time. There are people in Whitehall who think she's mad but are too afraid to speak out. It's become a reign of terror."

"It's been that for a very long time," said the Prince. "Some of us just weren't prepared to see it." He looked pointedly at Bainbridge. "I believe she's becoming paranoid," he continued, "beginning to see everyone as a threat. She's so determined to keep hold of that damn throne that it's curdled her ruddy mind." He took a sip of the tea; recoiled. "It's a bloody curse, you know."

Bainbridge feigned dismay. "It's not that bad, Your Highness. I had the leaves shipped over from your club."

They looked at one another for a moment, and then both creased into laughter.

"What's all this, then?"

She looked up to see Newbury, looking on from the doorway, perplexed. "Sir Charles's tea," she said. "It's awful."

"Well, I could have told you that," said Newbury, removing his overcoat, which he flung onto the sofa before slinging himself down, apparently equally unconcerned about the rodents. He removed his cigarette case, offered it around, and then struck a vesta and leaned back, blowing smoke from the corner of his mouth.

"You survived, then," said the Prince.

"I did," said Newbury, lightly. "A bit of a shock to the system, but at least it blew away a few cobwebs."

"Hmmm," murmured the Prince.

Veronica shook her head in exasperation.

"Well?" said Bainbridge. "Any news?"

"Angelchrist sends his regards," replied Newbury. Professor Angelchrist was the ostensible leader of the Secret Service and a dear friend to both Newbury and Bainbridge. Presently, he was on the run, working in hiding while attempting to avoid the Queen's exterminators.

"And he's quite well?"

Newbury nodded. "As fit as a fiddle. And twice as infuriating. He's moving from location to location, changing his appearance every two days. He doesn't think they're onto him yet."

"It's only a matter of time," said Bainbridge, "unless we get to them first."

"She'll never call them off," said the Prince. "Once she's let slip the hounds, she always allows them to have their fun."

"And a particularly tenacious hound it is, too," said Veronica. "Did the Professor have any more on August Warlow?"

Newbury shook his head. "Nothing that we don't already know. Ex-military, prides himself at executing orders, and has some particularly potent weaponry at his disposal. The corpses are still being found burned to a cinder."

"He certainly doesn't appear to do things by halves," agreed Bainbridge.

"So far, the targets have all been associated with the Secret Service?" asked the Prince.

"Aside from a handful of her own agents she suspected of moonlighting, yes," confirmed Newbury. "She doesn't yet seem to have added Miss Hobbes or me to her list, but it's only a matter of time. She must suspect the truth."

"And Sir Charles?"

"After he showed his face at the hospital during your . . . um . . . liberation, we must assume he's now a very high priority target too. For the Queen and for the police. As are you, Your Highness."

The Prince sighed. "Yes, I'd gathered as much." He puffed on his cigar thoughtfully. "And I think we must also assume that my siblings are equally at risk. If she really is as paranoid as I believe she is, she's likely to take measures to ensure they're incapacitated at the very least. Swearing their loyalty won't be enough."

Bainbridge nodded. "There are more of us than your mother could possibly imagine. We have agents keeping a watchful eye on the entire family, Your Highness."

"Arthur, too? I mean, there's not much he can do from the colonies, but all the same . . ."

"I shall make sure of it. We have a long reach. Arthur will be safe in Canada."

"Good, good," said the Prince. He didn't look entirely convinced. But then again, Veronica considered, who could be sure of anything when it came to Victoria.

She wondered what it must be like for the Prince, talking about his mother in such terms after what she'd done to him and still might yet do to his brothers and sisters. Had she once been a good mother? A caring, doting woman who had loved her children and looked to their well-being?

It was impossible to know. She supposed there was little normal about a family such as that. Not that she had any real sense of what "normal" was. Her own upbringing had hardly been conventional, and her relationship with her parents remained strained to say the least. Still, she supposed at least she hadn't tried to assassinate them. Yet.

"So, isn't it about time you outlined your grand plan?" said the Prince, glancing from Bainbridge to Newbury. "I mean, now I'm here, I presume you've worked out how you intend to install me on the throne."

Newbury leaned forward, lifted the lid on the teapot and dropped the butt of his cigarette inside. It hissed as it struck the liquid, eliciting a grimace of disgust from the Prince. Newbury looked as if he didn't care one jot. "As Charles intimated, we have an agent inside the palace. She's been tasked with feeding us information. To do this properly—to make it stick legally—we need something that can't be dismissed. Something bad enough to discredit her, or to encourage her to step down."

"Good God!" said the Prince, levering his ample bulk out of

the small chair. He glowered at Newbury, furious. "That's it? That's all you've got. What the Hell were you thinking, breaking me out of that place without even a *glimmer* of a real plan?" He jabbed at Newbury with the end of his cigar. "What we need is direct action. She's never going to go quietly. You already know that. We have to take her down. Use her own tactics against her." He turned to Bainbridge. "This man she has, Warlow. An assassin, is he?"

"More of an enforcer, by trade. But certainly, familiar with the application of violence, and currently operating for the Queen in that capacity."

The Prince waved his hand dismissively. "What matters is that she's using people like that against you. Against *us*. We need to do the same. It's the only way."

"Your Highness," said Veronica, choosing her words very carefully. "Let us speak plainly. You're advocating regicide. Of your own mother."

"Yes," said the Prince, through clenched teeth. "And none of this would be necessary if you'd allowed me to go through with it the first time. Can't you see? She's not my mother anymore. She's just an old woman who's outstayed her welcome in this world, and it's driven her to madness." He sucked on his cigar, crossed to the window, and stood with his back to them, looking out on the London night.

"Your Highness," said Bainbridge, in what Veronica knew to be his most diplomatic tone, "we have your own premiership to consider. If the Queen were to die in . . . difficult circumstances, the legitimacy of your own position could well be challenged in the courts. Especially if your stay in . . . your most recent lodgings were to become public knowledge. Appearances and all that. The crown heads of Europe must be placated."

The Prince turned slightly, peering at Bainbridge from the corner of his eye. "Are you certain you're a policeman, Sir Charles? You sound more like a damn politician with every passing day."

Bainbridge laughed, but the comment evidently stung. "One does what one must, Your Highness, to ensure justice is done."

"Yes, well. Let's hope justice bloody well hurries up and gets on with it, then, shall we. I hope this agent of yours is as good as you all seem to think."

"Oh, she is, Your Highness," said Veronica, without a moment's hesitation. She glanced at Newbury, who exhaled a long, slow sigh of relief. "She is."

CHAPTER 9

The old ones were the easiest, but also the worst.

It always seemed so anticlimactic. Perhaps it was because their lives were so easily extinguished, even when they tried to fight back; their feeble attempts to scrabble for a weapon, reaching for a poker from the fire or an old service revolver they could no longer reliably aim. One of them had even tried to draw an old sabre from its mount on the wall but hadn't been able to pull it free. He still remembered the sagging look of defeat upon the man's face. The rheumy, pleading eyes.

He supposed it must be something in their upbringing, the fact they'd spent their lives fighting for a greater cause, been recruited for their steely resolve and trained to never give ground.

It should have been a testament to their character, but to August Warlow, they always seemed so pathetic. It was all so undignified. If they could just accept their fate, the whole matter could be dealt with swiftly and cleanly, with minimal fuss. He knew they weren't obligated to make his job any easier, but surely, they must understand: this was always the fate of old agents. When had any of them been allowed to slip away quietly in their dotage? It just wasn't the way of things. They'd lived their lives by the sword, and so there was only ever one way in which those lives were going to end.

He'd lost track of how many he'd had to deal with now. Too many. Her Majesty was having a clear out, and he was her instrument, her weapon of choice. He didn't ask questions, didn't need to know why. He simply worked his way through the list of names he'd been given with determination and diligence, an approach that had already seen his standing with the Queen elevated beyond every expectation. Although he had no illusions–he might be her current favourite, but it was a tenuous position, and he'd have to work hard to maintain it. Thus, his readiness to do whatever was necessary to get to the end of the list.

He *had* gathered that many of the targets were those involved in what the Queen had called "extracurricular activities." Namely, the embryonic organisation referred to by its members as the "secret service," an independent group of agents with links to the police force and military. He guessed Victoria saw their rise in prominence as a threat and had deemed any of her agents involved in the organisation traitors to her cause.

To be truthful, though, he really didn't care. He'd enjoyed the Queen's patronage for several years now and planned to do so for as long as he was able. If this was what he had to do to keep himself there–well, that was just what was necessary. And when his own time finally came, which it inevitably would, he planned to accept it with all the dignity and clear-headedness he could muster. No feeble grasping for a rusty sabre for him.

This one tonight, though. He was something else. The man had never been in the Queen's employ, so far as Warlow could tell. Yet he'd obviously crossed her, in order to incur such wrath. His was the very first name on the list: Professor Archibald Angelchrist. And beside it, in thick black ink, a warning: TO BE CONSIDERED DANGEROUS.

Warlow wasn't sure about that–how dangerous could an old man be?–but he did know Angelchrist was a wily bastard. He'd been evading them for weeks. Constantly on the move, choosing different locations for every meeting, leaving no trace of his passing. How the bastard managed it, Warlow didn't know. The man was like some spider at the heart of a massive web that seemed to stretch from Epsom to Watford and beyond; a network of agents and followers who refused to give him up and continued to enact his will regardless of the very obvious threat such actions posed to their continued existence.

If the "secret service" was an organisation of spies, then Angelchrist was their spymaster, with all the requisite guile, cunning, and subtlety needed to thrive in such an environment. No wonder the Queen wanted him dead. Excise Angelchrist, and the "secret service" was like a body without a head.

They'd finally tracked him to this tumbledown house on the outskirts of Islington: a bleak, boarded-up old end terrace, with a visible hole in the roof through which ravens were freely flitting in and out of the loft. The neighbours—a rum collection of bohemian types, wearing dressing gowns that were freckled with spots of oil paint and god knows what else, and whose breaths stank of cheap gin—told him the place had been abandoned for over a year, left to rot after the owner had been shipped off to the workhouse.

In other words, the perfect hiding place for someone who didn't want to be seen.

He'd only found the place after he'd managed to persuade one of Angelchrist's spies to give him up. It had taken the man three days to break, and by that point, Warlow had almost abandoned the whole thing as a lost cause. There wasn't much of the poor bastard left to torture. In the end, though, the spy spilled his secrets as readily as he'd spilled his guts, and now Warlow was sitting outside atop the dickey box of his stolen hansom, hunched against the chill. At least the rain had stopped.

He checked his pocket watch. It was approaching eleven. He'd give it a little while longer. If he missed his window here, there was every chance the professor would move on to a different location and Warlow would be forced to start over again. He wasn't about to give up his chance for the sake of a warm bed, as tempting as it might be.

Not that the thought of loitering by the roadside for hours on end offered much in the way of appeal. He longed to be at home with his book and a hot toddy; to forget about the boltheads and the Queen's list, the death and depravity she had so rudely thrust into his life. Perhaps tomorrow, if he got this over and done with, he might head out to a music hall and lose himself for a few hours; take a night away from the horrors of his normal, daily life.

He sensed movement in the cab below and slammed the heel of his hand against the roof, causing a thunderous bang to reverberate throughout the vehicle. Within, the movement ceased immediately. Warlow nodded to himself in satisfaction. He could understand their restlessness. They'd been cooped up for hours, charged with energy, ready to do what was necessary. With any luck, they wouldn't have to wait much longer.

Warlow huddled over the reins, blowing into his cupped hands. He wished he'd brought something to read.

It was around half an hour later when the scuff of gentle footsteps sounded on the otherwise quiet street. The moon had slipped out from beneath the banks of dense clouds that formed a canopy across much of the sky, casting everything in a watery, silvery sheen.

Warlow peered out from beneath the cowl of his hooded cape, keeping his head bowed low so as to appear as innocuous as possible; just another London cabby, taking a rest down a quiet street before heading back into the never-ending melee of the capital's main thoroughfares.

Only, Warlow was anything but innocuous, and his passengers far removed from the revelling middle-classes who typically patronised such London cabs. He could sense them growing restless again; feel the hair at the back of his head prickling as it always did when they were anxious.

Finally, the man came into view. He was thin and reasonably tall, with a very slight stoop. His face was largely obscured beneath the brim of his hat, but from what Warlow could ascertain, he matched the description perfectly: clean shaven, old but not yet elderly, with a shock of white hair and a thin, lined face that had the appearance of crinkled writing paper. He walked with a sprightly gait and was dressed in a brown suit beneath a large woollen overcoat.

The man paused by the low front wall that ran around the perimeter of the overgrown garden at the front of the dilapidated house. He glanced left and right, looked up at the dimly lit window on the first floor of the neighbouring property, and then hurried up the steps to the door. Another furtive glance, and then he produced a set of keys, unlocked the door, and slipped inside. Moments later, the house was once again as silent as if no one had passed.

Warlow slipped down from the dickey box. He paused to take a deep breath. He steadied his hands.

This was a necessity. His duty to the Crown. And it would change things forever. For him, for the nation.

Carefully, he eased open the door. The three figures inside stirred, agitated, flinching from some unseen tormentor.

"It's all right," said Warlow, affecting his best soothing tone. "It'll be over soon." He hoped the professor wouldn't make a liar of him.

He motioned for the figures and, one by one, they exited the cab, clambering down onto the road. Warlow blanched at the sight of their pale, fish-like skin, their sunken eyes, the three bolts protruding from each head. Every man wore a leather harness over his shoulder, a bulky power pack on his back, a large glass-covered dial on his chest. Now they were out in the moonlight, he could see they were jittery, unable to stand still. That wouldn't last,

He glanced up at the house, then back at the boltheads. They were all staring at him, waiting for their orders.

"Come on, then. You know what you have to do."

He led them up to the front door, tried the handle. The old man had locked it behind him. He never seemed to miss a trick. Warlow would have to break it down, and that would raise the alarm, giving Angelchrist the opportunity to try to slip out the back. Well, he'd have one of the boltheads see to that. But they'd have to go in ready, and that meant lighting them up out here in the street. So much for being inconspicuous.

"Initiate," he said.

As one, the three boltheads swung open the glass covers on their chests and adjusted the dials, turning the arms to the extreme right. Almost immediately, arcing electricity crackled to life, blue light spitting and hissing between the bolts in their heads, stark and brilliant in the gloom. It danced along their arms, played across their fingertips, popped and spat over their teeth. The air smelled just like it did after a storm—fresh, clean. And that was what they were doing here, wasn't it? Cleaning up.

Warlow slammed his shoulder into the door. The wooden frame, softened with rot, splintered instantly. And then he was inside the dank, lightless hallway, the boltheads thundering in behind him, sparks dancing off the walls.

He motioned for one of the boltheads to continue down the hallway towards the kitchen, where it could cover the rear exit. He didn't care which—he'd given up trying to tell them apart or to assign them names. In truth, he barely even considered them human.

He kicked open the living room door. Nothing but the festering carcass of an old armchair, its innards dragged out by mice, and the stench of damp from the leaky bay window.

The dining room followed, equally as rank, and equally as empty. He indicated for the two remaining boltheads to follow him up the stairs, which groaned and threatened to collapse under his weight.

For a moment he wished he'd brought a gun. After all, the man was considered dangerous. But he hadn't wielded a weapon since this had all started, and he didn't wish to start now. The boltheads were the means by which his executions were delivered. If he had a gun, he might use it, and that might be something he wouldn't be able to live with.

The bathroom on the first-floor landing was empty, too— quite literally. The bath and toilet had been ripped out and not replaced, leaving only a cracked porcelain sink with a single brass tap, and a small mirror propped on the windowsill.

So, he had to be in one of the bedrooms. Unless he'd already decided to jump.

"Why don't we make this easy for once, Professor?" Warlow called, his voice seeming obscenely loud in the otherwise ringing silence.

He paused on the upper landing, cocking his head as he listened for a reply. There was only the crackling electricity of the boltheads. He started towards the first door, the boltheads obediently following like well-trained hounds. It slammed against the inner wall as he kicked it open. Inside, the room still clung to the peeling remnants of its previous life—a former children's nursery, complete with a mouldering, cobwebbed cot and faded splashes of once-vibrant paint on the walls. Damp had warped the floorboards and black spores bloomed across the ceiling. The whole place had the maudlin air of abandoned childhood. Warlow wondered what had become of the child who had once inhabited the cot, played with the festering toys. Whatever had happened, he didn't suppose it was a happy tale.

He moved on to the next room. Behind him the boltheads trailed electrical discharge, discolouring the flaking plaster and damp carpets in their wake. He could feel his hair standing on end as the air hummed with their presence.

The second room was also long abandoned—just a couple of planks of wood propped against the far wall that might have once been part of a bed frame.

That meant the professor had to be waiting in the final and largest bedroom. Warlow paused on the landing before the door.

"Remember what I said, Professor. We can make this difficult or we can make it easy. If I were in your shoes, I know what I would do."

He kicked the door open. A gun went off. The plaster on the wall just inside the door exploded in a cloud of dust and debris. Warlow strode in.

The man was sitting in a wooden chair by the window, a revolver held shakily in his fist. He was dressed in the same attire he'd been wearing when he'd arrived a few moments ago, having not even removed his coat and hat. He must have realised something was afoot. He fixed Warlow with a cool stare.

"You're making a mistake," he said.

"It's out of my hands," said Warlow, with a shrug.

"So says every hired killer the world over," said the old man. "But is it true? You always have a choice, August."

The use of his forename pulled him up short. Of course the man would know who he was. In fact, Warlow considered, he was surprised this wasn't some kind of elaborate trap, laid by Angelchrist to neutralise the man who'd been picking off his agents. It certainly didn't seem to be the case, however. The man was trembling as he tried to keep his weapon levelled on Warlow's chest.

"If you knew her," Warlow said, his voice level, "then you'd know there's never any choice."

The professor offered him a sad, regretful smile. "So, it's you or me?"

Warlow sighed. "No. That's not how this works, Professor." He motioned to the figures waiting out in the hall. "I really wish you'd opted for the easy approach. I'm sorry to say this is going to be unpleasant. For both of us."

The two boltheads filed into the room, grinning inanely, blue lightning crackling across their lily-white skin.

"No. Warlow—*please.*"

Warlow felt something snap inside of him. His patience, his temper, his resolve? He didn't know. But in facing this old man, alone in this mouldering old house, *something* had broken.

He glanced once more at Angelchrist, then turned and left the room, deciding for the first time since all of this had started that he didn't have it in him to watch.

Another shot went off. Then another, and another, until the man had emptied the chambers. He heard a sound like a soft whimper, a moan of realisation. That was another moment he'd come to expect. Those last few seconds before they died, when the veil fell away and they realised there was nothing they could do. That everything they'd fought for was meaningless now, as the devils closed in with the promise of torment and pain. In this, the professor was no different than any other man.

Warlow rubbed a hand across his face. The begging had started. It'd be over shortly. The boltheads had no capacity for empathy or understanding. No concept of mercy. Today, he envied them that.

There it was. The raw scream. The defiant roar. The last gasp of a man who'd been a hero to so many.

And then the stench of cooking meat. The strange, childish giggles of the boltheads. The foul taste in his throat.

He turned his back on the door. He didn't want to look. He already knew what he'd see. But it was done. It was over. The first name on the list was gone.

Professor Archibald Angelchrist was dead.

CHAPTER 10

"What'll it be, Perkins?"

"A large gin, Sergeant, if it's all the same to you."

Sergeant Quint eyed the young constable appraisingly. He was a tall, wiry man in his early twenties, with oily hair and patchy red bristles on his prominent chin. Quint barely knew him, but he had a reputation as a promising and diligent man. "Well, I suppose you are off duty." He indicated to the barman and ordered himself a pint of ale while he was at it.

The public house they were patronising—The George & Dragon—was on the corner of Crispin Street in Spitalfields, a particularly insalubrious neighbourhood known to the police for its gangs, pickpockets, and spate of revenant-related deaths, which, a year ago, had resulted in the area being briefly annexed while the army were brought in to clear the streets. Perkins, it seemed, was a local, and appeared to fit right in, even wearing his uniform.

That was the thing about London, Quint reflected: people looked after their own. Communities sprung up in the strangest of places, as the police and the solicitors rubbed cheeks with the gang lords and their foot soldiers. It was a game, and everyone knew they were playing it. Just because two people found themselves on opposing sides, didn't change the fact they grew up together, had history, and could still share a drink over common ground.

Places like this pub were the heart of it all. Neutral ground, where everyone was reminded where they came from.

Quint felt like a rank outsider; a man who'd waded well out of his depth. Still, he had a job to do, and there was no one else about to do it.

Inspector Foulkes had been tied up with this whole royal matter since they'd had word at the execution a few days earlier. Rumour had it he'd even been up to the palace and spoken with the Queen. Quint hadn't seen him long enough to ask the question, but he wasn't sure Foulkes was the sort of man to speak about it anyway. Especially as it concerned the chief inspector.

Quint had a hard time believing that Sir Charles would have gone and got himself involved in something like that. He'd always seemed like such a *sensible* man. A stick-in-the-mud, even. Kidnapping the Prince of Wales just didn't seem his style. Unless Quint had got the man wrong from the start. Foulkes certainly seemed pretty worked up about it. Yet Quint had noted that the inspector had failed to speak a word of condemnation against his friend and mentor. That didn't mean the man wasn't guilty, of course—just that it spoke of Foulkes's keen loyalty.

Quint wondered how it would all wash out. Whatever the case, it was Foulkes's investigation, and Quint wasn't likely to get a look in. Thus, here he was, in a stinking pit of a public house, about to question Perkins about an incident that sounded like it might somehow involve a man whom Quint already knew for a fact to be dead. Not for the first time that night he wished he'd just written it off, but that was the lot of a copper, wasn't it? To have stuff constantly buzzing around in their head, to overhear a story being recited over the tea canteen and knowing you weren't going to be able to get it out of your head until you'd looked into it yourself, just to be sure.

So, here he was, sipping foamy ale from a greasy pint glass and feeling the wary eyes of the gathered ne'er-do-well stabbing into his back. The sooner he got this over with, the better.

"Right then, Perkins. When you're ready—tell me again what you saw. And spare me no details. I don't want the short version. Nor do I want the embellished take you were giving the other fools back at the station."

Perkins looked sheepish. "It wasn't like that, Sergeant."

"I know exactly what it was like. I've been there enough times myself. They're a hungry lot and make no mistake—there for the blood and guts and salacious details. Never hurts to lay it on a bit thick for them, does it?" Quint took a sip from his pint; tried to repress a shudder. "But I'm not like them, Perkins. I want the truth. Just what you heard and saw, plain as you like. Ain't no one judging you here."

Perkins nodded, then took a long pull on his gin. Quint could see that he'd be standing another round before this was through. Well, another gin, at least. He put his pint back on the bar.

"There ain't really that much to tell," started Perkins, wiping his mouth with the back of his hand. "I was doing my rounds, like, about ten o'clock. It was a dark and dreary night, and the mist was coming on thick, swirling like some fancy woman's undergarments at a dan—"

Quint cleared his throat. "I said the facts, man."

"Oh aye, so you did." Perkins grinned. "Well, I was coming around the bottom of the lane down there," he indicated as though Quint could see through the pub wall to the street beyond, "where's there's a little snicket, like. A pass-through."

"You mean you were taking a short cut on your rounds."

"I never said that, did I? That's just what you're supposing." Perkins looked indignant for a moment, and then shrugged. "Anyway, I was passing the mouth of said snicket when I heard what sounded like a struggle."

"What do you mean by struggle?" said Quint. "What exactly did you hear?"

Perkins looked thoughtful. "Well, at first I wasn't sure." He lowered his voice. "You know, there are a few women around these parts who might be willing to help a fella out for a few coins, if you see what I mean." He glanced around at the clientele, then tapped his finger against the side of his nose.

"So, you thought it might have been a man copulating with a prostitute," said Quint.

"Not in so many words," said Perkins. "I thought they might have been fucking."

Quint took another sip from his pint. It was beginning to taste better. "And you thought you'd take a look?"

Perkins flushed. "Not like that, I didn't. The noises the woman was making, it didn't sound right. Like she was struggling. I wanted to make sure she was all right."

"Very good," said Quint.

"Aye. Well, it wasn't good, was it? Like I said, the fog was up, and the noise she was making, I'm not sure they heard me coming. The man, he had her on the cobbles, like, and his sticker in his hand."

"By sticker you mean . . . ?"

"A knife. A big one. He had a hand pressed over her mouth, and he was saying something to her, like he was trying to be nice, but the words didn't match the way that he was saying it."

"Can you remember any of it?"

"I'll never forget it, Sergeant. He said that she should just relax and let it happen. That too much stress would make her heart all tough and fibrous, and that he didn't want it that way. That it would taste all wrong when he ate it."

Quint eyed Perkins over the top of his glass. The man was visibly shaking as he recounted the memory. Quint wasn't feeling much better. How could it be the same man? He'd watched him dangling from a rope, just a few days earlier. But two insane killers with a taste for human hearts?

"What did he look like, this man?" Quint asked.

"Like the devil 'imself, Sergeant."

"What have I told you about exaggerating?"

Perkins looked offended. "I ain't exaggerating. It was the look in his eyes. He meant what he said. He was going to eat that woman's heart, then and there on the cobbles. I was sure of it."

"Yes, but what did he *look* like?"

"It's hard to say. Stocky, fair hair. But thin, like he hadn't eaten a square meal for a while."

"What was he wearing?"

"A dirty old suit, as far as I could tell. Caked in mud and worse, like he'd been down at the shores of the Thames or something, mudlarking." Perkins drained the last of his gin. He looked inquiringly at Quint, who nodded for the barman to fill it up again. The man had clearly been listening in to Perkins' tale, pretending to clean glasses behind the bar with a rag. Quint shook his head when the man asked if he wanted another beer.

"So, what happened next?"

Perkins raised his replenished glass in a salute, then took a swig. "I waded right in with my size nines. Startled him before he could hurt her. He came at me with the knife, but I clipped him round the side of the head with my truncheon, and he was off like a hare. I followed him for a few streets, but he was too quick by half. Lost him in the ruddy fog."

"And the woman?"

"Gone, too, when I got back. Can't say I blame her for taking off, mind. Not sure I'd have hung around long after being attacked like that."

Quint nodded. "And you've seen nor heard nothing of him since? No more encounters on your rounds? No more stories of people being attacked?"

Perkins shook his head. "Nothing, 'cept the usual. Drunken brawls and petty robberies."

Quint sipped thoughtfully at his beer. It wasn't much to go on. He supposed it could have been a copycat, someone who'd read about Parker in the papers and found himself inspired. That had happened before, more than enough times. Some people courted notoriety and would do anything for attention. Others idolised the villains they read about in the press; coveted them and their lives. Quint had never been able to understand it, himself; for him, there was enough darkness in the world already, without going looking for more.

"He was in here that night, you know," said the barman, placing a fresh pint on the bar before Quint, who, he realised, had just about finished his first one after all.

"Who was?" said Perkins.

"That fella you were just talking about. The one who said he wanted to eat that girl's heart."

"All right, all right," said Quint. "Let's keep our voices down shall we. We don't want the whole neighbourhood up in panic."

The barman laughed. "This lot? You're having a laugh."

Quint glared at him. "Well?"

"Not a lot to say, really. I thought he was an odd one when he came in. Sat at the bar over there," he gestured to the other end of the long mahogany bar, "and nursed half a pint for over an hour."

"Then how do you know it was him?"

"Because of the weird stuff he was spouting. Didn't say nothing about eating people's hearts, mind."

"Then what did he say?" urged Quint, his patience hanging on by a thread.

"You know, strange stuff. Like he was tapped in the head. Told me he'd been reborn. Something about doing God's work. He was reading a copy of that strange newspaper. You know: *The Wheel and Star*."

"*The Wheel and Star*?" said Perkins. "What's that?"

The barman shrugged. "It's a paper for them that are interested in the supernatural and the occult," he said, looking somewhat uncomfortable. "Like seances and tarot cards and old gods."

Old gods.

Quint felt a tightening in his chest.

"God's work? A preacher, then?" said Perkins.

"No, no. Nothing like that. Some foreign religion, or something–although he didn't look like a foreigner. He kept on saying the name. Mallerish, or Maderat or something."

Quint felt nauseous. "*Matherat,*" he said.

The barman clicked his fingers. "That's the one. You heard of them, then? They from Spain or someplace?"

"Something like that," muttered Quint.

"It's just like I told that other chap–there's no accounting for what foreigners think," said the barman, who was looking pretty pleased with himself for having finally wangled his way into the conversation with something useful.

"It's not like that–" started Quint, then suddenly changed direction as his mind caught up with his lips. "Hold on–what other chap?"

The barman had to think for a moment. "Oh, right. Yes. One of your lot, I think. Came in here yesterday asking all the same questions."

Perkins looked blankly at Quint. "First I've heard of it," he said, a little defensively.

"Did he give you a name?" said Quint.

"Now that you come to mention it, I don't believe he did. You're going to want a description now, aren't you?" He didn't pause for an answer. "You see, I know how your minds work." He tapped the side of his head.

"Well?"

The barman seemed to glaze over, as if casting his mind back to the previous day involved entering some mystical trance-like state. "An older man," he said, "wearing a hat and coat. Couldn't see much of his face, but I couldn't help but notice a few bristles sticking out from his chin where he'd missed a patch shaving. He seemed particularly interested in this Parker chap."

Quint looked at the man, incredulous. "Shit," he said.

The barman's description was a perfect match for the old gent who'd shown up at Parker's execution. The one who'd stood at the back, staring, and whom no one seemed to know anything about. How was he connected to all of this?

With a brief sigh of regret, Quint picked up the fresh pint from the bar and downed it in one.

CHAPTER 11

"Your tea, sir."

"Hmmm?" Newbury glanced up from the folder of papers on his lap.

"Earl Grey, sir. I thought you might be in need of refreshment."

Newbury smiled. "You know me too well, Scarbright. I'm quite parched. Please, find somewhere to set it down."

"Sir." The valet—as neatly turned out in his crisp black suit as ever—crossed to the small table before the hearth and, deftly dodging a tottering pile of dusty old tomes, carefully set the silver tray down. Then, wincing, he straightened up again, one hand unconsciously straying to his sore chest.

Newbury frowned. "Are you certain you're fully recovered, Scarbright?"

"Yes, sir. I'm perfectly well. The doctor has given me the all clear. My little . . . *escapade* is over and done with, and it's high time things returned to normal around here."

Newbury eyed him, dubious. "You do yourself a disservice, Scarbright. Having your chest forcibly cracked and an explosive device sewn into the cavity is hardly a 'little escapade.' I wish you would take some time to see to your own well-being as assiduously as you do mine."

It had been several months since the incident in question,

when, following the unexpected re-emergence of rogue former agent Dr. Aubrey Knox, Scarbright had been drugged and implanted with a small bomb, along with scores of others throughout the capital. Knox had intended to detonate the devices if the Queen—whose physical and mental condition he was intent on exposing to the Empire—did not reveal herself in public. Newbury and Veronica had managed to locate Knox and put an end to the sorry business before the deadline passed, and the bombs had all been safely removed.

Scarbright had been convalescing for eight weeks but had insisted on returning to duties the previous week, and Newbury was convinced it was boredom rather than fitness that had driven him back to work.

"I assure you, Sir Maurice—being here *is* seeing to my well-being. My mother, you see. She means well, but . . ."

"Ah, I see," said Newbury. His own mother had been far from the overbearing sort, but he understood all too well that impulse to coddle your loved ones following a substantial brush with death. It was an impulse he'd had to fight numerous times himself—and only then because he knew that trying to protect Veronica was the only sure means to drive her away. "Well, light duties, man, at the very least. If you're unwilling to continue your convalescence at home, you're very welcome to continue it here, on the strict proviso that you engage in nothing more strenuous than fetching tea, and that you spend at least half the day with your feet up before the fire, reading a good book."

"But, sir—" started Scarbright, clearly uncertain.

Newbury shook his head. "I'll hear nothing more on the subject. Not until I have word from a doctor that you're fit and well enough to be back to polishing silver, mending dinner jackets, and whatever else it is you do." He grinned.

"What about your meals, sir?" ventured Scarbright.

"Perhaps you could see to a temporary arrangement to bring in a part-time housekeeper? Someone who can offer us *both* a hearty meal and keep the larder stocked for the next few months. All under your supervision, of course."

Scarbright didn't look convinced, but nor did he broach any further argument. "Very well, sir. If you insist."

"I do, Scarbright. Just think—what would Charles say if he discovered I'd been mistreating you?"

"And how is Sir Charles, sir? I understand there's been some . . . difficulties of late."

Newbury offered a sad smile. "Not the same, is it, without him blustering in every few hours, claiming he needs my help. Funny how he always seems to turn up at dinner time, isn't it?"

"I wouldn't know, sir."

Newbury laughed. "He's well enough, Scarbright. But the least any of us knows, the better. He's a wanted man. His whereabouts remain unknown to us."

"Of course, sir."

"Ever dependable, Scarbright. Now, there is just one thing t—"

Down the hall, the doorbell trilled.

"Shall I answer that, sir?"

"No, no," said Newbury. "I'm quite capable of answering my own front door. Now, go and put your feet up, would you? We can have the White Friars send along dinner this evening. I'll see to the arrangements myself later."

The doorbell trilled again, more insistent this time.

"Yes, yes, I'm coming. . . ."

After stopping briefly in the hallway to light a cigarette, Newbury yanked open the door to find a short young man in a police constable's uniform standing on the lower step. The red-headed man—whom Newbury didn't recognise—looked up expectantly, shielding his eyes from the dappled morning sun.

"Sir Maurice Newbreet?"

Newbury eyed the newcomer. "It's Newbury," he said.

"Newbreet, that's what I said," replied the constable.

"No, I . . ." Newbury sighed. "It doesn't matter. What is it?"

"Are you him, then?" said the constable.

"Yes."

"Sir Maurice Newbreet?"

"Yes," Newbury ground out through gritted teeth. "How can I help you?"

"You're to come with me, sir."

"On whose authority?"

The constable frowned at this for a moment. "Well, it was Inspector Foulkes who sent me, sir."

Newbury nodded. God help them all if this was the future of the police force in London. "And where are we going?"

"Islington, sir. There's been a . . . um . . . crime committed."

"I gathered as much, Constable." A sudden thought occurred to him. *Islington.* "A murder?"

"Yes, sir," said the constable, in what he must have assumed was an approximation of a conspiratorial whisper.

"Name?"

"Jessop, sir."

"Not *your* name. The victim."

"I . . . um . . . I'm sorry, sir. I don't know. I was just sent from the Yard to fetch you. Haven't been over there myself yet. Got a carriage waiting down the street, see." He waved in the general direction of a waiting police engine. It was one of the newer, steam-powered varieties. Clearly, Foulkes wanted him there quickly. It didn't look good.

"All right. Run back to the carriage. I'll fetch my things and be with you in just a moment," said Newbury, flicking the butt of his cigarette over the constable's head, where it landed amongst the overgrown leaves in the front garden.

The constable seemed happy to obey this clear and direct instruction. "Very good, sir." He turned and hurried off down the street.

"Is everything quite well, sir?" said a voice behind Newbury as he closed the door.

"I fear not, Scarbright. It looks as though they've got to a dear friend." He edged past Scarbright to collect his jacket and hat from the stand in the hall, fighting back a wave of nausea.

"I'm sorry to hear that, sir. Not—"

"No, not Charles." He pushed his arms into the jacket and made for the door. "I'm afraid the White Friars is off tonight. You understand, I'm sure."

"Of course, sir."

"Very well. Now, go and put your feet up as you promised. I'll be gone for some time."

"Yes, sir. And sir?"

Newbury stopped on the garden path to look back at the valet, framed in the doorway, his features pale with concern. "Yes?"

"Be sure to mind your step."

"I will, Scarbright. I will."

The hollow feeling in the pit of Newbury's stomach intensified with every street as they neared their Islington destination.

Islington.

The place where Professor Angelchrist was hiding.

Had they found him? Had the Queen's killers finally tracked him down? Could Angelchrist be the victim Foulkes was so anxious for him to see? Why else would the inspector summon him across London in such a way?

Newbury sighed. *Too many questions.*

What would it mean for the future, for the Albion Initiative, if Angelchrist was dead? The plan was, after all, Angelchrist's brainchild. Newbury couldn't accept it had all been for nothing. Whatever was waiting for him at that mouldering house—for he was certain now that's where they were going—the plan would continue. It had to. He couldn't allow the Queen to win. Not this time.

The engine belched noisily as they trundled through the heavy morning traffic, barrelling past fist-waving cyclists and horse-drawn cabs, trolley cars and ground trains alike. Black smoke whooshed from the standing pipe at the rear of the vehicle, dusting everything in their wake in a fine layer of soot. Pedestrians lined the pavements, giving the roads a wide berth, jostling and elbowing each other out of the way. Newspaper salesmen bellowed on every corner, while flower girls hawked their wares, and the unscrupulous sold copper tins of "revenant repellent" to unwary tourists. It was a normal day in London, a pointed reminder that, no matter the hand wringing in Whitehall, the fierce debates raging in Parliament, or the subterfuge going on behind the scenes in the palace, Londoners just got on and did what they do best—lived their lives.

To most of these people, those like Newbury—knights and dukes and Whigs and queens—might as well have existed on another plane. They were as real as the characters in books or plays, and their deeds, while consequential to the Empire, were of little import to the majority of people who eked out their lives in the city.

Newbury leaned back in his seat, rubbing his temples with his thumbs. Perspective was a dangerous thing.

"Are you all right, sir?" said Jessop, piping up for the first time since they'd set off.

"What? Yes, yes, just a headache," said Newbury.

'We'll be there in a jiffy," said Jessop. He swallowed, looking a little green around the gills.

"First one?" asked Newbury.

The young man gave a nod.

"It gets easier," said Newbury. "Not that it should. You should always try to remember that they were a person once, like you or I, and afford them the respect they deserve, no matter the circumstances."

"I'll try, sir."

"Good."

The carriage juddered to a halt. Newbury peered out of the window as the driver climbed down from the dickey box. It was as he'd feared: they were sitting outside the dilapidated house that Angelchrist occasionally used as a bolt hole or meeting place. He opened the carriage door and climbed down, smearing his jacket with soot from the carriage's bodywork. He tried unsuccessfully to brush it off.

Two older constables were waiting by the front steps of the house, slouching against the railings. When they saw Newbury and Jessop approaching, they jumped to attention.

"Good morning, sir," said the man on the left.

"If only it were so," said Newbury. The two constables glanced at each other, unsure what else to say. "Is he inside?"

"Yes, sir. He's waiting for you."

Newbury touched the brim of his hat in acknowledgement, and then turned to face the old house. He'd been here several times before, for clandestine planning meetings, laying out the foundations of what would later become known amongst their circle as the Albion Initiative. He'd always said the place was full of ghosts. Now he was here to identify the dead.

Bracing himself, Newbury stepped inside, the young constable close at his heels. Immediately, the familiar, musty odours of damp walls and rotting wood assaulted his nostrils. Yet there was something else there too—something new. A burnt, rich stink. As if someone had left a joint of meat in the oven for too long and it had crisped to a cinder, filling the house with smoke.

"Foulkes?" called Newbury.

"Up here," came the echoing reply. Overhead, floorboards creaked with movement.

Newbury glanced at Jessop. "You can wait down here if you'd rather. There's no shame in it."

Jessop shook his head, once, and then gestured towards the stairs at the end of the hallway. "After you, sir."

Newbury crept up the stairs, his sense of dislocation growing. The world seemed to have narrowed until it included just the four walls of this house, the staircase, each small step.

He found Foulkes waiting for him on the upper landing, a tall, burly, familiar figure. He was wearing his large woollen overcoat, despite the clement weather, and his face was shockingly pale. His eyes met Newbury's, then flicked away. "I'm sorry, Newbury. I wasn't sure . . ." He rubbed a hand over his face. "I thought you'd want to be here. I know you were close."

"It's him?"

Foulkes winced. "We're as certain as we can be, given the circumstances."

"Show me."

Foulkes motioned for him to follow along the landing. He stopped outside a bedroom door. Here, the stench of charred meat was almost unpalatable, thick and oily at the back of Newbury's throat. "In there."

Newbury glanced back at Jessop, who was loitering further back on the landing, hands jammed in his pockets. "Give me a moment," he said to Foulkes.

He ducked into the room.

The body was on the floor beneath the window. The curtains had been pulled open, spilling great shafts of light onto the stark scene below. The room was bare and unfurnished, the wallpaper mildewed and peeling. It was a miserable place to die. Miserable and lonely. Newbury fought back a burgeoning sense of anger. Now was not the time. That would come.

He crossed to the corpse, crouching before it. The flesh was blackened and blistered, the face distorted almost beyond recognition. The man had died screaming, his gums and ears bleeding, his eyeballs boiling in their sockets. The flesh was seared where the electrical discharge had entered his body, so violent that it had puckered the skin, causing the muscles to erupt beneath the flesh. The hair was almost completely gone, and the clothes had burned and partially welded to the molten flesh. It was one of the worst things Newbury had ever seen. There was no question it was the work of August Warlow and his boltheads. And by proxy, the work, too, of Her Majesty the Queen.

"Oh, Archibald," he said, his voice low. "I promise you we'll see this through."

He turned at the sound of footsteps from the door. Jessop was standing there, just inside the door, wide-eyed with disbelief at the horror of the scene before him. He started to say something, but it came out as an incomprehensible noise.

Foulkes, just inside the door, patted the young constable on the shoulder. "Why don't you go and wait outside, Jessop. Sir Maurice will be along shortly."

"I . . . yes, sir," replied Jessop, before turning and hurrying from the room.

Foulkes heaved a heavy sigh. "What's going on, Newbury?"

"Murder," said Newbury, a little sharply. "He's been electrocuted. Assassinated."

"By whom? Similar corpses have been turning up all over the city, but I can't get a single lead or draw a single connection between them. If you've got any insight at all, please—help me."

"Someone is cleaning their house, Foulkes—someone very powerful indeed. Trust me when I tell you that you'd be better served to walk away. You don't want to be a part of this."

"Damn it, Newbury! I've always been a part of this. Can't you see that? Don't shut me out. You think you're helping, keeping me safe? You're not. All you're doing is making my job harder and preventing me from helping my friends. Whatever's going on here, *I'm on your side.*"

"Are you sure about that? Because there's no going back."

Foulkes glowered at him. "Where's Bainbridge? You know I don't believe a word of the charges that they're levelling against him."

Newbury crossed the room. He stood before Foulkes, studying the other man for a moment. "Let me ask you a question. This," he pointed at Angelchrist's corpse, "is it ever justifiable?"

Foulkes frowned. "Well of course not. That's why I do what I do. To bring people to justice. People who do things like this."

"No matter who they are?"

"You know this, Newbury. I'm a goddam *police inspector*. No one is above the law."

"No one?"

"Whoever is responsible for this—no matter who they are—should be brought to justice."

Newbury offered Foulkes a sad smile. "Then I think you should come with me."

"Where? Where are we going?"

"To see an old friend."

CHAPTER 12

Travers and Molesworthy, the two constables who had attended Parker's execution, were taking advantage of a brief reprieve in the weather to smoke cigarettes around the rear of the Yard when Sergeant Quint finally tracked them down. Here, the stink of damp horses and fresh manure was a pungent reminder that the Metropolitan Police Force had yet to fully concede to the oncoming tide of mechanisation that seemed to be washing over most of the Empire, and the capital in particular–Quint could barely walk the streets these days without catching sight of an automata in a shop window, or cross a road without some damnable steam-powered vehicle almost flattening him as it barrelled by. Worse, it seemed to be affecting people's home lives now, too–just the other day, his wife, Laura, had spent almost a week's wages on the purchase of an automated *whisk*. A whisk of all things!

It was a sad thing, what the world was coming to.

"All right, Sergeant?" called Travers, blowing smoke from the corner of his pursed lips. It hung in the damp air, formless and grey.

"Smoke?" said Molesworthy, offering up his crumpled packet.

Quint shook his head. "No, thanks. I don't."

The other two looked at Quint as if reappraising him following this apparently shocking revelation.

"What, not at all?" said Travers.

"Never. But I drink like a fish, so that probably makes up for it."

Travers cracked a grin. "Aye." The grin turned to a narrow-eyed glower of sudden suspicion. "But why're out here with us, if not for the smokes?"

"Got a case," said Quint. "Or at least, I think I have. Wanted to ask you boys for your help."

"What, *us*?" said Molesworthy. "Help *you*?"

"Well, if you're not interested . . . ," said Quint, turning away. "I was just thinking you'd appreciate the good word I'd be able to put in with your sergeant, is all."

He got three steps before Travers's voice cut in, urgent. "Well now, Sergeant Quint. Of course, we'd be only too happy to help, wouldn't we, Molesworthy."

Molesworthy took a long draw on his cigarette. "Of course, we would." Smoke billowed from his nostrils.

"See," added Travers. He perched his cigarette between his lips, folding his arms across his chest. "So, what can we do for you?"

"You were at the hanging the other day. Matthew Parker," said Quint.

"Aye, both of us were," said Molesworthy. "As were you."

Quint nodded. "Did you see what happened to the body?"

"Well, he danced about a bit on the rope," said Molesworthy, "before his lips turned blue like the rest of them." He flicked the butt of his cigarette across the gravel yard. "Never pretty."

"Yes," said Quint, trying not to reacquaint himself with the grisly memory, and failing spectacularly as he conjured the sight in his mind's eye, "I saw that much myself. I mean after they cut him down."

Molesworthy nodded. "Well, after the doctor checked him over and declared him dead, we wheeled him out back on a trolley while all the paperwork was all seen to."

"Surprising amount of paperwork, after a hanging," added Travers.

"And you had a constant eye on him while that was going on?" said Quint.

"Well, 'constant' might be stretching a little far," said Travers. "I can't say I'm overly fond of staring at corpses, especially when they've shit their own trousers like Parker had."

"Most of them do," said Molesworthy, with a knowing nod, as if he were some sage authority on the toileting habits of the dying and deceased.

Quint wrinkled his nose. "I'd heard that." He scratched his chin. "So, if the body had, say, *moved,* then there's a chance you might not have seen it?"

"Moved?" Travers chuckled. "What are you getting at, Quint? This case hasn't got something to do with the undead, has it? I might have to reconsider my offer to help. . . ."

"Or revenants," said Molesworthy, shuddering. "I'm not having anything to do with those bloody things."

Quint sighed. "To be honest, I don't know what I'm dealing with. You know I was one of the team that brought Parker in?" Travers and Molesworthy nodded in unison. "Well, there was something about him."

"A sick bastard," said Molesworthy. "All that 'Matherat' business and eating women's hearts."

"Yes. But more than that. A particular kind of madman. An *individual.* The sort you only come across once in a decade. Or so I've been led to believe. You know what I mean. The sort that sticks with you."

"Aye," said Travers, solemnly. "I know the sort. The ones that haunt you. That work their way under your skin."

"Yes. Well, then you understand. I got to know him. To know what made him tick, how and why he did what he did."

"And you want to make sure he was really dead," said Travers. "Makes sense."

"In a manner of speaking. Thing is—he was seen in Spitalfields the night before last."

Molesworthy laughed. "I think someone must have been on the gin."

Quint sighed. "I thought the same. Until I started asking around. There are multiple witnesses. He wasn't just seen—he tried to attack a woman, too."

"Must have been some other sick bugger," said Travers.

"Someone else who wanted to eat the woman's heart? And who said he was going to sacrifice her to 'Matherat'?"

Travers took another cigarette from his packet, balanced it between his lips, and struck a vesta. "Now that is odd, Quint. I'll give you that. But we saw the man hanged. We *all* did. The doctor pronounced him dead. So, unless there's someone out in Spitalfields with a nice line in necromancy, then I'm not sure what else we can do to help."

"Necromancy," echoed Molesworthy, with a shudder. "You want to be watching yourself, Sergeant. That's a dark business."

"What happens next?" said Quint.

Molesworthy and Travers exchanged a glance.

"Well, I rather think that's up to you," suggested Travers. "But if I were you, I'd leave it well alone."

"No, I mean after all the paperwork is done. You said you wheeled the body through to the adjoining room. What happens after that?"

Travers looked somewhat relieved to be back on firmer ground. "Ah, right. Well, the funeral service comes to collect them."

"Which one?"

"Heron and something, I think. You'd have to check. Old Hodges will know. Same firm every time. Some sort of standing arrangement."

"Hodges?"

"He's the pen pusher who sees to all that stuff. Put out to pasture in the basement by the powers that be. Earned a quiet life, apparently, after a pretty colourful career. Story goes that he once caught a murderer with a mousetrap, or some such nonsense."

Quint shook his head. He resisted the urge to prompt Travers to relate the story. He'd be there all morning if he didn't press on. "Thanks." A thought occurred to him. "Did Hodges attend Parker's execution? It's just that I noticed an old man in a hat, and wondered . . ."

"Oh, *him,*" said Molesworthy. "No, that's not Hodges. Hodges doesn't like to see 'em swing. Says it gives him indigestion."

Quint narrowed his eyes. "But you know this old man regardless?"

"No. That's just it," said Travers. "He's shown up, regular as clockwork, at maybe the last nine or ten executions. No one seems to know who he is, and he keeps himself very much to himself. Apparently, he's got all the right papers to be allowed into the gallery, though. I heard he's been cleared by Sir Charles himself."

"Odd though," said Quint. "Coming to spectate like that."

"Isn't it just," agreed Travers. He shrugged. "Sorry we couldn't be more help."

"Not at all," said Quint. "You've been very helpful indeed. Tell me—where will I find Hodges?"

"He's got an office in the basement," said Molesworthy. "Close to the site of the gallows."

"Thanks." Quint nodded his appreciation.

"Just you mind yourself, Sergeant," said Travers, as Quint turned to leave. "Molesworthy's right. You don't want to go getting yourself mixed up in any ugly business. Dead should stay dead, in my opinion."

"Oh, I wholeheartedly agree," called Quint over his shoulder, as he crossed the courtyard towards the main building, his feet crunching on the loose gravel.

Down here, in the bowels of the Yard, Quint always felt somewhat claustrophobic and hemmed in. He never reacted that way to the dank tunnels of the Underground, or when navigating the narrow alleyways and snickets that criss-crossed the arterial streets of the capital. It was only here, down amongst the glossy tiled walls, surrounded by the stink of dust and old polish, that he felt his hackles rising, like the walls were closing in.

Of course, there'd been that horrible business with Dr. Finnegan a few months back, when the whole place had to be shut down and fumigated to remove all traces of some dreadful contagion the man had contracted from a corpse—but it wasn't that, either, as nasty as it had been. Quint supposed his distaste for the place was more to do with what it represented. Down here was a place of ending.

He supposed in many ways it was a form of limbo—that anyone forced to exist down here had in some way entered a transitory state, waiting for the walls of their old life to crumble.

Just like Travers had said, old policemen came here to end their careers in the dark and quiet, away from the front lines. Criminals were brought here to await transfer to more permanent cells. Bodies were brought here for dissection and examination. And those who had committed the most heinous crimes came here to die, just like Parker.

To Quint's mind, nothing good happened down in these dingy corridors and rooms, and judging by the atmosphere, even the building itself seemed to know it.

Or perhaps it was just his imagination.

He found the door he'd been looking for. Hodges's name was engraved neatly in a small brass plaque attached to the wood: S. B. HODGES.

Quint knocked briskly, then swung the door open and stepped through.

"Did I say you could come in?" snapped the old man on the other side, who was stooping so low that his head was effectively buried in whatever ledger he was examining on the desk before him. He looked up, peering myopically through the thick lenses of his glasses. So, *this* was the famed pen pusher that Travers had mentioned.

Quint was taken aback by the state of the place. The room looked more like a library than an office—and one where all the books had been pulled unceremoniously off the shelves and heaped upon the floor in disarray. Dust swirled about his boots. He thought he could smell rodent droppings.

"Hmmm?" prompted Hodges.

"Um, sorry," mumbled Quint. "I didn't mean to disturb you."

"Didn't mean . . . ," echoed Hodges. He shook his head. "Well, you did, young man. If you'd shown a little patience and waited in the hall until I'd called you in, then I'd never have lost count."

Quint couldn't quite see what the difference was, between knocking and opening the door, but the man evidently wanted to make his point. "I see. Next time, I'll do as you ask."

"Yes, well," muttered Hodges. "See that you do." He pushed his glasses up to the bridge of his nose and sniffed. Loudly. "Now, what can I do for you, Sergeant Quint."

"You know who I am?"

"I *was* a detective, you know. And besides, it's my *job* to know."

"It is?"

Hodges drummed his fingers on the desk. "So . . . ?"

"Travers sent me your way. Said you'd know the name of the funeral service who collects the bodies of the . . . um . . . criminals who have been hung on the premises."

Hodges's fingers ceased their drumming. He cocked his head like a contemplative dog. "Travers, eh." He nodded slowly. "Interesting. Why would the likes of you be interested in the likes of them?"

"Travers?" said Quint.

"The *funeral service*," replied Hodges.

"It's for a case I'm investigating."

"What case? No case file relating to the funeral service in question has crossed my desk."

Quint recognised this for what it was—or at least what he *thought* it was—Hodges was angling for information. He'd probably been stuck down here for days with no one to talk to and didn't want to let his valuable snippet of information go too easily, not if he could draw it out, have a bit of fun with it and learn the gossip. Who could blame him if he was a little lonely down here, pushing paper day in, day out?

"There isn't a file, as yet," said Quint. "But there will be. I'm interested in what happened to the body of Matthew Parker after he was cut down from the gallows. Either he didn't die like we all thought he did, or we've got someone who looks very much like him attempting to re-create his crimes."

"Dead man walking, eh?" said Hodges. He moistened his lips with his tongue. He appeared to be missing several front teeth, and the tip of his tongue was yellowed with tobacco stains. "Strange business, that. Not the first time, neither."

Quint perked up at that. "It's not?"

"A couple of years back, now," said Hodges. He closed the ledger he'd been looking at with great ceremony, stirring a plume of dust. "Woman by the name of Shaw. Phyllis Shaw." He lowered himself into a huge captain's chair behind the desk, shuffling until he was comfortable. The chair seemed to dwarf him.

"Another prisoner who was hung?" ventured Quint.

"Sharp one, aren't you?" said Hodges, tapping the side of his nose with his finger and chuckling to himself. "Aye. And hung twice for her sins."

"Twice?"

"You heard me."

"So, she survived the first attempt."

Hodges nodded. "Not that we knew it at the time. She took the drop like all the others, hissing and spitting like a cat all the way up to the noose. She was a vicious one, that's for sure."

"What was her crime?" asked Quint.

"Boiled her sister alive in the bathtub for flirting with her husband."

Quint frowned. "That sounds . . . difficult to pull off."

"Not when you have one of those new-fangled tubs with the built-in heating element," said Hodges, with—Quint couldn't help feeling—something a little too akin to glee.

"I see," said Quint. "And you saw her hung?"

"Aye," said Hodges. "One of the last I did. Haven't the stomach for 'em, me. But we were certain she was dead. We cut her down and the doctor signed the death certificate. All standard procedures. They wheeled her out back and Herod & Co.—that's the funeral service you were asking about—picked her up and carted her right off to their morgue."

"So, what happened? How did she survive?"

Hodges shrugged. "The doctor made a mistake. She was badly bruised, but she wasn't dead. There was an inquiry, of course. I heard stories about an inadequately tied noose. . . ."

"She woke up in the funeral parlour, then?"

"No, no. She didn't even make it that far. She must have come to in the back of the cart they were transporting her in. Fought her way out of the wooden crate and up over the side. She was away down the street before any of them even realised what had happened. Gave old Herod a terrible fright."

"I don't doubt it," said Quint. Was this what could have happened to Parker? Another medical error. A poorly tied noose that didn't quite do the job. It was the only thing that made sense. But how could so many people get it so wrong? "What happened next?"

"They picked her up at the docks, trying to buy passage onto a ship to New York. She didn't have the right papers and was brewing up a stink. Almost clawed the eyes out of the ticket agent."

"So, she was brought back to try again."

Hodges nodded. "The gallows weren't as forgiving, next time around. Snapped her neck on the way down. Or so I'm told."

Quint shuddered. "And you think the same thing could have happened with Parker?"

"God knows," said Hodges. "I don't *think* anything. Who am I to speculate? But I don't see what else could have gone on.

Unless the mortician has been dabbling in the occult sciences, of course. . . ."

"Don't *you* start," said Quint. "I've had enough of that from Travers and Molesworthy."

Hodges snorted. "Doesn't surprise me. But then very little does, these days." He stood up, dusting his hands together, and then opened his ledger. "Right."

Quint watched for a moment, wondering if Hodges was going to say anything more.

After a moment, the man looked up from his ledger, frowned, and waved dismissively at the door. "Well, go on then. Sod off. You've got what you need."

Ah, there it is, thought Quint, grinning as he turned to the door. "Thank you, Hodges," he said, with only a hint of a laugh.

CHAPTER 13

"So, this Warlow character—he's working for the *Queen*?"

Inspector Foulkes was sitting heavily in one of the dusty armchairs in Julian Wren's living room, forehead furrowed in a deep frown, jaw clenched so tightly that the muscles bunched beneath his bristly beard. He looked decidedly on edge.

Bainbridge was pacing by the hearth, while Newbury and Veronica sat beside one another on the sofa. Veronica's hand rested lightly on Newbury's forearm, as if to steady him, or perhaps to discourage him from joining the discussion until the other men had finished what they had to say. The atmosphere was taut, palpable.

"Precisely that," said Bainbridge. "A fixer. A hired killer charged with eliminating anyone who has anything to do with the government department we refer to as 'the Secret Service.' Operatives, ministers, agents, administrators—they're all turning up dead, executed by Warlow's so-called 'boltheads.'"

"So *that's* what links all the victims," said Foulkes. "But why? Surely their goals are aligned with those of the monarch. Protecting the Empire and her subjects, upholding the law . . . ?" He trailed off.

Bainbridge chewed on the stem of his pipe. "That's just it. Were she in her right mind, she'd see that the Service in no way poses a threat to the monarchy. They're not—*we're* not—the enemy. Or at least we weren't, until she fashioned a conflict out of thin air. Now we're forced to act to protect ourselves."

"I don't understand," said Foulkes. "What's driving this?"

"Her Majesty's descent into paranoia is near complete. She cannot bear the thought that her pronouncements might be challenged or undermined in any way—that there are agents in the field who do not answer directly to her, who she cannot manipulate or control. There's been a clandestine war brewing for some time, between the Queen's agents and those she feels might pose a risk to her position. It's utterly unfounded, but the woman is beyond reason."

"Beyond reason? Sir Charles—you sound as if you're implying that she's no longer fit to rule?" Foulkes looked astounded at the very thought.

"That's exactly what I mean to say. If you'd seen what she's become, Foulkes, you might begin to understand the depths of her depravity. She clings to life to the exclusion of all else, eking out a paltry existence inside that gloomy audience chamber. She's more mechanical than human. She never sleeps, never engages with her family, her loved ones. I wonder now if she's even capable of such sentiment. She's nothing but a power-mad despot determined to hold onto her Empire at all costs."

"But you've worked for her for years. You told me as much. You and Sir Maurice both." Foulkes turned his gaze on Newbury, lost in incomprehension.

"Aye," said Bainbridge. "And shame on us for our part in it. We were blinded by our faith, our patriotism. We couldn't see how far she'd fallen. We did not *want* to see." He turned away, facing the fire, his back to them. "The things she's done, Foulkes. The things I've done in her name . . ."

"But now is the time to put things right," said Newbury, cutting in. "That thing in the palace is no longer the Queen. Not as I once knew her. It's an abomination that's taken her form, corrupted her from within. A shell of what once was. I feel no guilt at having served the Crown for the betterment of my people.

Those were not wasted years. But now, to turn a blind eye to her machinations would be to condone far worse than mere murder. It would be to endorse the suicide of an entire nation."

He fell silent, allowing his words to sink in. Foulkes looked as if he'd been punched in the gut.

"I concur."

Newbury looked around to see the Prince of Wales coming through the door from the adjoining room. He was smoking a fat cigar, regarding the scene in the living room through sharp, hooded eyes.

Foulkes scrambled to his feet. "Your Highness!"

The Prince waved him back to his seat. "We'll dispense with the ceremony, if you please. After all, it hardly seems appropriate, given our surroundings. What was your name again?"

"Foulkes, Your Highness. Inspector Foulkes, of Scotland Yard."

"Foulkes. Very well. Then I suppose that if Sir Charles is prepared to vouch for you, you have my trust in this matter, also."

"He's a good man," said Bainbridge. "He'll be a great help with what's to come."

Foulkes lowered himself back into the armchair. The ancient springs groaned. "What do you mean? What *is* to come?"

"We mean to remove the Queen from her position, to enable the Prince to take his rightful place as king," said Veronica. "To put a stop to all of this once and for all."

"You're talking about regicide!"

"We're talking about nothing of the sort," said the Prince. "We merely intend to encourage my mother to retire. A gentle nudge in the direction of her abdication. This sorry mess has gone on long enough. The truth is, Inspector, the Queen is dying. If it weren't for all the chemicals they're pumping into her, or the machines that inflate her lungs, she'd have been dead and buried long ago." He held up a hand to discourage any protestation from Foulkes. "I don't mean to imply that I wish her ill, you understand. Merely that the ministrations of these doctors have taken something of a toll on my mother's well-being. As Sir Charles has so colourfully explained, her mind is not what it was. I have no doubt that this whole business is the result of those same life-preserving chemicals, unbalancing her from within, clouding her judgement. What she needs is *care*, a place to rest and to see out her last days in peace. That place is not in the midst of a clandestine civil war."

"I see," said Foulkes. "And presumably Professor Angelchrist was the architect of this plan?"

Bainbridge winced at the mention of Angelchrist's name. He hadn't taken the news well when Newbury and Foulkes had first arrived at the house. Even now, he looked gaunt and drawn, his face under-lit by the soft glow of the embers in the grate. He clearly felt Angelchrist's loss acutely, both personally and professionally; it now fell to Bainbridge to assume command of the operation. It seemed their sponsors in the government were either dead or had grown remarkably quiet since Warlow's campaign against the Service had begun. There had always been an understanding amongst them that, should the Secret Service ever be compromised, the corridors of Whitehall would remain silent on the subject, invoking, if pressed, what they liked to refer to as "plausible deniability." Or, as Newbury understood it, outright lies.

"That's right. The Albion Initiative," said Bainbridge. "We'd always considered it a plan of last resort. A failsafe, if you like, to protect the Empire against a rogue monarch. We never thought we'd find ourselves neck deep in the midst of it."

"And now it falls to you?"

"It falls to *all* of us," said the Prince, before Bainbridge had a chance to reply. "I do hope you'll find it within yourself to help us, Inspector. The fate of the nation is, after all, at stake."

Foulkes seemed to shrink in on himself, buckling under the sudden pressure. It was a terrible thing to put on a man, but Foulkes was one of the best that Newbury knew. He would do the right thing. Newbury was certain of it.

"Very well," said Foulkes. "What do you need from me?"

"Good man," said Bainbridge, turning away from the fireplace.

"For now, nothing," said Newbury. "Your murder enquiry will go unsolved. The Queen will see to that. Make certain you do not push too hard, or you might discover she pushes back, harder. When the time comes, we'll need your help to take down Warlow."

"And Sir Charles? We cannot leave things as they stand. He's a wanted man." Foulkes looked to the Prince. "Surely the Prince could see to a pardon?"

"In time," said the Prince, "of course. But you must remember that I, too, am a fugitive, at least for the time being. My word in this matter is worthless and would only act to antagonise my mother further."

"Besides," added Veronica, "it suits our needs to have Sir Charles remain here, in safety. With the Professor gone, we need him free to operate without fear of interference."

Foulkes nodded. "So, my role is to keep the baying hounds away. I see."

"Thank you, Foulkes," said Bainbridge. "It'll all be over soon. A few more days while we get word to our allies, then we'll make our move."

"Very well," said Foulkes. He got to his feet. "I'd best be on my way. I've a murder investigation to stall."

"We'll share a cab," said Newbury. "I have an errand to run."

"And I need to get word to . . . um . . . Constance," said Veronica. "To appraise her of our plans." She glanced at Bainbridge. "You'll be all right here for a time?"

Bainbridge waved her away. "It's valuable work you're doing, Miss Hobbes. Be off with you. I shall remain with the Prince. We'll reconvene here tomorrow. Foulkes?"

"I'll be here," said Foulkes.

"Excellent. Then be on your guard, all of you. And remember—the walls have eyes. We can trust no one with this." He tapped the upturned bowl of his pipe against the mantelpiece, shaking free a shower of dottles. "No one at all."

CHAPTER 14

The card snapped down on the worn floorboard before him, revealing the image of a misanthropic figure with a tatty tricorn hat and a toothy grin, sitting by a set of crossroads with an empty wooden bowl on his lap.

The Thrice-Cursed Beggar. Hardly fortuitous. It joined *The Fallen Knight* and a reversed *Hierophant of Thorns* as part of a grouping. The signs were ominous.

Newbury sat back, rolling his tense shoulders as he regarded the brightly coloured cards before him. There were two more still to place. Nothing was certain yet.

He chewed his lip, thoughtful. Should he continue? He'd often wondered if the very act of consulting the *Crux Occultus*—of drawing a spread from the pack in this way—had the unwelcome effect of coalescing the future in a certain direction, like the gravitational pull of a heavenly body, dragging possibilities into its orbit. As if, by seeking a way ahead, a path through the gloom, he forced one such path to snap into tight focus, pushing all others aside.

Perhaps now, of all times, he needed the future to remain mutable. But that sense of surety, the conviction that what he was doing was *right*—he missed it terribly. It was a weakness, he knew, to require such a crutch. But the certainty of his youth had long given way to the cynicism of his middle age. Or perhaps it was just his experiences that had worn him down.

Long gone were days in which his faith was an unshakeable thing, when the word of the monarch had been enough to ensure his unfaltering—his *unquestioning*—obedience. When a single command had been enough to evoke his sense of duty, to enable him to put all his doubts and reservations aside. To blind him to the truth.

The visions had helped, as difficult as they were to bear. And he'd only carried their burden for six months. Amelia had lived with them for nearly *twenty years*. How the woman was still sane, he did not know. Now, though, she was a picture of health—following her encounter with the transformative spores cultivated by Julian Wren—and thus the need for his own, somewhat primitive treatment, had passed. The transference rituals had come to an end. Meaning his own clairvoyant seizures had ceased now, too.

It had been that acute loss that had driven him back to the *Crux Occultus*, a pursuit he had otherwise given up some years ago, unsure of its efficacy and concerned over its evident flaws. And yet here he was, sitting on the floor in his private study, the carpet rolled back to reveal the chalk-marked floorboards, the drapes pulled shut and the only light coming from a brace of white-stemmed candles he had placed upon the cold hearth. They guttered now in the draught from under the door. Scarbright was moving around in the hallway.

"I'll be down presently, Scarbright," called Newbury, hoping to head off any intended intrusion on behalf of the valet.

"Very good, sir," came the muffled reply. "I'll have a fresh pot of Earl Grey waiting." The shadows beneath the door shifted, and a moment later Scarbright was gone.

Newbury returned to the deck of undrawn cards. He reached for them, then hesitated, his fingertips brushing the filigreed back of the uppermost card. Then, coming to a decision, he drew it, flipped it, and placed it beside the others in the spread.

The Broken Chain.

His breath seemed to catch in his throat. He considered the card's meaning: *the end of things; a severance.*

The words of the terrified patient in Bedlam came back to him with startling clarity: "*It's all going to end.*"

Newbury moistened his dry lips.

But an end to what? Was the card's meaning literal or symbolic? Could it be that his remaining time was now being measured— that Warlow and his monstrous slaves would soon be clamouring at Newbury's door? Or was Her Majesty's time on the throne finally drawing to a close—was this indicative that the Albion Initiative might actually succeed?

Doubts tumbled through his mind. Perhaps it was something else entirely. His friendship with Charles. His ... *relationship* with Veronica. They were all of them playing a very dangerous game, and there was every chance *something* would go wrong. *The Broken Chain* might indicate any one such outcome.

Perhaps the final card would bring clarity.

He flipped it over; placed it with the others in a line.

The Squire and the Sword.

The picture of a peasant man in mediaeval dress, drawing a shining sword from where it was embedded in a large, grey stone. It was redolent of the fanciful tales of King Arthur—the boy made king by virtue of such a feat, drawing the blade from the anvil or stone to the incredulity of all.

The future King Edward, perhaps? Is that what it represented here?

Sighing, Newbury reached for the glass of Malbec he'd placed beside the candles on the hearth. The acrid wine seemed to coat his tongue as he swallowed, the slightly bitter taste of the laudanum tincture promising welcome distraction.

Yet the spread of cards before him were refusing to give up their truths.

The Fallen Knight. The Hierophant of Thorns. The Thrice-Cursed Beggar. The Broken Chain. The Squire and the Sword.

What story did they tell?

There was one man he knew who might be able to help make sense of it all: Aldous Renwick.

Newbury stood, abandoning the wine glass on the floor. "Scarbright?" he called, heading for the door. "I won't be needing that tea."

Aldous Renwick ran a small bookshop across town: a ramshackle affair, filled to bursting with dusty tomes and crumbling story papers, bundles of letters and illustrated plates; the literary detritus of years. Newbury loved everything about the place—the musty odour of the mouldering books, the higgledy-piggledy disorder of the bookshelves, the fact that the place rarely seemed to be inhabited by anyone *but* Renwick, whose strange implanted eye and shock of wild hair seemed enough to send any prospective customers scuttling back to Charing Cross Road and the safety of the more respectable outlets. One might wonder how Renwick made an income from such an ill-maintained venture, but Newbury well understood the truth—that the books were mere decoration, the furnishings that Renwick desired to surround himself with while he went about his real work—advising people like Newbury on all matters pertaining to the esoteric or occult.

It had turned into something of a small industry for Renwick, who worked out of a large back room where he brewed strange elixirs on a still made from glass bottles, rods, and gas burners, and kept all of his most essential volumes within close reach. He'd taken to writing small monographs on subjects such as "The Inner Spirit Life of the Beaker People of South-West Britain," "The Divine Paths of Ancient Man," "Landscape as Memory," and "Cernos: The Forgotten God." Newbury had read them all, and understood Renwick to be a true Hermeticist, combining his knowledge of both science and the spiritual into a holistic worldview that, while he didn't always agree with it, had proved infinitely insightful on numerous occasions. The last he'd spoken to Renwick, his friend was deep at work on a new study, involving the bodies of Anglo-Saxon people preserved in peat bogs and an attempt to distil their spiritual essence from their remains.

So it was that, upon arrival at the shop, Newbury was astounded to find an actual customer milling about inside, perusing the stacks.

The woman looked up as the bell chimed, and Newbury caught her eye, offering her a lopsided smile. She returned the smile with an amused expression of her own, before returning to her browsing.

Renwick, of course, was nowhere to be seen.

Newbury circled around the heaped stacks of books and rapped his knuckles against the wooden door behind the counter. When no one replied, he put his ear to the door. Something, presumably a new concoction, was bubbling away on the still. He pushed the door open and stepped through.

Renwick was sitting with his back to the door, a thin trail of wispy smoke rising from the tip of a cigarette he held pursed between his lips. As anticipated, the still was busily cooking up some unusual pink fluid–Renwick's answer to tea–and the room seemed even more cramped with books and curios than usual.

As Newbury stepped through the door, however, he was forced to dance hurriedly to one side as Renwick, spinning around in his chair, gave a little yelp and depressed the trigger of the crossbow-like weapon he held on his lap, which spat out a high-velocity bolt. It buried itself in the doorframe a few inches from Newbury's chest before fizzing and crackling with electrical discharge delivered via two trailing wires, still connected to the bolt that was wedged in the now-smouldering door.

"Newbury!"

"Aldous."

"Pull it out, quickly, before the fire takes."

"What?"

"The bolt! Pull it out of the doorframe. Do you know how flammable a shop full of books can be?"

Incredulous, Newbury used the sleeve of his jacket to pluck the deadly bolt from the scorched wood. He handed it back to Renwick. "You might have killed me."

"That was rather the point."

Newbury frowned. "You *meant* to kill me?"

Renwick blew smoke from his nostrils. "Not you. Someone else. I thought you were them."

"Right." Newbury shook his head. "You have a customer out there, by the way."

Renwick's remaining eye widened. "Blonde woman. Short. Hazel-coloured eyes?"

"Yes, that's the one. How did you know?"

"That's not a customer, Newbury. That's the person I was waiting for."

"You were going to *kill* her?" Newbury was having a hard time following.

"Of course!"

"Might I ask why you were so intent on murdering the only customer you've had in this shop for nigh on ten years?" asked Newbury.

"She's not a customer," replied Renwick.

"Then . . . ?"

"An assassin," said Renwick.

"An *assassin*?" repeated Newbury.

Renwick nodded slowly, setting his wild grey hair off in a performative dance atop his head. "Yes. It seems I have . . . upset some members of a Danish revivalist cult."

"You must have done more than *upset* them if they're sending assassins to your door, Aldous."

Renwick shrugged. "You know how these things are."

"I do," said Newbury, with feeling. He turned back to the door, reached for the handle. "Let's see about this assassin then, shall we . . ."

"Leave it," said Renwick. He stood, tossing the crossbow

device on the workbench and wiping his hands on the front of his leather smock. "She'll be gone by now. I suspect she'll try again tomorrow." He shrugged.

Newbury removed his hand from the doorknob. "You don't sound particularly troubled by the notion."

"What will be, will be," said Renwick. More smoke curled from his flared nostrils. "Tea?"

Newbury laughed. "No one could claim we lead boring lives, old friend." He pulled out a chair and dropped into it. "Make it the good stuff, would you?"

A short while later, they both sat with steaming cups, Newbury sipping Earl Grey, while Renwick sampled another glass beaker full of his odd pink brew.

"That's an impressive weapon you have there," said Newbury, indicating the crossbow with a nod of his head.

Renwick swallowed a mouthful of his drink, then gave a visible shudder. "I got the idea from Sir Charles's cane," he said, placing his beaker on the workbench between them, patting the crossbow with no small amount of pride. "A conducting bolt that delivers a short, sharp discharge of electricity. If the bolt doesn't kill them, the shock should be enough to stop their heart."

"How pleasant."

Renwick shrugged. "Needs must." He fixed Newbury with his implanted eye. The red dot seemed to swim in the black void of the socket like a lone star on a clear night. "But this isn't a social call, is it?"

"I don't suppose they ever are," said Newbury, "and for that I apologise."

Renwick gave a dismissive wave. "We all have our lives to lead. Now, what is it? I've rarely seen you so distracted." He leaned forward in his creaking chair. "Or so healthy, at least in recent months. You've stopped the ritual."

Newbury nodded. "No longer necessary. Amelia is healed. The exposure to Julian Wren's mutated spores appears to have had a positive, lasting effect."

"Fascinating," said Renwick. "And so . . ."

Newbury shrugged. "I read the cards."

Renwick smiled. "I could have guessed as much. And now you don't like what you saw?"

"It's not that. It's just . . . I'm unsure how to interpret the spread." He reached into his jacket and withdrew the five cards, tossing them over to Renwick.

Renwick studied them for a moment. "Yes, I see what you mean." He examined the cards again, one-by-one, then held up *The Fallen Knight.* "This one speaks for itself. You as caster must accept your own part in proceedings."

"Yes, but *fallen*?"

"The acorn must fall from the oak if it is to begin a new life of its own," said Renwick. "Don't be too literal in your interpretation. It merely means that you must prepare yourself to be cast far from what you have known before. What seemed solid may soon prove to be built on sand."

Newbury nodded. "All right. Then what of the others?"

Renwick held up *The Thrice-Cursed Beggar.* "Harder, this one, but at a pinch I'd say your new king is in for something of a surprise."

"How do you know—"

Renwick held up a hand to stop him. "A break-in at Bedlam, the palace suppressing the story. You, here now, with these cards . . ."

"Very well."

Renwick grinned. "This one," he said, "*The Hierophant of Thorns.* It speaks of a threat. A man or woman who whispers in the ear of those who would endow him with power. Grouped this way, with the other two cards—it suggests someone means you and your new king harm."

"August Warlow," said Newbury. "The Queen's bulldog. He's already come after Angelchrist."

"Then you should watch your back," said Renwick. "His placement in the spread means he's close."

"I shall be on my guard," said Newbury.

"No. It's more than that. You must be on the offensive. You must be ready to play the Hierophant at his own game. Anything less than that and you may find yourself ensnared in his thorns."

Newbury shuddered. "What of *The Broken Chain*?"

Renwick looked at the card and seemed to weigh it up for a moment. "Change is coming."

"But what sort of change?"

Renwick shrugged. "Change is not a bad thing, Newbury. Stagnancy is what ends empires and fells kings and queens. You of all people should know that. *The Broken Chain* might merely represent a freeing from the past—a breaking loose of those things that bind. Often, it is a sign of transgression and forward momentum—the choices from which you cannot come back. But that isn't inherently troubling. Or at least it shouldn't be. We all need to move on, sooner or later."

"I suppose we do."

"And then there's this," said Renwick, holding up the final card. "*The Squire and the Stone.* A warning to expect the unexpected. Not all will go as you or others have planned."

"Unexpected?"

"Yes," said Renwick. He reached over and plunged the tip of his cigarette into the flame of a burner, before taking another long draw on it, dry tobacco crisping as he dragged the smoke into his lungs. "Like the boy, Arthur, who claimed the throne by drawing the sword in the stories. Something you can't foresee."

Newbury laughed. "What's the point of a set of supposed fortune-telling cards that can't foresee anything?"

Renwick finished his cigarette and dropped the butt to the floor. "My advice is to not disregard anything. You're playing with fire, Newbury, and you know what that means. . . ."

"That I'm likely to get burned?"

"No," said Renwick, laughing. "That you're likely to burn the whole bloody place down around you."

Newbury stood, collecting the cards from the workbench. "Thank you, Aldous." Renwick nodded, but he'd already turned his attention back to the crossbow before him. "Be mindful of those assassins," added Newbury, aware how ridiculous the whole thing sounded—but then, with Renwick, ridiculous was a relatively normal state of affairs. "If you need me, you know where I'll be."

"In the midst of trouble," said Renwick, with a sly grin.

CHAPTER 15

The room was full of coffins.

New and unused, they shone with a patina of polish and brass, propped open so as to appear inviting, with plush, cushioned interiors and velvet-lined lids: empty, yet filled with the dreadful promise of future occupation. Sergeant Quint found them a stark reminder that even in death all men were far from equal—at least when it came to the quality of the box in which they would rot.

He walked the room, which was decorated to resemble a drawing room or parlour, taken aback by the sheer variety of options on offer—teak, mahogany, oak—none of them even close to the humble pine affair he'd seen his father buried in just a few years earlier. It seemed to Quint that Herod and Co. catered to a more salubrious class of deceased, well beyond the means of the humble policeman. So, what on Earth were they doing taking on contracts to handle executed criminals from the Yard?

He heard a polite cough from over his shoulder and turned to see a tall, thin man in a top hat. His jacket was unbuttoned, and he was wearing a smart waistcoat beneath, crossed with the silver chain of a pocket watch. He had a neat beard and a welcoming smile.

"It can be difficult to know what's best," he said, his voice soft and respectful.

"I'm sorry?" said Quint, baffled by the man's apparent non sequitur.

"Choosing a coffin," said the man. "So many different options, one can find it quite baffling. But perhaps I can help. Was the deceased a close relation?"

Quint laughed, eliciting a concerned look from the other man. "Mr. Herod, I presume?"

"Yes . . . but . . ."

"I'm not here to choose a coffin, Mr. Herod. Or to engage your services for a funeral. My name is Quint. I'm with Scotland Yard."

"You are?" said Herod, frowning.

"I am." He glanced around. "Is there somewhere more private we could talk? I'll try not to take up too much of your time."

Herod looked uncertain. "Well, yes, we could go downstairs, but I must—"

"Yes, yes, Mr. Herod. Please, lead the way."

"If you insist . . ."

Herod beckoned him to follow, passing through a discreet door at the rear of the showroom and down a flight of stone steps into a well-lit, tiled basement. The stink of carbolic stung Quint's nostrils almost as soon as he closed the door behind him, and as he approached the bottom step, his stomach almost turned. He'd made a grave error, cutting the other man off mid-sentence. Herod had brought him to a mortuary. What was more, there was a decidedly ripe human corpse laid out on one of three marble slabs—an elderly woman, naked and rotund, her lily-white face contorted in a horrible, rictus smile.

"Umm, excuse me for just a moment," said Herod, crossing to the slab to grab a white cotton sheet from a trolley, which he laid respectfully over the corpse. "There you are, Mrs. Monroe," he said quietly, as if the simple act of covering her had somehow spirited her away into the afterlife, like a stage magician making his assistant disappear with a flourish of silken cloth.

Quint swallowed back acidic bile. "So, this is where you prepare the bodies," he said, gesturing to the room.

It was a cavernous space, far larger than the building above would suggest, tiled in glazed white porcelain that had, in places, begun to fade to brown. It was equipped very much like the police morgue, with three marble slabs to accommodate multiple customers, drainage channels cut into the stone floor, and an array of workbenches and trolleys scattered around the edges of the space. They were heaped with vicious-looking tools and apparatus, some of which looked startlingly mechanical. A large double-fronted cupboard stood against the far wall, presumably to house supplies of chemicals and other necessary equipment.

"Yes. That's what I was trying to tell you," said Herod. "If you'd rather we went back upstairs . . . ?" The man seemed genuinely concerned. Evidently, Quint had singularly failed to disguise his revulsion. He was starting to wonder if he was really cut out for this policing business. Following a trail, searching out clues, narrowing down the pool of likely suspects–he revelled in all of that. But why did there always have to be so many *dead* people? He didn't think he'd ever get used to it.

"So . . . *Inspector* Quint?" said Herod, clearly feeling somewhat anxious about the reason for Quint's visit.

"Sergeant," corrected Quint.

Herod nodded. "What can I do for you?"

"I'm just following up a lead, is all, and I'm hoping you can help me."

"I'll do my level best," said Herod, straightening his tie, as if the thought of helping the police was a matter of some pride to the man.

"Well–I understand you have an arrangement with the Yard to . . . *deal with* the bodies of executed prisoners after their sentence has been carried out," said Quint.

"That's right," said Herod. "I'm proud to say that it's a long-standing agreement. We've handled such arrangements for Scotland Yard for some years."

Quint nodded. He glanced at the corpse of the woman on the slab, and then wished he hadn't. Even beneath the cotton sheet he could see that unsettling grin, almost as if she were laughing at her own terrible fate. Or at him. He fixed his gaze on Herod.

"They often come in like that," said Herod. "Poor things. It's our job—me and my apprentice, David—to try to make them presentable for the family."

Quint shook his head in disbelief. *Where would you even start?* "How . . ." he began, before thinking better of it and diverting his question in a different direction. He really *didn't* need to know. "I mean to say: what happens to the bodies after you collect them?"

Herod pushed a finger under the brim of his hat, scratching at an itch. "They're brought here for dressing and disposal."

"You hold funerals for them?"

"It depends very much on the circumstances. What the family requires . . ."

Or what they can afford, considered Quint. "I'm interested in a particular prisoner, a recently executed man named Matthew Parker. You'll have collected his remains several days ago."

"I remember," said Herod, his voice level. "We'd previously attended to some of his victims. He was a . . . *disturbed* man."

Quite the understatement. "Yes, he was certainly that," agreed Quint. "Did *he* have a funeral?"

Herod gave a brisk shake of his head. "No. There was no family or friends. Or at least none that wanted anything to do with him. His body was simply processed and disposed of."

"Buried?"

"Cremated," said Herod.

"Is that typical?" asked Quint.

"In those sorts of circumstances, yes—when there's no interested party. It's efficient."

Quint rubbed his chin thoughtfully. "Yes, I can see that," he said. "So, there's no evidence that the body was destroyed? Besides a handful of ashes, I mean."

Herod pursed his lips. His cheeks flushed, as if insulted. "What is this about, Sergeant?"

"I'm simply trying to ascertain what became of Parker's corpse, Mr. Herod. The thing is, a man matching his description has been seen in the area, and I merely want to rule out any complications."

"*Complications?* I can assure you, Sergeant, that corpses aren't in the habit of simply getting back up and walking off into the night."

"Not even those infected by the revenant plague?" said Quint.

"Ah, well. A different matter, perhaps. But that certainly wasn't the case with Matthew Parker. I saw to it myself. The body was collected from Scotland Yard and transported here in the rear of our wagon. Less than an hour later I had David help me to place it in an unadorned box–following instructions from Scotland Yard that there was to be no funeral ceremony–and committed it to the flames. It was all over rather quickly."

"And you checked he was dead?" said Quint.

Herod smiled. "He was most definitely dead, Sergeant. And if he wasn't before, I can assure you he was afterwards." His eyes flashed in amusement. "I am, of course, pulling your leg. You'll have to forgive the gallows humour. It's a necessary release, given the work we do."

"Hmmm," mumbled Quint.

"So, yes, I can confirm that the body was lifeless, just as the death certificate stated. Asphyxiation by hanging. We saw no need to perform an autopsy. The body was disposed of quickly and efficiently, leaving us more time to attend to more worthy customers." Herod glanced at Mrs. Monroe as if to underline his point. "Speaking of which . . ."

"Yes, of course," said Quint. "I'll leave you to your business. Thank you for your time." He indicated the stairs. "I'll see myself out." He started towards them, then stopped at the bottom and glanced back. "Tell me–what is it that led you to seek out the contract with Scotland Yard? You'll forgive me for observing that the sort of misanthropes and criminals who pass through our cells are a little below the standard of your usual clientele. . . ."

Herod shrugged. "It's good, clean money," he said. "And steady, too—there's no shortage of people ready to hasten their onward rush to the grave." He smiled. "Besides, it's my civic duty. *Someone* has to deal with the detritus, don't they?"

Detritus. No matter what they'd done, Quint wasn't sure he could ever see a person as that. "I suppose they do," he murmured, mounting the bottom step. "Good day to you, Mr. Herod. You've been most enlightening."

The fire was burning low in the grate when Quint arrived home later that day. Judging by the squealing coming from elsewhere in the small but warren-like terraced house, his wife was chasing the children off to their bath, so he decided to make the most of the opportunity, kicking off his boots and collapsing into his ratty old armchair by the hearth. He heaved a sigh of relief. He felt weary to his bones, and the chill, relentless damp felt like it had seeped beneath his skin. He tossed a couple of extra logs on the fire and eased himself back, stretching his toes and considering a brief nap.

He closed his eyes, felt his shoulders droop. The world seemed to retreat for a moment. All he could hear was the crackle and spit of the fire. Yet, no matter the ache in his legs or the crick in his neck, his mind wouldn't stop whirring like the workings of some overwound clock. Events surrounding the Parker case simply didn't add up, and he couldn't shake the notion that he was missing something. He'd seen the man hung with his own eyes. Herod had confirmed the body had been cremated. And yet days later, there Parker was, terrorising a woman in Spitalfields and threatening to eat her heart in tribute to his unholy god.

Someone was lying. That was the only conclusion. His gut told him it was Herod. The man had been strangely aloof at the funeral home. He'd relished Quint's discomfort down in the mortuary—almost as if he'd taken Quint down there on purpose, to unsettle him, throw him off his questioning. Or perhaps it was to serve as a distraction. It had worked, too. With the corpse of the old woman lying there, Quint had been dissuaded from paying too much attention to everything else.

He'd have to think on the matter. One thing was clear though: even if Herod was lying and Parker had somehow survived his execution—and Quint had to admit it was a huge *if*—there was no chance the man was still hanging around the funeral parlour. Whatever game Herod was playing, it would have to wait.

Establishing who was responsible for the attack in the alley was Quint's first priority. He had to ensure it didn't happen again. Whether it was Parker or someone mirroring his crimes mattered little unless he could stop them. He could go back to the funeral parlour and tear the place apart, but he wasn't sure it would help—not unless he could get Herod to talk, and that seemed unlikely. So, what *could* he do?

Quint sat forward, struck by a sudden idea. What was the name of that esoteric newspaper that Parker had been seen reading in the pub? *The Wheel and Star.* That was it.

Quint stood, crossed the room and snatched up a notepad and pen from amongst the disorganised mess of his bureau. He began scratching out the wording for a brief advertisement.

This'll snare the bugger.

CHAPTER 16

As the sun dipped below the skyline, Warlow took a moment to appreciate the warm patina it cast across the city: a burnt orange glow that spilled across the rooftops like liquid light, crowning the steeple of a nearby church and pooling on the ground near the foot of the cab. All around, the shadows were deepening and lengthening; the perpetual battle between light and dark, played out right there before his eyes. Within moments, dusk would fall, and it would be time to make his move.

Up front, the horses were getting jittery. He'd driven them hard on the way to Tottenham, until their mouths foamed and their flanks were lathered with sweat. He'd been anxious to get there early, to scope the place out while he had time. He couldn't risk any complications with this one. The stakes were simply too high.

The messenger had come around mid-morning, as he was still stirring from the pit of his bed. He'd been drinking the night before—to douse the screams and deaden the memories—and he still felt jittery and hollowed out. He'd been unable to hold anything down for days, and even now, he felt the hunger like a rusted blade working back and forth across his skin, rasping and uncomfortable; a constant, nagging companion.

The Queen had been her usual loathsome self: full of pomposity and lofty promises, all delivered with an undercurrent of threatened violence. Warlow had long ago learned to read between the lines when it came to Victoria and was under no illusions as to his usefulness—and his disposability. Yet today he'd seen something new. A chink in her illusory armour, a slight hint of regret. The words had not come easily to her, as she detailed his latest assignment: to hunt and eradicate the Prince of Wales, her own son.

Word had come that he was hiding out in an abandoned house in Tottenham, along with the disgraced police inspector, Charles Bainbridge. Warlow had met Bainbridge on a handful of occasions and had found the man singularly unimpressive. Just like the Queen, he was a bundle of airs and graces wrapped up in a Savile Row suit—a well-to-do toff with no substance, who'd clearly done nothing to warrant the position he'd been awarded. The way he'd looked down his nose at Warlow had spoken volumes. Warlow would have no difficulty putting the old fool out of his misery.

The Prince, however. Well, that was another thing entirely. This was the future king. A man who'd already spent time under lock and key in an asylum due to his ongoing disagreements with the Queen. To take his life . . . it seemed to Warlow like a new level of transgression, the breaking of a chain that could never be repaired. To kill a mother's son was one thing, but to alter the course of history was quite another. See this through, and he would doom the Empire to years—perhaps *decades*—more of Victoria's reign. And then who? There were stories, of course. A hidden child, kept away from prying eyes, fashioned in the very likeness of Victoria herself and schooled to rule when Victoria's husk of a body finally wheezed its final breath. But surely these were just stories, concocted by those seeking conspiracy where there was none, anxious to fill the void left by the Queen's retreat from public life?

Whatever the case, Warlow was here, now, sitting atop the dickey box of the same stolen cab that he'd used in Islington.

Beneath him, the boltheads were silent and still—a fact he found even more disconcerting than if they'd been bouncing off the walls as usual. Perhaps even their strange, dislocated brains understood the gravity of what they faced, what they would do this night.

And yet Warlow did not feel on the verge of greatness. Here, in the soft afterglow of the London sunset, he did not feel pride, his chest did not swell. There was nothing momentous about these passing seconds, minutes. There was just the cool breeze ruffling his hair, and the sick feeling in the pit of his stomach, the weight of what he must do heavy on his shoulders.

Tonight, he knew, the drink would not be enough. It might never be enough again.

He glanced up at the sound of a passing hansom. Two women sat side-by-side in the back, giggling at some shared amusement. A fleeting moment of passing intimacy. He felt a surge of envy, for the lightness of their expressions, the freedom inherent in their laughter. For a glorious moment he considered flicking the reins and turning the cab around, starting after them, riding the road away from the black horror he faced, chasing that burnt orange sunset right out of the city and away.

But he knew it was nothing but a passing dream. There was no escape, not now. He'd allowed himself to become mired, his boots sunken in the sticky mud. To thrash now, to try to pull away, would only help him sink all the faster.

He supposed, in some ways, that might be considered a blessing. It wasn't in his nature to give in, though. He'd fight to keep his head above the bog for as long as possible. Fight with every fibre of his being. And if that meant executing the Queen's commands—well, there was no higher power in the land. Surely that, in itself, was absolution enough.

He climbed down and unbolted the door.

Inside, the boltheads buzzed like angry bees.

Bees that knew exactly what they must do for their Queen.

♛

"It's a funny thing," said the Prince, "contemplating the weight of an Empire."

Bainbridge took a sip from his brandy and regarded the Prince over the top of his newspaper. "Is it a heavy burden?"

"All the heavier by virtue of the fact it's unwanted."

"Unwanted? It's not so long ago that you were hatching your own schemes to seize control from your mother."

The Prince smiled. "A spell in an institution provides a great deal of time for reflection, Sir Charles. I see now that I have a duty to my country—to my mother, too—but it is not a duty I relish. More, it is one I shall bear."

Bainbridge found himself wondering at the sheer ego of the man. It was all very well to sit there pontificating on the burden he was about to embrace, but this from a man who had hired a murderer to hunt down agents of the Queen as part of a plot to discredit her and take the crown. Bainbridge only hoped that, on balance, the trade he was about to make—one self-centred monarch for another—would work out in the country's favour. *That,* surely, was the real burden here.

A footstep sounded from outside the door. Bainbridge glanced at the window, but the curtains were pulled shut; a precaution against any casual passers-by happening to glance in.

"You told them to return tomorrow, didn't you?" said the Prince.

Bainbridge nodded, touching his finger to his lips. He beckoned for the Prince to stand, then waved him towards the kitchen door. "Remember the protocol we established," he hissed, his voice low. "They won't be expecting you to run that way. If I give the signal . . ."

The Prince nodded, backing towards the door.

Bainbridge yanked a poker from the fire, its tip glowing dark and red.

He took a step closer to the door. The wind rattled the window. A dog barked somewhere in the distance.

The door exploded.

Bainbridge staggered back as splintering wood showered the room, tiny lances that stung the skin of his cheeks, arms, neck. Someone barked a command, and figures rushed the opening, forcing their way in through the wrecked remains of the door. Figures with iron bolts embedded in their skulls and electrical light flickering like animated spider's webs across their pallid skin.

Boltheads.

Bainbridge turned to the Prince. "Go!"

The Prince hesitated for a moment, but then the reality of the situation seemed to crash into him at full force, and he took three steps back, before turning on his heel and charging out of the back door.

"I wouldn't bother trying to run," came Warlow's voice from beyond the doorway, where three boltheads had now clambered over the ruined door and a fourth was following behind. "I've got the place surrounded." His voice sounded eminently reasonable—as if they were discussing the weather forecast for the following day.

"Do you lay awake at night, Warlow, thinking of all the people you've killed for her? Is it easy, now, to take another life?"

One of the boltheads lurched towards him, and Bainbridge fell back, towards the same kitchen door through which the Prince had fled. He had to buy the future king enough time.

"It's never easy," said Warlow, from the doorway. "But it's *necessary.* I simply do what needs to be done."

"If you keep telling yourself that, eventually you might come to believe it," said Bainbridge.

The bolthead before him raised its hands, lightning dancing across its fingertips. The thing looked barely human, its mouth hanging slack, spittle running down its chin, its eyes flitting back and forth like a sleepwalker caught in the middle of a night terror.

Bainbridge raised the poker and brought it down in a fierce jabbing motion, ramming the hot end through the bolthead's left eye and on into the skull. The creature lurched manically as its brain boiled, blood and matter spraying down its face, showering the front of Bainbridge's suit. It collapsed, its body seizing, into one of its fellows, entangling them both and sending them sprawling to the floor in a mass of sparking, writhing limbs.

Bainbridge saw his opportunity and turned and ran. Behind him, he heard Warlow bellowing commands, and felt, more than saw, something explode in the kitchen, resulting in a clatter of copper pans and the smouldering scent of burning wood.

He followed the escape route they'd practised, slamming through the rear door and into the overgrown garden, where the unkempt grass and wildflowers would work to slow any pursuit.

Warlow hadn't been lying. Two boltheads had been lurking by the side passage, and they came after him now, sparking and fizzing in the wet undergrowth. But Bainbridge had a head start on them, and so long as his heart held out—it was hammering hard against his ribs with the sustained effort of his flight—he still had a chance of getting away.

He spotted the gap in the hedge, the one he'd cut two days previously, and slammed through into the neighbouring garden. He cursed as the hedge gouged furrows into his belly and the top of his thighs. He felt blood welling at the site of the wounds, but ignored it, charging across the neighbour's lawn and down the side of their house, emerging, panting, into the street. Behind him, more boltheads were now in pursuit, but as he'd hoped, they showed little in the way of ingenuity, still forcing their way into the Wren's house in order to follow his trail through the garden.

He charged down the street, counting the houses as he went. *One, two, three . . .*

And then skidded down the side path of the fourth house, into their large backyard. There, the Prince was waiting atop the dickey box of a steam-powered cab, wrapped in a tatty woollen overcoat with a hat pulled low over his brow. The cab's engine was already running, and the rear gates, which gave out onto a cobbled alleyway were open.

Lightheaded, his breath a dry rasp, Bainbridge covered the last few yards at a stagger, and then dragged himself up into the passenger seat, the Prince hoisting him the last of the way.

"Go!" he muttered, collapsing back into the seat as the Prince cranked the controls and the cab lurched into motion, shooting forward into the alleyway, just as the first of the boltheads appeared in the yard, electrical discharge leaping amongst the heap of metal cartwheels piled in one corner.

Moments later, the cab burst from the mouth of the alleyway in a cacophony of soot and smoke, and rushed away into the night, leaving Warlow, his boltheads, and Tottenham behind.

Warlow watched them go, charging off into the distance like the two women he'd witnessed earlier, buzzing with life, vitality, and freedom. Perhaps, in truth, he envied these men, too. The way they had cast off the yoke of conformity and followed their own paths, no matter how misguided.

He felt strangely light, as if, in failing to murder these two men, his burden had somehow been lifted, the matter taken out of his hands. He knew it was only a temporary reprieve, however. Now, he'd be forced to intensify his hunt, to seek out the others who might be assisting the Prince in his ploy. It was a short list, and he would find no pleasure in shortening it still.

First, though, he would gather the boltheads and report to the palace.

Her Majesty the Queen was not going to be pleased.

CHAPTER 17

"Is it done?"

"Yes. I've told her to listen out for the signal. It's written in the same cipher we used as girls, passing notes back and forth about Mother and Father. And boys, of course. There were always lots of boys."

Newbury laughed. "*Lots* of boys. Somehow that doesn't surprise me."

Veronica slapped his arm playfully. "I'll not have you cast aspersions on my character, Sir Maurice. It was all done in innocence."

"I'm sure it was," he said, in a tone that made it clear he thought anything but.

"Besides, I'm sure there were plenty of girls, too. . . ."

"Ah, best we don't get into that," said Newbury, his cheeks reddening.

"Oh, so what's fine for me . . ." She laughed.

They were sitting in a little restaurant called Rosalie's, just off Charing Cross Road. It was a favourite of hers, with a quiet, relaxed atmosphere and an exquisite menu of unusual continental dishes prepared by their French chef.

She'd decided it would do Newbury good to get out of the house for a while, and besides, they needed to be seen going about their normal business. Unlike Sir Charles, their involvement in the Bedlam affair had so far remained unexposed, but Veronica knew full well that, given their relationship with the chief inspector and the fact he'd been acting with another man and a woman, suspicion would soon fall upon them, if it hadn't already. To hide away would be to confirm such suspicions, so, despite the morning's shocking news, despite the fact that Sir Charles and the Prince of Wales were in hiding in a tumbledown house across town, and despite the fact they were plotting a coup that would conceivably change the course of history—they had ventured out for dinner at her insistence.

Veronica took a sip of her wine. Newbury was staring out of the window again, watching the milling passers-by. Outside, the streetlamps cast their soft, amber glow upon the pavements, like little traps that temporarily imprisoned anyone foolish enough to walk beneath them. Carts clattered on the roads, horses clip-clopped on the cobbles, and engines belched to announce the rumble of a passing ground train. She reached across the table, took his hand in hers. He looked up, surprised. "I'm sorry about Archibald," she said.

He squeezed her hand. "I know. Me too. He was a good man. A difficult man to like, sometimes, and perhaps a little zealous at times, but a good man, nonetheless. We're poorer for his loss." He broke a piece of bread from the slice on his plate and nibbled on it for a moment. Veronica noticed that he'd maintained his hold of her hand. "It feels odd," he said, after a moment.

"What does?"

"Being here. In a restaurant. Tonight. It feels . . . I don't know. *Wrong,* somehow. As if we should be doing something. As if life should have been interrupted somehow. A good man has died . . ."

". . . and the world just carries on. I understand. It's brutal, and wrong, but also, in its way, quite marvellous too. Life *never* stops. No matter what. Whether *we* as individuals live or die, whether we win or lose. No matter who sits on the throne or leads

Parliament, no matter the distant wars or the horrors perpetrated in the name of faith—the world just keeps on turning." She smiled. "You're always telling me that we can't slow progress. That whether we want it or not, things are going to change. New inventions are going to revolutionise the world. Society is going to adopt new norms. And the thing is—you're right. But just as we can't halt progress, we can't stop the world from carrying on without us, even when we wish it wouldn't."

Newbury sighed. "When did you become so wise?"

"I've always been this wise," said Veronica. "You just weren't paying attention."

"Oh, I assure you, I was. I've always paid attention." He squeezed her hand again.

Neither of them spoke for a moment.

"Well, I suppose we should think about ordering dinner," she said, glancing at the menu.

"Yes, of course," said Newbury, releasing her hand.

Veronica took another sip of wine. Something felt different, tonight. Something about the way Newbury was looking at her, the tone of his voice. His lingering touch. Perhaps, she decided, it was simply a response to what had happened to Angelchrist. Proximity to death always seemed to inspire intimacy in people—as if being reminded of their own mortality suddenly led them to grab hold of whatever, or *whom*ever, they could, to remind themselves they were still alive.

"The veal, I think."

"I'm sorry?" said Veronica.

Newbury laughed. "I said, I think I'll have the veal." His expression softened. "Is everything all right? You're worried about your sister, aren't you?"

"No. Well, yes, of course. But it's not that."

"Then what?"

"It's nothing. Don't trouble yourself. Honestly."

"Veronica . . ."

She took a long sip of wine. Was she really going to do this now? It was the worst possible timing. They stood on the precipice of an action that would define the rest of their lives.

Perhaps she'd been affected by Angelchrist's death, too.

"All right," she said. "I was thinking about . . . us. About what's going to become of us once this is all over."

Newbury shrugged. "I thought we'd already decided."

"We have?" Veronica's heart was thudding. Had she missed something, somehow?

"Yes, of course. I don't think I could bear to work for Prince Edward, not after what happened. Once it's over and things are settled, we sign up for the Service. With Angelchrist gone, it does complicate things somewhat, but I'm certain Charles will wa–"

"*Maurice,*" she said, cutting him off.

"What is it?"

"I was talking about *us.*"

"About us?"

"I'm in love with you, you fool, and if you still feel the same, then I thought perhaps . . ."

"Yes," he said, his voice cracking.

"Yes, *what?*"

"Yes, to everything," he said.

Veronica felt suddenly lightheaded, and she wasn't sure if it was the wine she'd drank, or the fact she'd forgotten how to breathe.

"Yes, to whatever you want," he said. "Yes, to *this.*"

Veronica drained the rest of the wine in her glass. Newbury grinned.

"Right then," she said. "It's decided. When this is over."

"Quite so."

"Good."

"So, what'll it be?"

"Hmmm?"

"The veal?"

"Oh, yes. I rather think so, don't you?"

"Over there. Pull over."

"Here, are you sure?"

"Yes, I'm sure. And be discreet about it."

"It's very difficult to be discreet, Sir Charles, in this monstrous excuse for a conveyance." The Prince cranked the brake as they entered the mouth of the alleyway and pulled the cab to a halt. The engine gave a final, wheezing rattle, and a cloud of black soot billowed from the exhaust vent. Bainbridge coughed and waved his hand before his face, trying desperately not to breathe it in. He looked across at the Prince of Wales, and the sight of the man—with soot-stained face and grimy overcoat, his battered bowler hat pulled down low and cocked to one side—was enough to make him hoot with laughter.

"What the devil is so funny?" demanded the Prince, sharply.

"I'm sorry, Your Highness, but you are something of a picture."

Grumpily, the Prince wiped his face on his sleeve, and succeeded only in smearing more of the black grime across his cheek. "I will add, for the record, that you're not looking too well turned out yourself."

Bainbridge looked down at the torn, bloody clothes, now powdered in oily soot and mud. He looked back at the Prince and grinned. "I freely admit it, Your Highness. You're right."

They looked at each other for a moment, and then both burst into laughter.

Bainbridge wiped his eyes. "I needed that."

"Indeed," said the Prince. "And for the meanwhile, I think it's best we dropped the honorifics, don't you? Plain Charles and Bertie should do it. It *is* my name, after all. We don't want to draw any further unwanted attention."

"Agreed," said Bainbridge. He slid down from the passenger seat and offered the Prince a hand. They moved a little deeper into the alleyway, standing amongst the pooled shadows at the foot of a factory wall. Beyond the wall, everything was quiet and still.

"Well, what's the plan?" said the Prince. "Presumably this Warlow character is unlikely to let us be. Especially if my mother has anything to do with it."

"Yes," agreed Bainbridge, "I rather think we're running short on time. It won't take him long to trace us, no matter where we go. Although how he found the Wren's house is still somewhat beyond me."

"A traitor in our midst?"

"Impossible. We've been too careful. If anything, one of us was followed."

The Prince nodded. "Plausible, I'll give you that. But it nevertheless suggests we'll need to be on our guard. Wherever we choose to go to ground, we'll have to be mindful of any comings or goings."

Bainbridge shook his head. "We're not going to ground."

"We're not?"

"No. It's too late for that. They're onto us. The longer we delay, the less likely we are to succeed. The only option is to strike now, while they think they have us on the run."

"*Now?*" The Prince sounded utterly appalled. "But we're not ready."

"Then we'll have to *get* ready. Our contact in the palace will be on hand to help get us inside. We'll have to make the rest up as we go."

"Make it up as we go?"

"Well, what is there to decide? As you outlined for Inspector Foulkes, the success of our plan rests on whether we can persuade your mother to make way."

The Prince scoffed. "You know her almost as well as I do, Charles. Do you honestly believe that she's going to agree to step down?"

Bainbridge chewed his lip. "No. I don't believe she will."

"And nor did Professor Angelchrist. Not for one second. When he planned this 'Albion Initiative,' he had only one end in mind. He knew full well that my mother would die before she abdicated. And so, it falls to us to see it through."

"You can't be serious," said Bainbridge. "I cannot condone murder. No matter the stakes. I'm a goddamn *policeman*."

The Prince nodded. "Yes, I rather thought you'd say that, so I've been giving the matter some thought."

"And?"

"And I believe we need to manufacture a medical emergency. To interfere with the machinery that maintains her life." He held up a hand for patience when he saw Bainbridge's scowl. "Nothing that will kill her, Charles. But enough that the doctors will be forced to hurry her off to some facility or other to preserve her life. I'll step in while she undergoes treatment, and in doing so, will see to it that she never leaves the facility. She can live out the rest of her days in comfort, while I serve as regent until her eventual death."

"It could work," said Bainbridge, warming to the notion, "so long as we're careful."

"It's not as clean as the alternative, but it does sit rather better, I think."

"Very well. Then we have a plan, after all."

"What now?"

"We'll find a local pub in which to clean ourselves up. From there, we can get a message to the others and arrange to meet them close to the palace in a few hours."

"A *public house*?"

"Don't sound so appalled. We can hardly go to my club." He led the way out of the alleyway and into the quiet street beyond. "Besides, you might find you develop a taste for it."

"Good Lord. I wouldn't count on it. . . ."

CHAPTER 18

"Foulkes. Thank God. For a while there I was worried none of you were going to make it."

Bainbridge was hunkered low behind a tight knot of privets and sycamore trees, about two hundred yards from the vast, dark edifice of Buckingham Palace. His knees were sodden with mud, he'd torn his jacket climbing over the wall, and he was shivering from the sharp, biting chill. He felt more alert than he had in days, his mind racing as he considered and rejected all the possible routes from here to the audience chamber, the various scenarios for how things might play out. His nerves were jangling, and his heart felt as if it were in his mouth. Grand treason had a way of doing that to you, he reflected.

Beside him, the Prince was kneeling in similar fashion, down amongst the dirt and fallen leaves, studying the palace with wolfish eyes. Neither of them were young or athletic men, but Warlow's attack at the Wren house had left them with little option, and Bainbridge was relieved that the Prince had risen admirably to the physical challenge, heaving himself over the estate wall and creeping with surprising agility across the grounds. And now Foulkes was here, too. Another reliable face.

He beckoned for Foulkes to join them. The other man seemed momentarily reluctant, but then shrugged and lowered himself into a crouch beside Bainbridge. His boots were already caked in thick mud.

"No sign of Newbury or Miss Hobbes?" whispered Bainbridge.

Foulkes shook his head. "Perhaps they didn't receive your message. I must admit, I was somewhat surprised myself. I'd only just returned from the Yard when the boy fetched up with your note. I thought we had more time."

"Events have overtaken us, Foulkes," said Bainbridge. "Our hand has been forced. Somehow, Warlow found the Wren house. We have to make our move tonight, before it's too late."

Foulkes's expression darkened. "Are you certain about this, Sir Charles? It's not too late to walk away, even now. Hand yourselves in at the Yard. It would be a matter of moments to clear you of any wrongdoing."

"It's too late for that," said the Prince, interrupting before Sir Charles could answer. His voice was low, steady. Resigned. "If there was another way, I would take it. But *someone* needs to put a stop to my mother's scheming before she drives this country into the ground, and the responsibility for that falls squarely upon my shoulders."

"Besides," added Bainbridge, "she's not the type to forgive and forget. I've learned that from bitter experience. There's no going back, Foulkes. Not now. Things will never be the same again." He considered for a moment. "But listen—you're a family man. I can see how conflicted you are. You didn't sign up for any of this. *You* can still walk away. Newbury only brought you into it because he felt you deserved answers, and because you've been such a true friend to us all in the past. You're a good man, Foulkes, and whatever you decide, I'll understand. If you want to turn around and leave, I won't stop you."

Foulkes glanced back the way he'd come, as if contemplating the idea. An owl gave a shrill call into the night. "It's tempting, I'll give you that. But I'm here now. I'll see this through."

"Good man, Foulkes," said Bainbridge, gripping the other man's arm.

The Prince shifted his position, rustling the carpet of fallen leaves. "Well, it doesn't look as if Newbury or Miss Hobbes will be joining us," he said. "More's the pity. I've had my disagreements with Newbury in the past, but I wouldn't wish to exclude him from seeing the look on my mother's face when it dawns on her exactly what's happening. He's earned that, if nothing else."

"Yes, well, let's save the gloating for when it's actually done, shall we? There's a long night ahead of us yet."

"As you say," muttered the Prince.

"So, what's the plan?" asked Foulkes. "We can't very well go marching up to the front door."

"No," said Bainbridge, a sudden idea taking shape in his mind, "but *you* can."

"*Me?* What can I do? They don't even know me here."

"Precisely!" said Bainbridge. "You can serve as a distraction. Create a commotion—explain that you're a police inspector and claim that you've seen the Prince and I at a pub near Marble Arch, dressed as cab drivers. The Blacksmith's Arms. We were there earlier, and the barkeep will corroborate your tale. You'll even find the engine we used to escape Warlow parked in an alleyway close by. Meanwhile, me and Bertie can slip around the side and give the agreed signal to our contact inside."

"Which is?"

"A tune to be tapped out on a particular drainpipe. That'll get us inside, and with the rest of the household distracted by our supposed sighting, we can slip through to the audience chamber and confront the Queen."

"It's far from the most ironclad plan I've ever heard," said Foulkes. "And damned risky."

Bainbridge laughed. "Point to anything about this endeavour that isn't risky, man! But what we're doing is *right*."

"I don't doubt it," said Foulkes. "Fine then. I'll do it." He stood, smoothing the front of his suit.

Flustered, Bainbridge grabbed his arm and pulled him back down behind the bushes. "Not yet!"

"What? Why?"

Bainbridge glanced at the Prince. "I just want to give Newbury five more minutes. Agreed?"

"Agreed," said the Prince. "But then we go, irrespective of whether they're here or not."

Bainbridge glanced at Foulkes, but the other man was staring off into the distance, pale and silent.

He doesn't want to be here, considered Bainbridge. *He doesn't want to be a part of this. But he's doing it regardless.* That, to Charles's mind, was the measure of a good man.

Perhaps, he decided, *there's hope for us all yet.*

To Amelia, there was nothing quite so satisfying as a good book; the opportunity it provided to lose oneself in the imagined world of another, to pretend for a time to be a player in someone else's tale, to travel to far-off cities or fantastical realms, to scare yourself silly with the sort of bleak, esoteric fiction that was considered utterly unladylike in the "right" sort of society.

During her tenure in various London asylums—when she wasn't undergoing thought-deadening therapy or suffering from a successive chain of clairvoyant seizures—Amelia had learned to escape into the pages of such stories, to imagine herself far away from the four bland walls of her cell, across oceans or deserts from the terror of the treatment room. To her, words had become a safe harbour, a steadying force for good, and she did not doubt that it was her ability to cling onto these conjured realities that had kept her sane throughout those many troubling years.

So it was now, too, living within the walls of this ridiculous, pompous palace, keeping up the pretence of her alternative life.

To her, Constance Markham was just like a character from one of her books, another person she could pretend to be when times became difficult and she longed for home. Constance was the one who had to deal with that ridiculous toad of a man, Trimbey, or fend off the unwanted yet charming advances of the young footman, Chappell. Constance was a mask, a guise, and Amelia only let it slip at night, when she was curled up in bed, reading by the soft glow of a reading lamp.

This, she had claimed to Trimbey, was the reason why she had volunteered to sleep alone in this small, dank cupboard of a room at the very end of the servant's quarters—because she feared a shared dormitory would be unfair on her fellow workers, who might be kept awake at night because of her prolific reading habit—which, in itself, she claimed to be a symptom of persistent insomnia. The real reason, of course, was so she was close to the outer wall and the iron drainpipe that ran by the window on the upper floor, just above the small room.

Of course, she was aware of the risks that taking such a room might present—the unwanted intrusion of male servants hoping to take advantage of her loneliness—but from her first night there until this one, she had taken to shifting the heavy chest of drawers across the door to block entry whenever she took to her bed. She was, she considered, beginning to regain much of her lost strength.

Now, she was propped up on one elbow on her bed, dressed in her nightclothes, deep in the midst of Le Fanu's salacious novella, *Carmilla*. She'd long ago learned not to be repelled by such tales of depravity and horror, having, she supposed, been somewhat desensitised by her experiences in real life. Having witnessed true horror in its many human forms, fantastical tales of monsters, vampires, and evil, uncaring gods seemed somewhat pale in comparison.

Still, the book was enjoyable, and she would thank Newbury for the loan of it when at last she was able to speak with him again.

She started at a knocking sound and, for a moment, thought there was someone rapping at her door, but when it sounded again a moment later, she realised it was coming from outside. She set the book down upon the pillow and sat up, listening intently.

It couldn't be, could it?

Veronica's note had suggested at least another day or two before they'd make their move. Surely, they couldn't be here, now. She waited, holding her breath, straining for every sound.

The crunch of footsteps on gravel. A cleared throat. And then it sounded again, six short, sharp knocks upon the ringing iron of the drainpipe.

Oh, God. This is it.

She exhaled. Mouth suddenly dry, Amelia got to her feet, hurriedly grabbing her dressing gown. Why now? She wasn't ready! She hadn't practised her patter in case she was interrupted wandering the halls. She'd have to think on her feet and hope that the rest of the staff were already asleep.

Something must have happened to force their hand. That suggested real danger. If the Queen was on to them, then nowhere was safe. They were taking her down now, before things escalated.

They were taking down the Queen of England.

She could hardly believe that it was finally happening, this scheme that had seemed so unreal for so long, that had consumed them all for months. In a few hours it would all be over. First, though, she had to play her part.

She slipped her shoes on, tied the ribbon at the front of her robe, and took hold of one end of the chest of drawers blocking her door. Slowly, cringing at the sharp grating sounds it made as she dragged it across the flagstones—rude and extraordinarily loud in the otherwise silent room—she pulled the hunk of furniture out of the way.

The knocking sounded again.

"I'm *coming*," she hissed beneath her breath.

She opened the door and peered out. The passageway was silent and empty, the lights all extinguished. She could hear a commotion coming from somewhere deeper in the house. Raised voices. People arguing. Hopefully, whoever they were, they'd been too involved to hear her moving furniture.

She stepped out into the corridor, pulling her door shut behind her, careful to release the handle slowly so as not to make another sound. All of the other doors appeared to be closed. Light was seeping out from beneath one at the far end, dusting the flagstones—Jenny and Madeline's room. Two of the kitchen maids.

Amelia passed softly through the gloom, her nightdress swishing around her ankles. It was cold, and her breath fogged before her face. She would have to be swift. She'd open the door, hurry them inside—Sir Charles, Newbury, Veronica, and the Prince of Wales—and then flit away again, back to her room, to continue the pretence of Constance until such a time that word came that it was safe.

She'd quarrelled with Veronica that she should be there at her sister's side for the denouement, that there was strength to be had in numbers, but both Veronica and Newbury had argued that it was more important to protect her cover in case something went wrong and they needed someone on the inside to aid their escape. After all, the only members of the court who could identify Amelia were the Queen herself, and her doctor, Warrender. To everyone else, she was simply Constance, the maid.

Behind the kitchen maids' door, the two women were talking in hushed tones. Amelia steeled herself, keeping to the far side of the passage to avoid her shadow spilling under the door. A misstep now could ruin everything. She couldn't hear what the two women were discussing and didn't much care; neither had been particularly welcoming since her arrival. If they were to catch her creeping around now, she had no doubt that Trimbey would hear about it in the morning.

She slipped past, rounding the bottom of the steps. As she did, one of the women emitted a shrill laugh, and Amelia jumped, heart racing, certain that she'd been spotted. But the door remained shut.

Steadying her breathing, she mounted the steps, then hurried on up, taking them two at a time. She reached the dog leg, peered around to see the coast was clear. Onwards, then, to the main doorway that led into the palace proper.

She loitered there for a moment, listening, watching, allowing her eyes to adjust to the change in the texture of the light. The arguments were still ongoing elsewhere in the building. Here, though, there was no one else around. From the top of the steps she could see the outer door where the others would be waiting. All she had to do was take a few more steps, then slide open the bolt. That was it.

So why did she suddenly feel so terrified?

This was the culmination of all the time she had spent here in the palace, all the times she'd been forced to bite her tongue in Trimbey's presence, to scrub laundry or fold sheets. And yet, for some reason, it felt as if she still had unfinished business.

Whatever it was would have to wait.

She stepped out into the hall, feeling suddenly exposed. Ten steps to the door. She counted every single one. Numb fingers slid the bolt, turned the handle.

Outside, a cold wind was stirring the distant treetops of the grounds. She stood there, framed in the open doorway, dressing robe whipping about her in the breeze. The cold stung her cheeks, made the hairs on the nape of her neck prickle uncomfortably.

There was no one there.

Amelia took a step out into the gravel. She glanced to the right and saw to her surprise that the two strange carriages were back, parked outside the same door where she'd found them the other night. The same two men were standing around smoking cigarettes, their backs to her. She ducked back into the shelter of the doorway, her eyes flicking in the other direction. Two shadowy figures stood to the left of the window, by the drainpipe that ran above her room.

Only two?

"Constance?" One of them hissed. His voice was so low it might have been nothing but the breath of the wind.

"Yes," she returned. "You'd better hurry."

The man who'd spoken stepped forward; she glimpsed his features in the silvery moonlight. Sir Charles Bainbridge. *Then the other must be . . .*

Amelia swallowed at the sight of the Prince of Wales as he hurried after Bainbridge. Both of them were caked in mud and soot, and Bainbridge looked as if he was carrying some minor wounds.

She stepped aside to let them pass, pressing a finger to her lips before gently shutting the door.

Bainbridge paused on the passage beyond, glancing back. "Thank you," he mouthed, with a taut smile.

"Veronica?" she replied in similar fashion.

Bainbridge shrugged, and she nodded to show she'd understood. He looked as baffled as she was by her sister's absence.

With one last glance back at the Prince, Bainbridge turned and set off into the gloom, his cane clasped tightly in his fist like a bludgeon. The future king followed after him without a single word.

Satisfied that there was nothing more she could do for them now—besides being ready if they needed her—Amelia retraced her steps, back down the stairs, around the dog leg and on into the servants' quarters.

The light was still on in the kitchen maids' room. She rounded the bottom of the steps, steadying herself on the banister. Her legs felt like jelly. She was trembling. But she'd made it. Only a few more steps to go, and she'd be back in the relative safety of her room, where she could wait out the next hour or so while Bainbridge and the Prince did whatever they had to do.

As before, she crept along the passageway, skirting the light from under the door. Then she was past, and . . .

. . . the door to her room was ajar.

Her heart seemed to stop with a sudden jolt. She was certain she'd closed it behind her.

She paused for a moment, her mouth dry. Then, reaching out her hand, she pushed it open.

Trimbey was standing beside her bed, flicking through the pages of her book. He looked up, eyes narrowing at the sight of her in the doorway. "This is racy stuff," he said. "Not at all what I'd deem appropriate for a young lady such as yourself, Constance." He closed the book, dropped it back on her pillow. "Now, perhaps you might be good enough to tell me where you've been."

Amelia cleared her throat. "I simply had to a pay a visit to the water closet, Mr. Trimbey," she said, attempting to keep the quaver out of her voice.

"The water closet." He tapped the edge of his shoe against the chamber pot beneath her bed. His grin was wicked, knowing. "What if I told you that I didn't believe you? What if I said that I think you were poking around where you're not wanted again, hmmm? A little maid who's got ideas above her station." He crossed the room to stand before her, uncomfortably close, so that she could feel his hot, sour breath on her face. "What would you say to *that*?"

Amelia felt anger welling up inside of her—a burning, fiery rage that seemed to originate in her chest, radiating out into her limbs, burning away any last vestiges of the chill, of the nervous energy that remained. "I'd say, Mr. Trimbey, that neither a woman's *toileting* habits, nor her choice of reading matter, had anything at all to do with *you*." She stood aside to make way. "Now, if you'd kindly get out of my room. I'd like to return to my bed, and if I were forced to raise the alarm, I have *no doubt* that your presence here at this hour would be viewed as entirely inappropriate by your superiors."

Trimbey sniffed, and then cleared his throat, before stepping out into the passageway. "Don't think that this is the end of the matter, Constance. I know you're up to something. I can smell it." He started off towards the stairs. "I'll find out what it is, soon enough."

Amelia watched him go. Then, when he'd been swallowed once again by the gloom, she stepped into her room and closed the door, before pulling the chest of drawers back into place. After catching her breath—determined not to give anyone the satisfaction of an overheard sob—she shed her nightclothes and dressed hurriedly in a blouse and pair of culottes she'd borrowed from her sister. Then, taking a small leather bag from the bottom drawer, she began throwing in her small stash of belongings, ready to make a run for it.

She'd done what she came here to do, and she wasn't going to hang around the miserable place any longer than was necessary. She wouldn't give Trimbey the satisfaction.

CHAPTER 19

Sergeant Quint's thighs were aching, and he was desperate for a piss. He'd been in the same position for almost two hours, and the cold breeze blowing in through the broken windowpane was playing havoc with his bladder. Not to mention the crick in his neck. God, he felt old.

He'd chosen the position for its clear view of the door, but the decision had been predicated on the thought that the zealous murderer Parker might actually show up, following the taunting advert that Quint had left as bait in *The Wheel and Star*. Of course, the man was a no-show, and so Quint had been forced to crouch here in the darkness for much longer than he'd anticipated.

Despite this, he wasn't ready to give it all up for lost just yet. If he were Parker, he'd have played things cautiously, too, refusing to turn up on time for the rendezvous in case it was a trap. Nevertheless, Quint was gambling on the hope that Parker wouldn't be able to resist the temptation of finding out more about the person who'd invoked the name of his god, and fully expected that the man was even now scoping the house from outside, waiting to catch a glimpse of the other players in this most unusual game.

Assuming, that was, that the man in question even *was* Parker. He still wasn't clear how the killer might have survived being both hung *and* cremated, unless there really was something about this so-called Matherat, to which Quint wasn't prepared to give any credence whatsoever. He put little stock in the supernatural, and while he wasn't entirely a non-believer—he'd heard his fair share of woeful tales from respectable men at the Yard—he believed firmly that it was the stock in trade of a policeman to deal purely in the rational. Facts were Quint's currency, and at the moment, the facts did not add up.

He only wished the man would hurry. Otherwise he was going to have to piss on the floor, and the people he'd borrowed the building from (a Quaker society who'd evidently fallen on hard times and were glad for a couple of pounds towards repairs for their meeting hall) wouldn't be best pleased to have to clean up after him the next morning.

He made the mistake of trying to think about something else, picturing the hearty dinner that he'd passed up in his urgency to get across town in good time. His stomach growled, empty and angry. Maybe he'd have to think about calling it a night. Just another quarter bell before he—

Quint started at the tinkle of broken glass, coming from across the other side of the hall. The sly bastard was coming in through a window, rather than risking the door. Quint cursed. They'd set up in the wrong place. Now they'd have to hope he hadn't brought a torch. Still, at least he'd find it a lot harder trying to leave the same way when the net finally closed on him.

A soft thud denoted Parker's arrival inside the building. Boots crunched on broken glass. Quint could hear the man's ragged breath, even from across the hall. The man seemed to linger for a moment beneath the window—probably waiting for his eyes to adjust to the gloom. He raised his arm, and something glinted in his fist. A knife. A big one. So, he wasn't taking any chances. Either that, or he'd come here with the express purpose of murdering the person who'd placed the advert in the newspaper.

Quint glanced from left to right but could see nothing of the three constables he'd brought with him. Good men, one and all, and so far, they were sticking to the plan. Quint needed to reel the bastard in before they made their move to make sure there was no possible opportunity for escape. To do that, Quint needed him closer.

Taking a deep breath to steady his nerves, Quint cleared his throat.

Parker–it *had* to be Parker, didn't it?–froze on the spot. He looked around, suddenly nervous, then glanced back at the broken window.

No. Don't. Hold your nerve.

Parker took a step back towards the window. Quint could feel the opportunity slipping away. If the killer made it out into the street before they stopped him, he was in the wind. There was no way he'd fall for another trap like this. Quint knew he had to do something.

"Blessings of Matherat be upon you," said Quint, his voice tight and tinged with nervous energy.

Parker spun on the spot, his blade slicing the air. He hunched his shoulders, as if flinching away from Quint's voice. "Who's there? How do you know that name?"

"I, too, hear the call of Matherat."

"That's . . . that's imp . . . impossible . . . ," stuttered Parker. His eyes were wide, his mouth gaping, like he couldn't take it in.

"No!" said Quint, emerging from behind the stack of crates where he'd been squatting. His muscles burned, and he thought his bladder was about to burst. "Not impossible. He speaks to me. Does he speak to you?"

Parker banged the heel of his empty hand against his temple, as if trying to bash the unwelcome thoughts away. He stepped forward, brandishing his knife. He'd seen Quint, now; two silhouettes, dancing in the gloom. Quint circled carefully, arms raised, hands up before his chest–both to show that he wasn't carrying a weapon, and to be ready if Parker made any sudden moves.

"But Matherat is *my* god. He belongs t . . . t . . . to me. Not you, not anybody else."

"Is that because Matherat isn't real, Parker?" said Quint. "Because he's just some fucked up figment of your twisted imagination, the means by which you justify the horrible things you do to people to please yourself."

"No," growled Parker, rushing forward, swinging his knife in a wide arc before him.

Quint stepped back, out of arm's reach. He could see now, without doubt, that the man was Parker. The red welt around his throat would have been enough of a giveaway, but the cold, dead eyes were the same as the ones he'd seen at the gallows, too. The exact same ones he'd seen at the scene where they'd arrested him, his lower face dripping in arterial blood.

"I knew that the advert in the paper would bring you here," Quint said. "That you wouldn't be able to resist finding out who had set up a meeting to preach Matherat's name."

"Don't you say that," hissed Parker. "Don't you even *think* that name."

Quint was circling around towards the crates again now, and Parker was keeping step with him, blade shaking in his outstretched hand. There was no doubt in Quint's mind that the man was insane—and what was more, that he would do to Quint what he had done to the others if given even the slightest opportunity.

"How did you do it?" said Quint. "How did you get away?"

"I'm blessed," said Parker. "I'm his chosen one. I cannot die."

"That seems a little unlikely," said Quint. "Despite the evidence to the contrary."

"You're a filthy policeman," said Parker, lurching forward, the tip of his knife brushing the front of Quint's shirt as he skipped back to avoid the stabbing blow. "You're the one that found me, that locked me away and stopped me doing *his* work."

"I am. My name is Quint."

"You were there, that day at the gallows. Gloating."

"I wasn't gloating," said Quint. "I just wanted to make sure you were dead."

Parker laughed, and the sound was like the warble of a bullfrog, low and distant. Quint glanced up, searching the darkness for any sign of his constables, to make sure they were ready.

Parker saw it, that flick of the eyes, and leaped. Quint turned, too late, and felt the blade slide into his upper arm with a blossom of pain, as Parker fell upon him and they both crashed heavily to the floor. Quint tried to roll, but Parker's full weight was on top of him, pinning him down, and his arm blazed in agony, lolling uselessly beneath him.

Parker was in a frenzy, teeth gnashing as he tried to bite at Quint's face, but Quint had managed to work his other hand free and grabbed his assailant by the throat, forcing his head back as he continued his savage assault.

"Hurry up!" bellowed Quint, frantic, as Parker reached for the knife still buried in Quint's other arm, yanking it free in a flash of white pain, blood gushing down Quint's forearm, soaking his sleeve.

The knife glinted as Parker raised it, eyes wild—and then his weight was lifted off Quint's chest, and the three other policemen were wrestling Parker into submission, clapping cuffs around his wrists and ankles.

Quint fell back, flat against the floorboards, his breath shallow and uneven. After a moment the lights went up and a concerned, clean-shaven face appeared above his. "We've got him, sir. But we'd better get you to a hospital to see about that wound. All right if we move you now?"

Quint shook his head, then forced himself to sit up, groaning. He looked at the young constable. "I'm all right, Overton. Just a scratch. Fetch something to bind it, will you?"

The young man looked startled, but then nodded and hurried off to see what he could find.

Quint eyed Parker, who was now sitting slumped against the heap of crates, all the fire gone out of his eyes. The knife had disappeared, taken by one of the constables, no doubt.

Quint could taste blood. He realised he must have bitten his lip in the fall. "Tell me," he said, "what happened?"

Parker raised his head. He grinned. "I already told you. Matherat won't let me die. After your lot tried to hang me they left me for dead, but I came around in the back of a wagon. My lungs were on fire. I could barely swallow or turn my head, but I was alive. I laid there for a while, waiting.

"The wagon took me to a funeral parlour, like they were still going to see it all through. As if I really was dead and they were going to stick me in a coffin and cremate me. But that's not how it went." Parker gave a sickly grin.

"Well?" prompted Quint.

"The drivers handed me to a man they called Herod, who jabbed me with a syringe of something to make me more compliant—after I tried to scratch out his eyes." Parker laughed. "Afterwards, he threw me in a cell, where a score of others like me were being kept prisoner."

"Others?"

Parker shrugged. "Sorry bastards, the lot of them. Like they'd been rounded up off the streets."

"Criminals?"

"Well, they weren't sporting rope burns, if that's what you mean. I was only there for a few hours before they came to get us, some more men with wagons made up to look like big, posh carriages. They started to chain all the prisoners to each other, leading them into the wagons, but I wasn't having any of that. I killed one of the drivers, ripping his throat out with my teeth. They were so shocked they didn't even come after me when I did a runner."

Quint chewed his lip in frustration. So, Herod had lied to him. What a surprise. No doubt they'd disposed of the dead driver the same way they claimed to have dealt with Parker's body—via the crematorium. But what was Herod up to? Where were all those people coming from, and being taken to? And was the police doctor involved? He surely must have known that Parker was still alive after his hanging. In fact, the equipment had to have been rigged to ensure his survival. How high did this go?

Quint felt dizzy from the possibilities. He wanted to lie down again, but someone was doing something to his arm. He turned to see Overton there, kneeling on the ground, tying what looked like a strip of old curtain around Quint's arm.

"What . . . ?" he said. But the world seemed suddenly woozy.

"It's all right, sir. You've lost a lot of blood but you're going to be all right. We'll have you to a doctor in no time."

Quint nodded, and the motion set off a burst of dancing stars before his eyes. He rocked back, resting his head against the worn floorboards. He'd just rest for a moment. Just a few minutes. . . .

CHAPTER 20

Inspector Foulkes, it seemed, had done an admirable job with the promised distraction, if the raised voices, bellowed commands, and scurrying guards were anything to go by. It seemed to Bainbridge as if the whole palace were mobilising to search for him and the Prince. Only, they were mobilising in very much the wrong direction. As guards and agents swarmed to the Marble Arch, Bainbridge and the Prince's path to the Queen lay relatively clear.

He'd been through the plan a thousand times in his mind's eye, and, knowing the interior layout of the palace as he did, had chosen the route with the utmost care, considering all of the hidden nooks and crannies within which they might conceal themselves to avoid detection.

It had worked, too, with one exception—he hadn't anticipated that the old man, Sandford, might still be on duty.

Sandford had been in the Queen's service even longer than Bainbridge, first as a valet or groom—the stories differed every time he told them—then later as a butler to the various agents in her employ. In such a way, Bainbridge had come to know him as a warm and generous sort, and more than once he had helped steady the chief inspector's nerves after a particularly heated exchange with Her Majesty, or offered him a quick nip of brandy to help take the edge off a chill. He must have been approaching his eighth decade, and was stoop-backed and liver-spotted now, his silver hair reduced to thin, oiled threads that no longer managed to cover his freckled pate. What he was doing here at this hour, sitting in his armchair, eyes closed, an open book perched on his lap, Bainbridge had no idea. He should have been asleep hours ago.

Bainbridge and the Prince were close now, too. Across the small room was the door to the Queen's audience chamber, and beyond that, mired in perpetual gloom, the monstrous woman herself. Yet any alarm from Sandford risked bringing the whole endeavour crashing down around their ankles. There were still plenty enough guards in the palace to subdue the two of them, even with Foulkes's false trail.

From the other side of the doorway, the Prince pointed at Bainbridge's cane. He then jabbed his finger in the direction of the dozing valet, as if to suggest that Bainbridge should use it to subdue the old man.

Bainbridge shook his head. There were some lines that shouldn't be crossed. They'd just have to try sneaking past without waking him. He ducked through the doorway. He'd taken three steps before he heard Sandford's warbling voice.

"So, it's true, what they've been saying. I'd hoped it was all a terrible misunderstanding. Not Charles Bainbridge, I said. Not him. He was always such a good boy. Loves his country. Respects the old ways. He wouldn't go doing something like that."

Bainbridge turned to see the wily old valet was watching him with rheumy eyes, a revolver propped on his lap.

"But now here you are, sneaking about with Bertie and up to no good."

"Put the ruddy gun away, Sandford," said the Prince, impatient. "You're really going to try and shoot me for visiting my mother?"

"Don't you do that, Bertie. Don't you lie to me. I may be old, but I'm far from stupid. I know what's going on here. And it's incumbent on me to put a stop to it." He stood, shakily, the revolver still hovering between Bainbridge and the Prince.

"This isn't what you think it is, Sandford. We need to put things right. The Empire is unravelling. She needs to be stopped, for her own good as much as ours."

"I won't let you hurt her, Charles," said Sandford. "I know things haven't been going so well. That she's not the woman she once was, full of life and joy and love. But she's still the Queen of England. The Empress! And she still deserves our respect. If anything, I blame myself. I let her down, steered her wrong after Prince Albert died. But I'll see her right now." He waved the revolver shakily. "Please don't make me do what needn't be done."

Bainbridge took a step closer, ignoring the weapon. He put a gentle hand on Sandford's shoulder. "We're not here to hurt her, Sandford. I promise you that. But don't you think she's done enough? She's lived most of her life on that throne, with all the pressure, pain, and misery that comes with it. She won't give it up because she doesn't think she *can* give it up. But surely, she deserves a rest? A chance to step away from it all, to be a grandmother."

Sandford wouldn't meet his eye. "But it's not right, is it? Taking it all from her."

"You've seen what it's done to her, Sandford. You know she isn't well, that she's not thinking straight. What those machines have turned her into. Someone needs to help her. To share the burden. That's what the Prince is here to do. That's all. He wants to let the doctors look after her while he takes on the responsibility of running the Empire. This isn't an usurpation. It's a kindness."

"You really believe that?"

"I do. I think we'll all be a lot happier this way."

Sandford lowered the gun. "I hope you're right. I won't know how to live with myself if you're not."

"I'm right, Sandford. I wouldn't be here if I thought otherwise."

Sandford gave a short, sharp nod and shrugged away Bainbridge's hand. "Go, then. Do what you have to do. But try to remember: she wasn't always like this."

Bainbridge had to admire the man's stoicism, his loyalty to the woman Victoria had once been. He knew what she'd become, perhaps even knew of some of the horrors she'd perpetrated, but he still couldn't believe there wasn't something left in her to be redeemed. Bainbridge thought it was a lovely, if somewhat naïve, idea.

He glanced up, indicating the door with a nod of his head. The Prince visibly steeled himself, standing taller, puffing out his chest. He hadn't seen his mother since she'd committed him to Bedlam, so this was going to be far from the happy reunion most parents might hope for when their children return to the nest.

Together, the two men went inside.

The velvet darkness of the audience chamber was absolute.

Bainbridge had been led to believe the Queen no longer slept, a symptom of the chemical infusions that were slowly pickling her brain, but wondered now if that was just another simple falsehood he'd been foolish enough to accept, a myth perpetuated by the court along with all the others. That was the thing about Victoria, there was no longer anyone close enough to her to see the truth and discern the reality of the woman from the enigma she had fabricated.

Now, though, there was not even the timid glow of her hooded lantern to penetrate the gloom. Just the foetid stink of soiled clothes and sweat and the familiar, wheezing burr of her breathing machine.

"Mother?"

The Prince's voice echoed in the cavernous space, repeating like a mocking echo.

No response.

Bainbridge considered going back to Sandford to find a lamp. But then a thought occurred to him and he unsheathed his cane and twisted the haft, igniting the electrical coil within. He held it above his head as it spat and sparked, casting a penumbra of thin blue light around him and the Prince. It did little to banish the inky murk, but for the first time he sensed the true scale of the room, where the distant, unseen walls hinted at rows of neat alcoves.

From the darkness ahead came the slow, solemn creak of wooden wheel rims.

Bainbridge turned towards the sound, raising his sparking cane aloft.

A wet, cackling laugh. A hacking cough.

A vesta flared like a distant star, and the hooded lantern flickered to life, seeming to hover in the darkness, suspended in the air itself.

Victoria shifted, leaning forward into the orb of light, her plump, leathery face peering out at him like some grotesque, errant spirit.

"Oh, *policeman*. You truly have outdone yourself. All that grand ambition, all those lofty ideals, those plans to forge a new agency, a force for good. What use were they in the end, hmmm? All they have brought you to is *this*." She spluttered into her fist, dark blood dribbling down her chin. "Although we admit there is a delicious irony in the notion of a man of the law turning common criminal."

"Mother. Stop this."

Victoria turned her gimlet-eyed glare on her eldest son. Bainbridge could see that he was trembling but whether from fear or rage, the chief inspector couldn't be sure.

"Silence!" she hissed. "You have no voice here, *traitor*."

"Mother–"

"You are no child of mine."

The Prince took a step forward. "You *will* listen to me. Your time is at an end. I cannot permit you to continue with this grotesque performance. You bring shame upon our house and name. You rule naught but an empire of decay. There is a reason all of your children have fled."

"Not all of them," said Victoria. "Just those unworthy of us."

"Your Majesty," said Bainbridge. "I implore you—it's time. While your legacy remains intact. It's time to let go, to rest. You've done enough."

"So, this is how a fanatic justifies a coup. With talk of kindness. Yet the company you keep tells an altogether different tale. You align yourself with one who seeks bloody revolution. A man who has already plotted to overthrow us once, and who demonstrated no compunction in attempting to murder your friends in pursuit of his goal. Or had you forgotten our son had sanctioned the murder of your supposed friends, Sir Maurice and Miss Hobbes? We may no longer be the model monarch, Sir Charles, but at least we are not a hypocrite."

"No," said Bainbridge. "I do not believe that you are. Nevertheless, you have allowed yourself to forget the true purpose of your reign: your responsibility to the lives of your people. They starve, and they die, and you sit idly by in your gloom-ridden chamber without a moment's care. I have tried to understand you, Your Majesty, but I cannot fathom what it is you have become. You seem only to see the world as chaff with which to line your own nest, a thing to be owned and controlled. But control is not enough. The people need a leader. They need something to believe in again."

"And you think *he* will give them that?" she scoffed. "A jumped up, petulant child who's never forgiven his mother for keeping him from his 'destiny.' A jealous little boy who never had to grow up. Forgive us, Sir Charles, if we fail to see how your so-called 'Albion Initiative' changes *anything*."

"It changes everything," said Bainbridge, with a conviction he didn't feel. While he was loathed to admit it, even to himself, there was a kernel of truth to her words. Prince Edward was a far from perfect replacement. But he had to believe that the man could be better than this ghost of a woman before him.

Victoria gave a showy sigh. "Well, we must admit, this evening is turning out to be quite the disappointment. We had expected more of you than this . . . paltry showing. Have all of your friends and allies deserted you in your hour of need? Are they all dead, like Professor Angelchrist?"

Bainbridge gritted his teeth, refusing to rise to the bait, to reveal his anger at the mention of his murdered friend. To give her the damn satisfaction.

A thought occurred to him: the latent policeman's brain, still looking for inconsistencies, for little idiosyncrasies, for clues. "You . . . expected us?" he said, with a sudden stab of doubt. How could she have anticipated their arrival? Was she simply trying to wrongfoot him at the crucial moment?

Of course, she must have assumed he'd broken the Prince out of Bedlam for a reason such as this. But how could she possibly have known that they would make their move that night? It went against everything they'd been planning. Unless . . .

"Oh, of course. You see, you've been usurped, Sir Charles. We found we had a vacancy in need of filling, and we do like to keep a tame policeman on a leash. Don't we, Inspector?" The shadows stirred to the left of Victoria's bizarre chair. "Come now. Don't be shy."

Footsteps. Heavy, even, steady.

Bainbridge's heart sank. He felt as if the world had suddenly shifted three steps to the left, leaving him unsteady and unable to find his footing.

It can't be. Please, don't let it be.

A figure emerged from the gloom. A tall, bulky silhouette. Familiar.

Oh, please . . .

The man stepped closer, so that the soft blush of the Queen's lantern light caressed his pale, bearded face.

Not this. Not you. Not now.

The man fixed him with a hollow stare.

"Foulkes."

Foulkes had betrayed them. His *friend* had betrayed them.

It all made sense now—how Warlow had known to find them at the Wren house. Why Foulkes had rushed to meet them, why he'd agreed to provide the distraction. He must have set the guards off on their wild goose chase before coming directly here to warn the Queen, allowing Bainbridge to think they were safe. Luring him deeper into the trap.

The bastard.

"I'm sorry, Charles. She has my *children.*"

Bainbridge could see the sorrow on Foulkes's face, the deep creases of pain as the man tried to contain his emotion. This was not something he'd done easily, or out of choice.

Not that it mattered now. And there was still time, still—

"Give me that."

The Prince lurched suddenly towards Bainbridge, grabbing for and twisting Bainbridge's wrist. The move was so unexpected that Bainbridge reflexively released his hold on his still-sparking cane, pulling free of the Prince's vicelike grip. It was a deft move, and the Prince pivoted smartly, catching the falling cane by its handle so that he might wield it as one might wield a rapier in a fencing match. He took a step forward, the crackling tip wavering just a few feet from Victoria's heaving chest. The bellows wheezed as she emitted another wet laugh.

"And so, you once again show your true colours, boy. Kill us, would you? Your own mother?"

"You've said it yourself—I'm no child of yours. Not like this. Not after what you've become. Father would be disgraced."

At this, Victoria's eyes narrowed, and she leaned forward in her chair, spittle flecking her lips as she spoke. "He was twice the man you are, *boy,* and he'd never have tolerated your insolence. Your disloyalty would have broken his heart years ago if he'd survived to see it. Perhaps it was for the better that he didn't."

The Prince took another step forward. "Don't think that I won't do it. For England. For the Empire."

"For yourself," spat Victoria.

"Remember our agreement, Your Highness," said Bainbridge, still rubbing his wrist. He didn't like the way this was going.

From nearby, Foulkes looked on, his face ashen, unwilling to play a part in whatever was about to unfold.

"Our agreement?" laughed the Prince, bitterly. "Really?"

"It's not our place. We cannot be judge, jury, and executioner. That way madness lies. That way we end up like her."

"Not our place?" muttered the Prince. "I'm the goddamned *king*!"

"Not yet, you're not," said another voice from the darkness, "and if you kill her, you never will be."

"Who in the name of Hell?"

"Hell is right," said Bainbridge.

He watched lightning spark in the gloom—threads of fierce blue light spitting and hissing as they danced across the pale scalps of three, four, six, *ten* boltheads, standing in a long line behind the Queen's chair. At their head was Warlow, a commander on the field of battle, ready to lead his troops on the last charge to victory. "The moment that cane moves another inch towards her, my boltheads will move against you in turn. Your rule will be but a footnote in history, your only command a single exhalation."

"Are you all mad?" bellowed the Prince. "Can't you see that, for the good of us all, *she must go*?"

"I see only the ravings of a matricidal madman and his scheming colleague, hungry for power and prepared to take it at any cost."

"You're wrong, Warlow. You'll see that soon enough," said Bainbridge.

"Perhaps I will. But for now, Sir Charles, I must act as my conscience dictates. Lower the weapon, Your Highness. This is a stand-off you can never win."

Cursing wordlessly, the Prince slammed the cane upon the ground, shattering the generator mechanism, so that the spinning coil slowly wound down to a stop, the spitting discharge of electricity petering away to nothing.

Bainbridge hung his head.

Victoria cackled with glee. "Another failure to chalk up amongst so many others, *policeman*." She turned her head, calling over her shoulder to Warlow. "Take him to the cellars. He may yet prove a useful source of information about his traitorous friends."

"And the Prince?" asked Warlow.

"Oh, we have something very different in mind for him," she replied, with an air of reptilian satisfaction that made Bainbridge's skin crawl.

"As you command, Your Majesty."

Bainbridge didn't see any use in putting up a fight. It was already too late. Foulkes's betrayal had seen to that. The Albion Initiative had failed. *He* had failed. He only wished he had the means to warn Newbury of what would come next. With Angelchrist already dead, the Service would fall apart, dismantled piece-by-piece, corpse-by-corpse. And this monstrous Queen would live on to shape the future in whatever fashion she chose. At least he wasn't likely to be alive to see that future.

Three of the boltheads formed a loose circle around him and, together, they began shuffling towards the door. Warlow followed behind, a wicked smirk on his lips.

"Oh, and Warlow?" called the Queen, as they neared the door.

"Yes, Your Majesty?"

"The girl, too. This 'Constance Markham' who conspired with these traitors, see to it that she does not trouble us again."

"It would be my pleasure," said Warlow, with a low, satisfied laugh. "Consider it done."

Not Amelia, thought Bainbridge, his guts twisting. *Not her, too . . .*

CHAPTER 21

The wait was excruciating.

Amelia had been sitting for almost an hour, perched on the end of her bed, dressed in her travelling clothes with the small leather bag by her feet. The door to her room was now propped slightly open, the chest of drawers pulled aside once again. When the call finally came, she hoped to move quickly.

Yet she'd heard nothing. The raised voices elsewhere in the palace had died away long ago, disappearing into the London night, and there'd been no further calls of alarm, no word from Sir Charles or Inspector Foulkes, no sign of Newbury or Veronica.

She got to her feet, unable to shake off the nervous energy of the last few hours, the anxious voice at the back of her mind whispering unwelcome thoughts. What if something had gone wrong? What if they'd failed, after all this planning, all this effort? They wouldn't get another chance, not like this. What if something had happened to Veronica? Why hadn't she come with Sir Charles as they'd agreed? Could the Queen's agents have got to her first?

Amelia realised she was pacing, and stopped instead by the door, listening intently for any sound that might help provide a clue as to what was going on.

Nothing.

Then—a door opened with a creak. Footsteps. Lots of footsteps. Getting louder. The hint of a voice. A man's voice. Familiar, weaselly: Trimbey. She strained to discern what he was saying.

"... rl in question is Constance Markham. I caught her sneaking about earlier tonight when she should have been in her room. I'll show you—her room is just this way."

The footsteps—at least four sets—were at the top of the stairwell, leading down from the main floor, where she'd let Sir Charles and the others in a short while earlier.

She had to think quickly. They were coming for her. Did this mean the coup had failed? That they knew the part she had played in it? Or simply that Trimbey, petty-minded as he was, intended to seek revenge for her earlier admonishment? She supposed it mattered little either way. Getting caught up in something now could prove disastrous. She had to get out before they cornered her down here in her room.

Amelia snatched up her bag and stepped out into the passageway for the second time that night. She could hear the men more clearly now, descending the stairs around the dogleg.

"I *knew* there was something up with that one. She just isn't like the other girls. Always plotting something, you know?"

Who was Trimbey talking to?

Amelia was trying not to panic. Down here, she was effectively cornered. There was no other way out of her room, and the only exit from the passageway was the stairs. There was nowhere else to hide, except the other rooms, which were all occupied.

She steadied her breathing. The light was still on in Jenny and Rosemary's room. That in itself would usually incur Trimbey's wrath, but he clearly had other things on his mind.

She considered her options. It was a desperate ploy, and there was every chance the women would give her up. But, if she stayed where she was, she was trapped regardless.

Decision made, she raced down the corridor, grabbed the door handle and threw herself into the kitchen maids' room.

Carefully she closed the door behind her, just as the footsteps started down the main staircase.

The two women—who had both turned to stare at her with shocked incomprehension—were laying side-by-side on one of the twin beds, arms wrapped around one another in what had evidently been a passionate clinch. They hurriedly pushed each other away, disentangling, smoothing the fronts of their nightdresses.

Amelia raised her finger to her lips, urging them to remain silent while the footsteps sounded noisily on the other side of the door, and the pleading look on her face evidently did the trick, as Rosemary's shocked aspect quickly turned into a deep frown.

"What the hell are you playing at, Constance?" hissed the woman. "You can't just come barging into other people's rooms like you own the place."

"It, umm, wasn't what it looked like," added Jenny. She ran her hand through her hair, bit her lip.

"I don't care what it looked like," said Amelia. "I'm happy for you."

"You are?" said Rosemary, her expression softening. "You won't tell Trimbey, then?"

"Trimbey! That's who I'm hiding from."

Raised voices sounded from down the passageway. They'd evidently discovered she was no longer in her room.

"You're hiding from Trimbey?"

"Quickly, put out the light!"

Jenny nodded, twisting the knob on the lamp. The room was plunged into darkness. Amelia stood with her back pressed to the door. She was certain Trimbey would hear her heartbeat, thudding through the wooden panels like the beating of some dreadful drum.

More footsteps, hurrying this time. Voices retreating back up the stairs.

Amelia waited at least a minute before she spoke again, finally letting out a long breath. "I think it's safe now, you can put the light back on."

The soft glow seemed to swim up out of the darkness, like a star being born. The tiny pinprick brightened until the lamp was an orb that banished the night. Both women were still staring at her.

"What happened?" said Jenny. "What did you do?"

"I didn't do anything," protested Amelia. "I went to the water closet, and when I came back, he was in my room, standing over my bed. I told him to get out and he stormed off. That was about an hour ago. But he obviously wasn't going to take no for an answer. He was coming back, but I've packed a bag and I'm going. I can't stand to be around him any longer."

"You're leaving?" said Rosemary.

"He's left me no option," said Amelia. "He's made my life a living hell."

The two women glanced at each other. "We thought it was just us," said Rosemary. "That he'd found out somehow and wanted to make a point. Especially with Jenny being coloured and all." She wouldn't meet Amelia's eye. "I must say, it's something of a relief to know he's the same with you, too."

"A man like that," said Amelia, "he's probably the same with all of us. Just look out for yourselves." She turned to the door.

"You're really going, just like that?" said Jenny.

"I can't stay here. I've got somewhere to go. But listen—please—if he comes down here looking for me, don't tell him you saw me."

"That bastard ain't getting nothing from us," said Rosemary. "Now you go and do what you have to do. And mind yourself on the way."

"Thank you," said Amelia. She slipped out through the door.

Out in the passageway, the coast was clear. Quietly, she crept to the bottom of the stairs, just in case Trimbey and the others had left a guard. There was no one there. She hoisted her bag onto her shoulder and hurried up to the dogleg, careful that her boots didn't scuff on the stone.

Another quick check, but the way seemed clear. All she had to do now was make it out through the same door she'd let the others in through. Once she was out in the grounds, she could make for the cover of the trees, and then on over the wall and away. She'd head straight to Veronica's house, try to find out what had happened. Things here clearly hadn't gone to plan, but there was nothing she could do about it by herself. Her only hope was to get away.

She reached the top of the stairs, where they opened out into the hallway. Here, a cold breeze brushed her cheek, causing her to shiver. The door to the outside stood open.

Amelia broke cover, running for the door, and then through it, into the yard. Her feet crunched in the gravel. She glanced to the left and right. The strange carriages were still parked by the other door to the right. To her left, she could see lanterns approaching, presumably carried by Trimbey's men, returning from a search of the grounds. Ahead, the path through the grounds would be treacherous in the dark, but she'd have to try her luck. She had no other cho—

"Constance?"

Her mouth was suddenly dry. She turned, forcing a smile.

"Mr. Chappell." The junior footman and sausage roll thief.

He was eyeing her with genuine concern, having just emerged from the doorway in her wake. "What's going on? What are you doing out here at this time of night? If Trimbey catches you, he'll have your guts for garters."

"I . . . um . . . I just needed a little air, that's all."

"I saw you running. And you're carrying a bag and wearing your civvies." He crushed the still-smouldering tip of the cigarette he'd been smoking, tossing the remnants away amongst the gravel. It was starting to rain. Amelia felt a droplet strike her cheek, cool and startling. Perfect. Typical. She turned to glance the other way. The lanterns were getting closer.

"Look, I have to go. I'm sorry."

He reached out, took hold of her wrist. His grip was gentle. "Whatever it is, I might be able to help."

"I doubt that very much."

"Try me, Constance."

She sucked in a deep breath. She didn't have time for this. The rain was now pattering steadily upon her head and shoulders, trickling down the back of her neck in cool runnels. "It's Trimbey. He's after me."

"After you? What do you mean?"

"I mean he's searching the Palace and grounds for me, and I need to get away, *now*. He wants to hurt me, Tom. There are people coming. I'm sorry. I have to go."

She made to pull away, but he held onto her wrist, his fingers slipping on her wet skin. "*Hurt* you? Jesus, Constance. What's going on? Why would he want to *hurt* you?"

"I don't know, all right, but he was in my room earlier and now he's looking for me, and I need to *go*." She yanked her wrist free of his grip.

"Let me help." He puffed out his chest, as if trying to make himself look more impressive. "I want to help."

"Then buy me time. Tell them I went the other way." She started to back away, heading for the grounds.

"No! I mean, yes, of course, but don't go that way. There's more of them out there. At least three groups of them. I thought they were looking for an intruder on the grounds. They'll find you if you try for the walls or the gates."

"Then where?"

"If you really want to get out of here, those wagons. They'll be leaving shortly. Same time every night. They load them up with some sort of cargo and ship it out through the main gates. You can hide inside and slip out later when they get wherever they're going."

Amelia glanced at the carriages, then back towards the grounds. She could see several people now, silhouetted against the night by the lanterns they were carrying, their shoulders huddled against the pelting rain. "All right," she said. "And thank you." She leaned forward, brushed her lips lightly against his wet cheek, then turned and hurried off down the side of the building. Behind her, she heard Chappell clearing his throat in embarrassment.

The carriages were parked just as they'd been the other night, close to the door through which the drivers collected their mysterious cargo. She slowed as she approached, pressing herself against the wall. A quick glance back the way she had come told her Chappell had gone to engage with the guards. Perhaps she'd misjudged him. Perhaps he was a good man with honourable intentions, after all. Aside from his propensity for pilfering late night snacks, of course.

She edged along the wall, anxious but trying not to inadvertently give herself away. There was no sign of the carriage drivers. She assumed they were probably inside, smoking, drinking, and laughing again. She hoped beyond hope that they were.

Someone shouted across the yard, and she saw more bobbing lights amongst the trees, coming from the direction in which she'd been intending to flee. It was quite probable that Chappell had saved her life. Assuming, that was, she managed to make this harebrained escape plan work, and the vehicle's drivers didn't discover her. That, though, was a problem to face at a later time. First, she had to get inside one of the carriages.

The nearest of the two stood with its rear doors open. She inched closer to peer inside. More of the same unusual log-shaped objects lay inside. She estimated there were around ten of them, heaped on top of one another in haphazard fashion. The same musty odour prickled her nostrils, but there was no other clue as to what the rolls contained. Another thing for her to worry about later. Raindrops drummed on the carriage roof.

She heard laughter emanating from the open doorway and realised that her earlier estimation had been right. This was probably the nightly ritual of these drivers—collect their cargo, then share a glass or two of gin with the palace staff before going on their way.

She considered hopping up into the back of the carriage and laying down amongst the log rolls, but her instincts told her that they'd probably left the doors open for a reason and may yet have a small amount of cargo to load. It was a certain way of getting herself caught.

Instead, the second carriage would be a better proposition. The doors of that one had already been closed, suggesting it was fully loaded and ready for despatch. There was less chance of them opening it up again to check inside. The only problem was that it was parked on the other side of the open door. She'd have to walk right past the drivers—who she could now sense were standing just inside the doorway—without being seen.

The rain was falling hard, slicking her hair to her scalp and causing her culottes to stick to her thighs. It ran down her face, stinging her eyes, dirty with London grime. She wiped her face on her sleeve, for all the good it did.

More voices from behind her. She dared not look back. Chappell had obviously done all he could, suggesting he'd seen her run off into the trees, but it wouldn't be long before they were swarming the area again, rain or not.

She had to move, and she had to move now.

Amelia forced herself to walk, slowly and steadily, making a direct beeline for the other carriage. She could hear the men talking and hoped beyond hope that they had their backs to her as she crossed the slanting shaft of light from the open doorway. She didn't look, didn't want to jinx anything by testing fate. If she looked, they were real and if they were real, they were more likely to see her and raise the alarm. Better to ignore them, to just keep on walking like there was nothing else in the world but her and the carriage.

Five more steps. Three more steps. One more step . . .

She was there, and she slipped around the rear of the vehicle, out of view of the door.

So close now.

Slowly, she reached for the handle. It clicked open as she turned it, and the rear door eased aside without a sound. Inside, this one was stacked even higher than the other, with around twenty of the log rolls, all similar in size and shape. Her job, for the next while, was to become another of those strange logs—to slide in amongst them and await the opportunity to escape.

She threw her bag in, then hoisted herself up after it, sliding around as she tried to wriggle further in on her stomach, her clothes uncomfortable and clingy with damp. Then, twisting around, she reached down and pulled the door shut behind her, thrusting herself into sudden, intense darkness. She settled down amongst the hard, unforgiving rolls, dragging two of them on top of her, just in case the drivers did decide to do a final inspection.

Then, the only thing left to do was hope, and wait.

CHAPTER 22

The moment he opened the door, Newbury knew that something was wrong.

It wasn't so much that there was anything untoward in the hallway—only a blossoming, deep-seated sense of disquiet, an instinctive alarm that the atmosphere felt unsettled, out of sorts.

Bainbridge would have laughed at him, teasing that he was giving credence to old wives' tales of second sight or "unnatural sensitivities," but it wasn't that. More, that Newbury had become so well attuned to the character of his home that any change in its timbre rang out like a clanging bell.

Someone uninvited has been here.

He stepped inside slowly, pulling the door shut behind him. The lock appeared unmolested and the hinges undamaged. If someone *had* been inside, they'd exercised great caution, and even greater skill. The lock, Newbury knew from experience, was unpickable by anyone without an expert eye and the correct tools. He'd had it fitted for exactly that purpose.

Inside, the house was silent. He'd given Scarbright the night off and suspected the valet was still at the pub, catching up with some of his old school friends. Thus, the house had stood empty for most of the evening, meaning the intruder had had plenty of time to work. It stood to reason that they'd probably already left, but he'd have to proceed with caution regardless.

Newbury had come directly home after dropping Veronica at her house that same night, brimming with a warm sense of hope for the future. Even the sudden downturn in the weather hadn't been enough to dent his ebullient mood. He barely remembered the carriage ride after bidding her goodnight–his mind so fixed on the possibilities that were suddenly opening up to him. Things that, just a few weeks ago, he had scarcely thought possible. A future without the bleak, ongoing oppression of the Queen. A future by Veronica's side.

Welcome thoughts that would have to wait for another time.

He considered his options. An intruder would have one of three purposes: firstly, to find evidence of suspect behaviour that could be used against him, such as anything that could link him to the Secret Service and the Albion Initiative; secondly, to steal some rare esoteric text or belonging; lastly, to attempt an arrest or assassination. None of them could be discounted.

He decided to start in the drawing room, not least because of the loaded pistol he kept on the mantelpiece there, tucked behind his tobacco jar. He shrugged out of his jacket and flung it over the coat stand, folding back his shirtsleeves. Then, cautious but determined, he strode down the hallway and pushed open the door.

The room had been methodically turned over. His precious books had been pulled from the shelves and strewn across the floor like a sea of dead birds, covers open and leaves flapping in the draught like lifeless wings. The damage, he knew, was irreparable, and his anger surged into near rage. All that work discarded like so much flotsam. Rare tomes that could never be replaced, years' worth of carefully filed notes spilled and chaotic. Drawers, cupboards, the writing bureau all stood open, too, similarly abandoned, their contents abused. The drinks cabinet had been raided, and several bottles were overturned, their lids removed so that their contents had run out upon a stack of leather-bound books.

This, Newbury understood, was not the result of any real search. The person who had committed this atrocity was not looking for something. No, this was simply an exercise in spite, a tactic designed to unsettle Newbury, to anger him so that he would be wrong-footed and not thinking straight when the perpetrator made their real move.

So, something else is coming.

Carefully, wincing as he was forced to tread on the spines of several precious books in the process, Newbury picked his way over to the hearth, where he could now see the cooling ash of several burned books and papers. The bastard had been thorough. This was going to take years to put right.

The objects on the mantel had been disturbed; the cat skull had been picked up and slammed back down, so that several of the teeth had broken loose; his tobacco jar had been opened and left with no lid; several pictures had been toppled and smashed. He checked behind the tobacco jar. The loaded pistol had gone.

Newbury cursed. He'd have to try the study upstairs for one of his rapiers. He backtracked to the door, took one last, maudlin look at the chaos of his life's work, and then pulled the door shut behind him.

Back out in the hallway, he drew a deep breath, tried to steady his nerves. He wanted to rage, to kick at the walls and bellow at the sky for the injustice of what had been done, but he knew that was exactly the response the perpetrator was intending, and he refused to give them that satisfaction.

There were only a handful of people who could hurt him so deeply–Veronica, Bainbridge, Scarbright, Amelia. Camilla Karswell, perhaps. And the Queen. This had to be the work of the latter. She was sending him a message. She knew that he was involved in Angelchrist's Secret Service. A warning, then, that his card was marked. His name was on her list.

If that were the case, though, why not send Warlow and his boltheads, as she'd done for Angelchrist and the others? Execute him immediately to eliminate the threat. Was she toying with him, enjoying the chase, relishing the thought of his face upon seeing such devastation wrought upon his work? Or was Warlow simply busy elsewhere, and this was the handiwork of some other loyal agent working in Warlow's stead? He'd made as many enemies amongst her followers as he had friends over the years—those who took exception to his methods, who considered him a dangerous influence on the monarch with a habit of dabbling in things that should better be left alone. He could think of any one of a handful of such fools who would delight in such repugnant work.

He crossed to the bottom of the stairs, listening. Still nothing; not a single creak of a floorboard or the hollow groan of a door being opened or closed.

He started up the stairs, the treads bowing slightly under his feet. He walked with his neck craned, watching the landing above, beyond the rails. All was still and dark.

He reached the first landing and took a moment to ensure there was no one lurking in the bathroom there. Venturing up here was risky if there was still someone hiding below—they could effectively cut off his exit route, as the only other way down from the first and second floors was the windows. In his time, he'd been forced to deploy such methods to make good an escape or to stay on a suspect's trail, but he was getting older, and more brittle, and he risked doing himself some permanent damage if he were forced to employ them again.

He edged around the loose floorboard outside the spare bedroom door—another he'd chosen not to have repaired for want of any other early warning signal for anyone venturing up here without permission—and then, noting that all of the doors remained closed, including the access door to the attic, he crossed to the study door at the far end of the landing.

He tried the handle. Locked. Now, that was interesting. Had they tried and then failed to gain access? Or had they naïvely assumed the drawing room was the only repository of his work?

Newbury slipped the key from his pocket and turned it in the lock. Then, slowly, he pushed the door open.

It was dark inside, the only light spilling in from the electric bulb in the hallway behind him, but it was evident from his first glance that the room had been subjected to the same disarrangement as the room downstairs. More bookcases toppled, this time without even the pretence of a search. The meticulously prepared chalk circle on the floor had been purposefully scuffed and disfigured. Specimen jars had been shattered, spilling their acrid contents over every surface. A preserved human heart lay squished by the window, as if from under a boot. A sheep's brain lay crumpled and broken where it had been dashed against the wall. The violence of the scene was truly shocking. This had been committed by a man harbouring true hate.

Most notably, the cards of the *Crux Occultus* had been tossed on the ground in a fluttering wave, landing just inside the open door. Most were face down, some of them torn, but staring right up at Newbury were two familiar images: *The Fallen Knight* and *The Broken Chain.*

So, this is where the chain is broken.

He stepped inside, realising too late that he hadn't considered why the intruder had bothered to lock the door again after they'd finished wrecking the place—another tactic designed to throw him off guard. He turned, reached for the handle, just as something—a fist—came swimming out of the gloom, striking him hard across the jaw.

He went down, groggy, knees buckling as he fought to remain conscious. He knew this was it. If he passed out now, he was dead. He had to fight. There was too much at stake for him not to.

Newbury roared, coming back up, using his legs to propel him from the ground, grappling the intruder around the waist and bringing them down heavily, too. They crashed through a toppled display case, splinters of broken glass snagging his skin as they rolled.

The woman—he could tell by the grunt of surprise she'd emitted as she fell—thrashed her body and pounded at the back of his head with her fist until he was forced to let go, rolling away, scrabbling to his feet. He was standing by the window, and he grabbed for the curtains, yanking one of them sharply so that the pole tore free of the wall, spilling moonlight onto the scene.

The woman snarled, glowering at him from across the room. She had neat black hair, scraped back in a taut bun, and was wearing a form-fitting black blouse, with matching black culottes and boots. Her skin was dark, her mouth drawn in a tight sneer. She was bleeding from a gash on her cheek.

"Agent Bakshi," said Newbury. "I see you redecorated."

"You traitorous bastard," she spat. "Wallowing here amongst your unclean rituals and godless filth. You're a disgrace to the Empire."

"I'm a necessity, and *she* well knows it," said Newbury.

Bakshi moistened her lips, pacing in a semicircle through the wreckage of his study, arms poised as she searched for an opportunity to strike. "Perhaps you'd managed to pull the wool over her eyes before, but not now. She sees you for what you are. We all do."

"And she sent *you* to eliminate me?"

Bakshi laughed. "Just consider how far you've fallen," she said, "that you weren't even worth sending Warlow for."

"Oh, I take it as a compliment," said Newbury. "That woman has always underestimated me."

"No," said Bakshi. "I rather think she had the measure of you all along." She launched herself, then, striking left, then right, then left again, delivering a flurry of successive blows that left him reeling, unable to even raise his arms in time to defend himself from the percussive blows. He staggered, rasping for breath, tasting blood.

Bakshi was laughing. "I thought so. All talk and no—"

A jab to the gut knocked the wind from her lungs, and then Newbury was shouldering her over, slamming her against the back of a fallen bookcase, so that she grunted in pain. He punched again and she rolled, launching a spilled volume of the *Ars Magicka* at his head. He ducked, and it struck him hard in the side of the neck, causing him to stagger back again, struggling for breath.

And then she was up and upon him, raining more and more of those devastating blows, striking his gut, his chest, his groin. He fell, hitting the wall and sliding to the ground, reeling from the pain and dizziness.

Her hands closed around his throat, and he raised his arms, trying to push her away, clawing at her face. But it was no use. She was stronger than he'd ever be, and so filled with hate that he knew she'd never stop, that even when he was dead, she'd still keep on squeezing, just to show him how much she despised him and everything he stood for.

Panic came like an onrushing tide as he tried to breathe, bucking and wheeling, but her grip was a vice, unshakeable and deadly.

His vision was swimming. Darkness was closing in like a narrowing tunnel, so that all he could see was her grimacing face, her wide, piercing eyes, her blood-streaked brow.

Something went bang, and he knew it was over—that this was the sound of his own death, his ears popping with the pressure exerted by the dreadful woman. He thought then of Veronica, of the promises he had made that would now be unfulfilled, of the life he so longed for that he would never get to lead.

He watched as Bakshi's grinning face slid away out of view. His eyes fluttered shut.

Something hard and sharp stung his cheek, and he drew ragged breath, feeling sweet, cool air flood his lungs.

He hacked, reaching for his throat, coughing as his breath returned in short, shallow gasps.

What . . . ?

He opened his eyes and looked up to see Veronica standing over him, his pistol—the one from the mantel downstairs—gripped in her hand.

Bakshi was lying dead on the ground a few feet away, blood still welling from the puckered wound in her chest, her eyes still open, face still contorted in a victorious grin.

"I . . . ," he croaked, before breaking off into a hacking fit.

"It's all right," said Veronica. "Take it slowly." He could see that she was trembling.

"How?"

Veronica shrugged. "They'd been to my place, too. Just the same. After you dropped me off, I found everything had been overturned, drawers emptied, pictures smashed. There was no one there—I thought they might have been here, too. I hailed a cab and came straight over."

Newbury rubbed his throat. "Thank goodness you did."

Veronica glanced at Bakshi's body. "The look in her eyes . . . They really do hate us, don't they?"

"They can't see what we see," said Newbury. He reached out and took the pistol from Veronica's hands. "They don't want to believe the truth, even though it's staring them in the face. And so, they carry on, following her commands, doing her bidding. Because if they don't, they have to admit that they were wrong, too. That they've spent years of their lives dedicated to a corrupt cause. It's too much for some people to bear. And so, they turn on us instead for speaking the truth. Better that than accept it for themselves. Better to live with the lie."

"You almost sound like you *understand*. She would have killed you."

"I understand how it feels to hide from betrayal. I think we both do."

Veronica turned away. "I suppose we do. But right now, we need to be practical. They're onto us. They won't let this lie."

Newbury nodded. "More of them will come. We need to go. To hide."

"The Wren house?"

"No. Too risky for us all to be under one roof. I have somewhere else in mind." Newbury held out his hand and Veronica helped him to his feet. "There are bags already packed in the dining room. We can be there within the hour."

"But what about the house? About . . . *this*?" She indicated the body on the floor.

"A problem for another time," he said. He moved to the door, then hesitated. "I need to leave word for Scarbright, too. He won't be safe here, either. We have a code—if the attic window is ever open, he knows not to come inside. Would you . . . ?"

"I'll see to it," said Veronica.

Newbury smiled. "You rescued me. Again."

"That's what love is, isn't it? Rescuing one another, over and over again."

Newbury laughed. "Yes," he said. "I suppose it is."

CHAPTER 23

The carriage juddered to a halt.

In the back, beneath the mysterious cargo, Amelia gave a sudden start. The dark, close atmosphere coupled with the monotonous rocking motion of the wheels and the crash from the adrenaline of earlier that night had almost lulled her to sleep. She cursed herself, flexing her numb limbs. She'd lost all sense of time but guessed she must have been hiding there for an hour or more, nestled amongst the strange log-shaped bundles in the pitch darkness.

She stilled her breathing, listening for any sounds that might give her a clue as to their location. A horse stomped its foot and snorted. A bird hooted. Then voices. Two men, their conversation receding. She recognised one of them as the man she'd spoken to during that first night in the rain. The drivers. She strained to hear more but couldn't pick out much of their conversation.

". . . night . . . nas . . . business . . . Jim."

". . . ver and done. . . . we . . ."

They were walking away from the carriage. Now was her chance. Stifling a yelp of pain as she rolled free of the two bundles she'd pulled over her earlier, she wriggled towards the door. The muscles in her left leg were cramping and her feet were burning with the sharp prickle of pins and needles.

She willed herself to move. For all she knew, the carriage

could be opened at any moment, and while she'd managed to get this far, away from the guards at the palace, she didn't fancy her chances against two burly male drivers, or worse, a gang of their compatriots. She didn't have Veronica's schooling in the defensive arts, or her upper body strength. Not that she was in the habit of comparing herself to her sister—more that she was aware of her own limitations and didn't want to take any unnecessary risks.

Carefully, so as not to make a sound, she reached down and turned the door handle. The rear carriage door opened, and she held it there for a moment, peering out through a gap of about an inch.

Outside, it was a cold, crisp night. Wherever they were, there was no lighting, other than the silvery glow of the moon, deepening the shadows. She could see some sort of stone building or construct, flanked by what appeared to be the statue of a winged angel, its hands held open by its sides in supplication. She shivered at the sight of it, eerie and blank-faced in the gloom.

She listened but could hear nothing beyond the snorting horses, and so, gingerly, she swung her legs down and around, then pushed the door slightly further ajar and slid down. The edges of the bundles scratched at her back. Her feet encountered stone paving slabs. She reached back for her bag, dragging it out behind her, and then edged out from behind the door. She pushed it shut.

She was in a cemetery. The building she'd seen was a tomb, and the angel a nearby grave marker. The area was littered with angels that erupted at jagged angles from the loam. A forest of the divine, petrified by man to preside over the dead. She turned on the spot. The cemetery stretched away in all directions. Narrow lanes criss-crossing the fields of the lost. This was Highgate, she realised, where the great and the good came to rest when they died. The creed of all London was buried in its strata.

Around her, the gravestones were as eerie sentinels, some grown tired and listless, their charges long forgotten, others still proud and erect, watchful. Others still had been ill-treated by the ivy that scampered up their sides, a groundswell of reclamation dragging the stones back to the earth, rendering the names of the dead near-indecipherable. Oblivion by nature. She supposed it was only fitting.

She heard the tread of boots and crept away from the carriage, edging behind the wall of a nearby tomb. From here she'd be able to watch what the men were doing so she'd be better informed when she reported back to Veronica and Newbury later. Whatever was going on, it was clear the palace didn't intend for anyone to know about it.

One of the drivers appeared around the side of the carriage. The young man wore an oiled overcoat and flat cap. He had a distinctive hair lip and striking blue eyes. He was about to open the rear doors of the carriage, when the other man called him back, and he shook his head in exasperation, doubling back the way he'd come. She listened to their brisk exchange as they decided to unload the other vehicle first.

Hugging the wall of the tomb, Amelia circled around the other side, treading lightly and keeping to the shadows. The soft loam sucked at her boots, and she couldn't help but imagine what that ground contained, the things it had seen, the history upon which she walked. She found a position by the rear corner of the crypt, peeking out from behind a stone lintel. Above her, grotesque statues leered, tongues lolling from their fanged mouths, eyes wide and staring.

From here she could see the two men lugging the bundles one by one over their shoulders, fetching them from the back of the carriage to disappear inside one of the other nearby tombs, a large domed structure, flanked by Corinthian pillars at all four corners. The double doors at the front of the tomb had been propped open and the men were evidently piling their cargo inside. It was brisk, methodical work. She got the sense they'd done it dozens of times before, if not more.

She continued to watch until they'd emptied the first carriage, and then started in on the second.

What were they doing? What was hidden inside these rolls they were fetching down from the palace every night? And why hide them in a tomb at Highgate Cemetery? She supposed it was as good a hiding place as any. The base for a smuggling operation, perhaps. She wondered if the two men were part of a larger gang, and others would come later to collect the strange deposits. She resolved to take a look just as soon as the two men had finished.

It didn't take them long to unload the second carriage–the one she'd ridden here in–and unlike at the palace where they'd hung around to jape with Trimbey and his cronies, here they seemed anxious to get away. Muttering something about "paying off the night watchman before taking the wagons back to Herod for another load," the two men locked the door to the tomb–placing the key on an out-of-the-way ledge around the corner of the structure–and then returned to their vehicles. A few moments later, they were trundling away towards the exit.

Rubbing her arms to stave off the chill, Amelia emerged from her hiding place the moment they were out of sight. She hurried over to the ledge, retrieved a rather large, ornate key, and approached the door to the tomb. The entire door was forged from banded sheets of heavy iron, with a clunky lock mechanism that must have dated from early the previous century. That would seem consistent with the discolouration of the marble of the tomb's construction and the weathering of the sculptured faces, their noses worn and soft, as if she were seeing them from far away, or out of focus as in a hazily remembered dream.

With an effort, she turned the key in the lock and heard the mechanism click. She tried the door, but the hinges were stiff and seemed unwilling to cooperate. With a heave, she wrenched it open. The squeal of the hinges pierced the night. A flock of birds, startled, burst from a nearby treetop, taking wing.

Glancing after the carriages—still out of sight—Amelia ducked inside the tomb.

The place reeked of age, and death, and being there, in the gloom, knowing that the structure had once been built to house the corpses of some rich London family, Amelia shuddered. She felt as though she were trespassing, as though the dusty skeletons of the dead might rise unbidden from their niches at any moment to challenge her and drag her down into their terrible domain. She thought perhaps the stories she'd been reading had impacted her imagination, after all.

Yet here there was no white-robed Carmilla, no restless spirits. Just row upon row of the same log-shaped bundles, laid out in neat, towering aisles. She walked amongst them for a moment, trying to estimate how many there were. One thousand? *Two* thousand?

What were they doing here? And what was the Queen's role in it all?

The light was thin and watery, and the tomb went back further than she'd imagined from the outside. In fact, as she approached the rear wall she saw that a set of steps led down to an excavated cavern below. She had no torch or lantern, but she did have a book of vestas in her coat pocket, and so, steeling herself against what she might find down there, she lit one with a loud rasp and descended the dank steps to see what was below.

Here, the musty odour was nearly overwhelming, and she was forced to bury her nose and mouth in the crook of her arm. She could see the rows of log-rolls continued to either side, but the sense down here was claustrophobic, hemmed in.

The vesta had nearly burnt down to a stub, singeing her fingertips, and she dropped it, shaking her hand to dull the pain. She struck another, and in that momentary flare, got a true sense of the scale of the chamber. It was *huge*. Roughly hewn from the bedrock, it sloped away into what looked like endless darkness, deeper and deeper beneath the cemetery. She lit another, and another, dropping them by her feet, allowing them to burn while she tried to take it all in.

The cavern was *full.*

Every inch of it packed with towering piles of rolled canvas bundles, as far as her eyes could make out, in every direction. The heaps in the chamber above were just the tip of the iceberg. Whatever was going on here had been going on for a very long time indeed.

Amelia stood there for a moment, her heart sinking as the light guttered and blinked out. It was time she faced what she'd been suspecting all along, but didn't want to admit, not to herself, not to anyone. Because to give it voice was to make it real, and the thought of it was simply too horrible. Yet, despite it all, she had to know.

She turned and hurried back up the steps to where the moonlight slanted in through the open door, passing the swirling dust motes she'd disturbed on her way in. She crossed to one of the bundles nearest the door, presumably one of the few brought in with the latest shipment. It took her a few moments to worry the tightly knotted twine that bound the canvas sheets loose, her fingertips bloodied and sore, but finally she was able to yank the twine free and peel back the canvas sheet.

She almost wished that she hadn't.

The dead man's face glared up at her accusingly. His eyes were hollow sockets, his skin leathery and taut. He seemed somehow desiccated, as if all of the fluid had been leached from his flesh, reminding Amelia of the Ancient Egyptian mummies she'd seen on display at the British Museum as a child. His brittle lips were folded up, away from his yellowed teeth, and his tongue was a black, shrunken strip in his mouth. His hair was still dark and vibrant, mussed, but formerly kept in a neat, lacquered side parting. She could see the outline of his skull through the papery skin.

She ran outside.

All those people. Tens of thousands of them. More . . .

This was an act of genocide. A horror beyond comprehension, beyond measure. Worse than she could have possibly imagined. At the thought, she vomited on the grass. She hadn't eaten, and the bile gushed in a thin, acidic stream, burning the back of her throat.

All those people.

She got to her feet, brushing herself down, hugging herself. She'd ridden in the back of the carriage amongst those same corpses. She felt horribly unclean. But it wasn't the proximity to the bodies that made her feel that way. No, the thing she wanted to scrub away above all else was the terrible sight of all those bundled, nameless corpses, piled high beneath the tomb, stretching away into the darkness. All those lost people, stolen from their families and hidden here, beneath London, like some perverse mine, the bedrock seamed with human death.

She let out a sob, and fell to her knees in utter despair.

All those souls. All those lives. People who had once walked the city just like her, their futures now stripped away, stolen. People who had once had names. Families. Lovers. Aspirations. Dreams.

The loss was beyond measure. Beyond imagining.

How could anyone be so cruel, so heartless? How could anyone be a part of this and still live with themselves?

Amelia remained there for a moment, huddled on the grass amongst the tombstones, a living grave marker for the legions of the dead.

But then a single thought seemed to cut through the morass of emotions.

What would Newbury do?

He'd put a stop to it. He'd do whatever it took to end this nightmare. He wouldn't stop to wallow. He'd see it through to the end.

She got to her feet. The men had gone. But they'd spoken about paying off the night watchman before leaving to see someone called Herod. Perhaps there was still time to catch their trail, to follow them to the other end of this macabre chain and decipher exactly what was going on so she could end it.

She would bring it to the attention of the new king. She had to believe that he, King Edward, would be better than this. That everything they were fighting for was worth it. She only hoped their ploy had been successful—that, as she'd fled the palace in the chaos, Bainbridge and the Prince had managed to unseat the murderous Queen.

Amelia pulled the tomb door shut and pocketed the key. Then, her mind made up, she set off running in the direction of the two carriages.

CHAPTER 24

Bainbridge *wanted* to tell Flora the truth.

Keeping it from her felt wrong, inciting a sharp, physical pain that seared like a needle, jabbing behind his left eye. He tried to pull away, to leave, but no matter which way he turned, she was standing there in front of him, her expression full of sorrow. He'd disappointed her, he realised that. He'd let her down in the worst possible way.

This wasn't like her. The Flora he had loved all those years ago had always worn a calm, happy expression, had always been so patient and forgiving.

So why couldn't she see? All of this was for her own protection, to keep her safe! She'd already died once. He couldn't allow it to happen again.

He'd always promised not to keep anything from her, to never shy away from difficult truths, to hide. It had been a fundamental tenet of their relationship and ensuing marriage, and it was a promise he had always kept, right up until that first time she'd died.

Now, though, her disapproval hurt more than any other wound could. A cut so deep that he thought his soul might be flensed from his body.

"I'm so sorry, Flora. I'm so, so sorry."

"Well?"

"I can't. If I tell you, they'll kill you. They'll come for you in the night like the others. I won't allow them to do that. Not to you. Not even if it means we can't be together."

"It's no use," said Flora. "He's a tough old bugger."

"What do you mean?"

"I think we'd better put him out again before we break him. We'll try again in a few hours. We'll get it out of him eventually."

Bainbridge couldn't make sense of what she was saying. "Flora? Flora? I don't understand. Come back. *Please.* Please come back."

But she was walking away. He coughed down a sob. His eye was hurting again. Why couldn't she understand? She'd always listened to him before, always trusted him. Why wouldn't she trust him now?

"Flora?"

But she was gone.

"All right," said a man's voice. He thought he recognised it from somewhere, but he couldn't place it. "God, I think we've lost the eye. He didn't even scream."

"Warrender? Is that you? What the hell are you doing in my house? Where the devil are you? Come here, where I can see you."

"I'm putting him under."

"You're doing what? What the hell are you talking about, man? Where's Flora?"

A cold flood, like iced water rushing through his veins. Haziness. Silence. Peace.

Then blackness.

It was approaching one o'clock in the morning and Sergeant Quint was beginning to have second thoughts about his plan.

Had he taken a blow to the head while dealing with the murderous Parker? What on Earth had possessed him to head straight over here, to Herod's funeral parlour? He could have waited until the morning, briefed Foulkes, and led a team over to carry out a full, meticulous search of the premises.

Instead, he'd come alone in the middle of the night, thinking that he might be able to catch them unawares in whatever nefarious business they were carrying out here.

He supposed it made sense to strike while the proverbial iron was hot, before Herod had seen the morning papers and learned that Parker had been recaptured. This way, the unsuspecting warden of the dead wouldn't have a chance to cover his trail.

Which was all well and good, save for the fact that Quint was almost dead on his feet.

He wasn't used to all of this scheming and gadding about. He'd always been a methodical man, more measured in his police work, rarely given to bursts of frenetic action or violent encounters of the sort he seemed to be enjoying of late. And enjoying was, he admitted, the applicable word. Quint had never felt quite so exhilarated as he did earlier that evening when he faced down Parker at the meeting hall. There was, it seemed, something to be said for the more hands-on side of the job. He could see now why it had always appealed to men like Sir Charles Bainbridge.

Still, embracing a previously neglected side to his work and poking around the exterior of a funeral parlour at one in the morning were, perhaps, two different things. Rather than recapturing that exhilarating feeling from earlier, he suspected all he'd managed to catch was a head cold. Or possibly a fever. Definitely a chill of some description. At least his arm had stopped throbbing. The wound had—thankfully—proved to be superficial, if somewhat messy. It was now bandaged up tightly, and he'd taken a welcome tincture for the pain before venturing back out.

He shivered and turned the collar of his coat up as he crept around the side of the building, trying to locate an entrance that would lead down to the mortuary area where he'd interviewed Herod earlier. The cold felt as if it were seeping into his bones, and, just to make matters worse, a fog was now beginning to descend on the city, tendrils thickening like the limbs of some strange, serpentine beast. He longed for his bed.

Still, he was here now, and he knew his instinct had been right, even if every fibre of his being was protesting about it.

Around the rear of the building two black carriages had been parked beside a cellar door, similar to those through which his local pub would take delivery of new casks each week—wooden panels banded with wrought iron for strength. The carriages looked glossy and well maintained, such as those used by the gentry, but upon closer inspection he realised they were of an unusual construction, with double doors opening at the rear and no passenger compartment. More like cleverly disguised wagons than the carriages they purported to be.

Quint presumed it was some disguise employed during funeral services: a form of specialised hearse used to ferry coffins about incognito. Regardless, the carriages were all locked up and the cellar doors were closed. As one would expect at this ungodly hour.

Still, at least he'd found the access point to the lower level. Judging by the shape of the building, the cellar doors had to lead down to an area of the basement close to where he'd been.

He heard a noise, somewhere to his left. A footfall. Gentle, but close. The sole of a boot scuffed the paving slabs.

Quint turned just in time to see the coattails of a slight-looking figure disappearing around the other side of the building. A quick glance told him that no lights had come on anywhere else in the property, so it had to be someone else poking around. Or else he was being followed.

Intrigued, he pursued the woman around the corner. For he was sure, judging by her size and build, she *was* a woman running for the cover of some nearby trees.

Evidently she had seen him and realised that she'd aroused his suspicions. She glanced back over her shoulder, her face pale in the moonlight. A few steps more and she'd be swallowed by the fog.

Quint stopped, skidding to a halt. There was something familiar about that face. Something that had lodged in his mind. . . .

"Stop!" he hissed, keeping his voice low so as not to draw the attention of anyone inside the parlour. "Miss Hobbes, please stop!"

The woman came to a stop. Slowly, she turned on the spot, staring at him with wide eyes. She looked thinner than he remembered, and she'd done something to her hair, but he was certain it was her. He took a step forward. "You won't remember me, Miss Hobbes, but my name is Quint. Sergeant Quint, of Scotland Yard. We worked together, briefly, in the aftermath of the Lady Armitage affair. And again, with that Seaton Lock business, a few years back." He held out his hands to show that he meant her no harm, then fished out his warrant card, brandishing it for her to see.

"I'm sorry," she said, taking a step towards him. She glanced at the warrant card.

"Don't worry, Miss. I wouldn't have expected you to remember me. I was just a constable back then, fetching and carrying and the like. But I remember you were kind to me, even then."

The woman smiled. "That sounds like her."

Quint was lost. "Pardon? I fear we might be talking at cross purposes."

"My sister," said Amelia. "You're talking about my sister, Veronica."

"But then . . ." Quint trailed off. He supposed that would explain the hair. And the similarity in appearance. "I wasn't aware . . ." He cleared his throat. "My apologies, ma'am. She's an admirable woman, and you and her . . . well, the resemblance is uncanny."

The woman nodded. "Used to happen all the time. I'm Consta–" She seemed to catch herself. She studied him for a moment longer, evidently weighing her next words with care. "Amelia," she said. "Amelia Hobbes."

"An honour to make your acquaintance," said Quint, all

considerations of the cold now gone. He stepped closer and shook her outstretched hand.

"If I might ask—what is a policeman doing here at a funeral parlour at one o'clock in the morning?"

Quint considered this for a moment. "Following a lead," he said. He frowned. "And if I might reflect the question back at you, ma'am—this seems a rum place indeed for a lady such as yourself at this hour."

"It does, doesn't it. Then I'll let you in on two further secrets, Sergeant. Firstly, I am certainly no *lady,* and secondly, I, too, am here to follow a lead."

"You are? Then you're working with your sister and Sir Maurice?"

"In a manner of speaking."

"And you have an interest in Herod & Co?"

"I have an interest in why they're involved in depositing thousands of dehydrated corpses at a tomb in Highgate Cemetery, and the nature of their connection to Buckingham Palace."

Quint stared at her for a moment.

Thousands of dehydrated corpses? Could that really be right? She didn't *look* like a woman given to hysteria. But surely this had to be an exaggeration. He supposed the only way to be certain was to investigate further. "Then I think, Miss Hobbes, that you and I should talk," he said.

She nodded. "I must admit—this is a welcome surprise, Inspector. It's been something of a trying day, all told, and anyone who holds Veronica in such high regard . . . well, I can think of fewer better marks of character."

Quint's mind was still reeling. "You did say *thousands* of corpses?"

"I've seen them myself," said Amelia. "I, umm . . . well, let's say I've been following the drivers of those wagons. They've gone now, but they came here directly from Highgate, after depositing several bundled corpses that they'd collected from Buckingham Palace. I'm led to believe they've returned the wagons here to collect more fresh corpses in the morning."

"More fresh corpses . . ." Quint was trying to piece it together in his mind—the story he'd heard from Parker, and now this . . . It just didn't seem to add up.

Buckingham Palace?

"Look, I don't mean to question the validity of your statement, Miss Hobbes, but did you actu–"

"Shhh!" she cut in. "Did you hear that?"

"Hear what?"

She waved him quiet.

There. The tinkle of broken glass, coming from the other side of the building. How had he missed it? She grabbed his wrist, dragging him off in the direction of the sound.

"Don't you think we should app–"

"*Shhh.*" She squeezed his wrist so sharply that it hurt.

Quint wondered for a moment exactly how he'd ended up in this position, in the orbit of this remarkable young woman. One moment he'd been searching for a means of ingress to the mortuary, the next he was being dragged around by the arm and informed that the case he was investigating involved thousands of bodies and, somehow, Buckingham Palace. His head was whirling. And then:

"You!" he barked, upon rounding the corner and seeing the old man from Parker's execution, right there in front of him, attempting to climb into the funeral parlour through a broken window.

The man scowled at him from beneath bushy grey eyebrows. "Quiet, man!" he hissed. "Do you want to bring the whole place down upon us?"

"No, but, I . . ." He snatched his arm free from the grip of the Hobbes woman. "Who are you, and what the hell do you think you're doing?"

The man sighed. "My name is Professor Archibald Angelchrist, young man, and I'm trying very much to save the lives of the several unfortunate people being held inside."

Quint gaped.

"Now, if you and Miss Hobbes would be kind enough to assist me, I believe we can have the matter resolved in quick order."

"I . . . but . . . you're *dead*!" said Quint. The news had been doing the rounds at the Yard all day. Foulkes had been the one assigned to the case. Another murder of the type plaguing the London gentry. Members of Parliament, government agents, newspaper barons. And in this case, one of Sir Charles Bainbridge's greatest allies, and a key advisor to the prime minister. Although, if this man before him was to be believed, it appeared Foulkes had been mistaken.

"Apparently not," said Angelchrist, tartly. "Now are you going to help me, or just stand there gaping?"

Quint glanced back at Amelia, who shrugged, evidently as perplexed by the matter as he was. Then, shaking his head, Quint went to help Angelchrist up through the window before he and Amelia followed the man inside.

CHAPTER 25

"My thanks to you, Miss Hobbes. Your daring escapades this night have provided me with a piece of the puzzle for which I have been searching for some time. Namely—evidence of the Queen's direct involvement in these unconscionable deaths."

"I have no doubt she's behind it. After what she sanctioned at The Grayling Institute . . . what they did to me and the others there . . ." Amelia hung her head. Whatever had gone on had evidently left a deep and unforgiving scar.

Sergeant Quint stood watching Amelia and the professor as they hurriedly laid out their stories. His head was swimming as he tried to take it all in. Never in all his years at the Yard had he heard such a bizarre and, frankly, despicable tale.

"Sir Maurice has appraised me of the details, my dear," said Angelchrist, laying a gentle hand over Amelia's. "I intend to ensure that nothing of the sort ever happens again. That's the point of our initiative—of everything we do. We must protect the people of this Empire, even from those who would have us believe they know best. Especially them."

"I'm just glad to see you're alive," said Amelia. "From what the sergeant has told us, it seems the rest of the world believes quite the opposite."

Angelchrist looked pained. "Alas, there's little cause for

celebration, as grateful as I am to be here. For me to survive, another poor soul had to die."

"Who, then?" asked Quint, finally finding his voice. The whole matter was growing more and more incredulous by the moment. Nevertheless, everything finally seemed to make sense. It was clear neither Miss Hobbes nor Professor Angelchrist we're attempting to mislead him. Indeed, so far, their testimony had only served to corroborate or explain his own findings. Yet the scale of the deception behind it—involving the Queen of England, no less—was difficult to even conceive. Instead, he was focusing on the smaller, more manageable questions. "Who was it they found in Islington?"

They were inside the mortuary area of Herod's parlour, where, thankfully, no fresh corpses had been laid out upon the slabs this time. They'd been comparing notes in hushed tones, and the professor—somehow risen from the very grave—had been outlining his case against the Queen. The evidence was damning, to say the least.

"A man named George Foster. Terminally ill with cancer, with no family, and bearing enough of a resemblance to pass for me to any casual observer, or to those who've not spent too long in my company." Angelchrist rubbed his hand over his face, evidently pained. "One of several such men I employed to serve as misdirection. To masquerade in my place, visiting my usual haunts throughout the city, adopting my established habits. None of them were meant to die, you understand—more that they were engaged to act as decoys, throwing the Queen's men off my trail." He sighed. "Alas, the ploy seems to have worked a little *too* well. I very much regret the manner in which Mr. Foster met his end."

"And all of this," said Quint, "it's why you were at Parker's execution? Why you've been asking questions around Spitalfields? You knew they weren't going to kill him, didn't you?"

"I had my suspicions," confirmed Angelchrist, "but I hadn't been able to prove anything. When he escaped and turned up alive, back to his old tricks—well, it was another piece of the puzzle confirmed."

"So, the doctor is faking the death certificates at the executions and someone working with him is sabotaging the hangings to ensure the victims survive," said Quint, working through the chain of reasoning. "The 'bodies' are brought here, where they're held for a time, before being shipped, still alive, to Buckingham Palace. Something happens to them there, and then later, desiccated and wrapped in canvas—and thoroughly dead—they're taken to Highgate Cemetery to be disposed of inside a subterranean tomb. And this has all been going on for some time."

"That's about the size of it," confirmed Angelchrist. "Except, the executions can't be the only source of people," he added. "There are too many bodies for that, if Miss Hobbes's testimony is correct, which I do not doubt. They must be filtering people through this funeral parlour from a variety of different routes. People snatched from the rookeries, imported from the colonies, the workhouses, the streets—people who won't be missed."

"But why?" said Amelia. "What possible purpose could the Queen have for all these people? And why murder them in cold blood?"

Angelchrist grimaced, revealing his distaste. "I'm not quite sure. But it's a huge operation. They must be providing something she wants or needs. If it were a matter of merely culling the population, removing those she deemed undesirable—well, there are tidier ways to go about such heinous crimes. Ways that wouldn't implicate her directly."

"And why would she be saving the lives of criminals at the gallows, only to kill them later?" added Quint. "That makes no sense. There has to be more to it." He looked at Amelia. "You saw nothing else that might hint at the reasoning behind this monstrous industry?"

Amelia shook her head. "If I had, I'd have already gone to my sister. Whatever it is, they're keeping it well hidden. It explains why they got so jumpy when they caught me poking around the carriages, before I knew they were bodies."

"Well, we have what we need to convince the government to act. I need to secure this . . . repository at Highgate, just as soon as we're done here."

"What can I do?" asked Amelia. "I won't sit idly by and allow this to continue. I won't stand for any more deaths. Not a single one. Even if Sir Charles and the Prince have been successful at the palace, I feel duty bound to expose this horror. And we cannot yet be certain that they *have* been successful."

Quint nodded. "Whoever turns out to be behind this, for whatever reason, I want to see them brought to justice." He massaged the back of his neck. Not for the first time that night—or morning—he wished he had a stiff drink. "Even if that person is the Queen of England."

"All right," said Angelchrist. "I think I know how you can help. But it's dangerous. Your sister wouldn't thank me for it."

"My sister isn't here."

Angelchrist grinned. "That's the spirit. First, though, we have a job to do. If I'm right, Herod is holding people somewhere down here, ready to make a fresh shipment to the palace in the morning. We need to find them and set them free." He glanced around, looking for any obvious signs of a concealed compartment or door. "You've been here before, Quint. Where could he be keeping them?"

Quint wracked his tired brain. "Upstairs is just a showroom full of empty coffins. We're in the right place. It would have to be down here somewhere."

He began a slow circuit of the mortuary, searching for any clue. If Angelchrist was right and there really were people being held here, it would largely confirm everything the two of them had said.

Amelia was examining a locked door at the rear of the room. The handle was rimed with frost. Quint approached. "Cold storage," he said. "Nothing could survive in there for very long. They keep the temperature low to preserve the bodies."

She nodded and continued her search elsewhere.

"Although . . . come to think of it, that must be a huge cold store. Consider the size of the building. Could there be something on the other side? Another set of rooms, inaccessible without going through the refrigerated area?" Both Angelchrist and Amelia had come to join Quint before the door. The sergeant glanced at Amelia. "It's all right to say you told me so."

"Open it up," she said.

"We don't have the key."

She rolled her eyes. "Step aside."

Quint did as he was told.

Amelia rolled her shoulders, eyeing the lock.

"Are you sure that's a good idea?" ventured Quint.

Amelia ignored him. She was counting under her breath . . . "Three, two, one . . ."

She barged the door.

The force of her shoulder against the door snapped the old lock. The rusted hinges shattered and the door clattered noisily to the tiled floor.

The two men glanced at one another. Angelchrist raised an eyebrow.

"Impressive," said Quint, with a low whistle.

The silence, when it returned a few seconds later, seemed stark, as Amelia, standing in the doorway, rubbed her arm, her breath fogging before her face. Quint could feel the chill coming off the ice heaped inside the opening.

They ventured over the threshold.

Here, the dead were laid out in a series of shelf-like cubbyholes that lined the walls, like so many books, their stories waiting to be told. Quint tried not to stare at them as they traversed the strange microclimate of the cold store, heads tucked low, hugging themselves against the frigid atmosphere. Ice crystals glittered on the cheeks of a middle-aged woman, dusted the moustache of an elderly man.

This, then, was the fruit of Herod's genuine labours: the bodies he prepared for the genuine funerals he continued to conduct alongside the grotesque operation with which he had become entangled.

Sure enough, a second door stood opposite the first, in the far wall of the cold store. Quint tried the handle and almost recoiled at the sharp, biting chill of the metal against his palm. It, too, was locked.

Amelia put her hand on his shoulder to motion him aside, but he shook his head. "I'll see to this one." He took a step back, following her lead. He rolled his shoulders, counted down from three . . .

. . . *three, two, one* . . .

The sergeant launched himself at the door, throwing his weight behind the movement. The door shook in its frame, but didn't budge, causing him to rebound sharply, staggering to maintain his footing. Embarrassed, he righted himself, trying to ignore the welling pain in his upper arm. He cleared his throat. "Let's just try that again, shall we?" He stood back, making ready for another attempt.

"Hold on," said Amelia, trying but failing to keep the amusement out of her voice. "This one opens the other way." She hurried back through to the mortuary, returning a moment later with a mean-looking hammer, looted from amongst the mortician's tools. She crossed to the door, lifted the hammer and then struck the handle sharply. The frozen metal shattered with a single blow, sending fragments raining to the tiles beneath. A few seconds later and she was wrenching the door open to reveal another room beyond.

"Remind me never to get on your wrong side," muttered Quint.

The thick, mingling aromas of sweat, urine, and faeces emanating from the room struck him like a wave. It was dark in there, and it took a moment for his eyes to adjust to the sight.

Almost a dozen terrified people huddled against the back wall, some standing, others on their knees, one lying prostrate on the cold floor. Their clothes were filthy, and they stared at the group with exhausted, bloodshot eyes. They were all adults, of varying age, a mixture of men and women of assorted ethnicities. One of the men was jabbering in what sounded like Spanish. Some of them were marred with dark bruises across their faces and forearms.

"Please," said a woman in a torn grey dress, "we've done nothing wrong. Please let us go." Her plea was so weary, so lacking hope that it tore at Quint's heartstrings.

"It's all right," said Angelchrist, stepping forward. "We're not part of this. We're here to help. We're going to get you out. Can you walk?"

"Yes," replied the woman. Several of the others agreed, nodding vigorously.

"Good, good," said Angelchrist. Quint could see the dismay written in the deep lines of the professor's face, the appalled horror at what these people had been reduced to, and Quint knew then, without doubt, that whatever happened next, he would fight alongside this man to see this ended. He had a notion that such a position might put him on the wrong side of the law and his colleagues, but he understood now why Sir Charles Bainbridge had made the choices he had, why a man like that would risk everything, even his life, to help put a stop to this terror. It was the only honourable thing to do. The sight of these poor people filled him with anguish.

"Come with me," said Quint, motioning for the prisoners to follow. "I'll show you the way out. You're going to have to climb through a window, but once you do, you get away from here as quickly as you can. Understand?"

One of the men, dressed in little more than tattered brown rags, fell to his knees as Quint's words seemed to sink in. With grimy hands he wiped at the tears flooding down his face, his body wracked by waves of fitful relief. A black woman in a worn grey dress rushed to the man's side, sliding her arm around his shoulders, holding him close and still. He rocked there for a moment, his breath whistling through broken teeth.

These people. They're desperate and forgotten. Victims in more ways than one. Victims of an Empire that barely recognises them.

"Yes, yes. Thank you," muttered another man, hurrying forward, clasping Quint by the sleeve of his jacket. He clung on as if he was never going to let go. "Thank you."

Quint forced a smile, but he felt no cheer. What he was seeing here was heinous.

"Who are you?" said a tall, thin woman, her voice heavily inflected with what sounded to Quint like a Russian or Eastern-European accent.

"I'm a police officer," said Quint, his voice almost cracking at the sight of more and more people gathering near the doorway, their dirty faces now transformed into shining beacons of hope. "From Scotland Yard. I'll see you out of here, now."

"Go, then. Follow Sergeant Quint, all of you," said Angelchrist. "Come along!"

The people charged forward in a rushing tide, as if the chains that had been holding them had suddenly been broken and they were no longer bound. Even now, though, desperate, scared, and malnourished, these people treated one another with respect, with no pushing or shoving as they filed through the door behind him, no screaming or shouting or claiming dubious priority over one another.

Better manners, Quint considered, *than half the shoppers on Oxford Street.*

It was only the work of moments to see them out through the window through which he and the others had gained access earlier. He'd counted eleven of the sorry beggars, and he listened now to the sound of their retreating feet with something akin to satisfaction. Whatever use these people were intended for, they were free now. Someone was going to be *very* disappointed.

He heard the others coming back through from the cold store and turned away from the window, only to find himself staring down the barrel of a shotgun that was clutched in the hands of an irate-looking Herod.

Cold fear trickled down Quint's spine.

"What the hell have you done?" barked Herod. "You've damned us all!"

CHAPTER 26

The door exploded.

Newbury—who had, somewhat remarkably given the circumstances, been asleep with his head on Veronica's lap—sat bolt upright, reaching immediately for the pistol that he'd left on the dust-matted coffee table. The bruises around his throat from Agent Bakshi were now a livid purple, bright and sore, and she saw him wince with pain as he got to his feet, covering the door with the gun.

Of all the places for them to take shelter, this would have been Veronica's last possible choice: Aubrey Knox's former residence in Ladbroke Grove—the house where Knox had lived and worked before being declared rogue, and the scene of some of his most horrendous crimes. Last time they'd been here, during what she'd come to think of as the "Big Ben Affair," they'd uncovered an underground laboratory where Knox had been carrying out a programme of highly unethical eugenics, performing wicked surgeries on a host of unfortunate souls who'd then been left to fend for themselves in the sewers following Knox's arrest. These victims, now shunning life amongst the London masses, had formed a loose community amongst themselves, building a kind of shanty town down there in the tunnels. Tunnels that were still readily accessible from a hatch in the dining room floor.

Nevertheless, that was why Newbury had selected the place,

she knew—the opportunity for a quick exit. It appeared to have been a well-judged decision, too, if the noise coming from the hallway was anything to go by. There was just one thing that was troubling her. They'd only been there for a few hours, just long enough to take a short rest and eat a simple meal. They'd taken a circuitous route from Newbury's house, doubling back on themselves and switching cabs twice. It was almost impossible to conceive that they'd been followed.

"How did they find us so quickly?" she said, grabbing the bags and backing towards the door that led to the adjoining room.

"They must have known where to look. They'd never have dreamed of searching for us here otherwise. They must have a man on the inside. Someone who knows our plans, our likely hideouts. Or else we're too late, and they've already got to Charles."

"Correct on both counts," said a quiet voice from the hallway. The man sounded smug, but Veronica could tell it was an affected confidence, as if he was engaged in playing a part, fulfilling a role in some garish West End stage show in which he was destined to act the villain. "Although I tried a few other places first. Made quite a mess of them, too."

"Warlow?" she asked Newbury, who nodded in affirmation.

A figure stepped into the room, and Newbury's pistol barked. The stink of cordite filled the air. The figure—a bolthead, by Veronica's reckoning—dropped to the ground, a wet, red hole in the centre of its forehead. Its head was wreathed in wild, sparking electricity. It looked just like the patient they'd met in bedlam, with metal spurs jutting from its skull and strange, pallid skin that had an almost translucent quality. An abomination, more than a man. An experiment of the sort carried out by Knox. It twitched as the electrical discharge caused its muscles to spasm. The floorboards blackened beneath it.

Out in the hall, Warlow laughed. "Very good, Sir Maurice. But how many bullets do you have? Because my boltheads will just keep on coming, all night if they have to. Her Majesty has charged me with 'dealing with the Newbury problem,' and I intend not to disappoint her."

"Don't you realise, Warlow—you already have. Nothing you do will ever be good enough for her. She'll string you along, of course, keep the monkey dancing for as long as she can. But eventually she'll tire of your tricks, or happen upon a more useful tool, and you'll be discarded just like the rest of us."

"Perhaps," said Warlow. "Or perhaps I'll do things differently. Perhaps it's the other way around and I'm just using her to get what I want."

"You sound just like I did, Warlow. Young and stupid."

"What? So, you're suggesting I give it up and walk away? That I put my hands up and walk in there so we can join forces?"

"Walk in here and I'll shoot you," said Newbury, through gritted teeth. "For Angelchrist and the others you've murdered."

The timbre of Warlow's voice changed, becoming softer, more considered. "I don't suppose you'd believe me if I told you that was a most regrettable business. But that's the truth of it. I don't really have the stomach for this kind of work. Needs must, however, when duty calls."

"Duty? What about your duty to the people of the British Empire, who deserve to be free of her tyranny? What about your duty to those she's killed?"

Warlow laughed. "And you think your plan to supplant her with the Prince of Wales was any better? One in, one out. They're all the same. You wouldn't have changed a thing, Newbury, except the person sitting in the chair."

Newbury glanced at Veronica, and she read the dismay on his face. Warlow had spoken about the plan in the past tense. Not only was he aware of it, it seemed he and the Queen had already put an end to it, somehow.

"So, you found them, then? Charles and the Prince?" called Newbury. He was backing towards Veronica, making ready to run, keeping Warlow talking in the meanwhile.

"Oh, yes. Your man Foulkes has been most forthcoming. I see why you keep him around—a truly helpful sort. Knows which way up his bread is buttered. And no doubt Sir Charles is giving up the rest of it as we speak, naming names, outlining all the details of your so-called 'Albion Initiative,' the bits that Foulkes wasn't able to give us earlier."

"He wouldn't," said Veronica. She looked to Newbury, mouthed the word "Foulkes?" She couldn't believe for a minute that the man had betrayed them as Warlow claimed. But then . . . Warlow was *here*, and apparently had the others in custody. *Someone* had told him where to look. Could Foulkes really have been the one to give them up?

Newbury had a haunted look in his eyes. "Get to the trapdoor," he hissed. "We'll lead them into the sewers."

"But—"

"Go!"

Veronica knew when an argument was lost. She turned and ran into the dining room, kicking aside the Turkish rug with the edge of her boot. The cobwebbed trapdoor was just as they'd left it after their previous visit; incised into the floorboards, with an inlaid iron ring with which to lift it open. She did so now, hoping that the sound of its creaking hinges hadn't carried as far as Warlow and his minions in the hall.

Behind her, Newbury was still talking, buying her time. She kept thinking of Bainbridge, held captive, probably in some dreadful, barbaric dungeon beneath the palace, subjected to ministrations of those amongst the Queen's followers who knew exactly how to extract the sort of information they wanted from him. The thought brought budding tears to her eyes. Hadn't they already lost enough?

What of Prince Edward, too? Returned to captivity in Bedlam? Pumped full of chemicals to make him pliable, compliant? Tortured, too, for his part in all this?

And what of Amelia, trapped in that dreadful place with

nowhere to turn? Thankfully, Warlow hadn't mentioned her. Did that mean she was still safe, that her role in things had yet to be discovered? Veronica hoped so, for all their sakes. She wouldn't be able to live with herself if anything happened to her sister, not now, not after finally getting her back. It had been hard enough to agree to the plan in the first instance—now the thought of the danger faced by Amelia was almost too much to bear.

She tried to stem the black tide of despair that was threatening to overwhelm her. There was still hope. There had to be hope. It was incumbent on her and Newbury now. And that started by ensuring they survived the night.

She tossed the bags down the flight of stone steps and then, with one last glance over her shoulder, hurried down after them.

The subterranean laboratory was gloom-ridden and filled with the macabre rejects of Knox's work—which she now had no doubt had been sanctioned by the Queen, and only denied by the palace after the truth regarding the horrific programme had come to light. Hulking figures, the remnants of humans who had been experimented upon, floated in upright glass tanks, suspended in clear, viscous fluid. Some of them had begun to rot, whilst others seemed almost perfectly preserved. Their shadowy faces were peaceful in repose. Most were criss-crossed in ropey scars, their limbs and torsos bulky and misshapen, swollen by whatever compounds and surgical procedures the insane doctor had applied.

Just the thought of the man filled Veronica with cold dread. She'd nearly died at his hands, had witnessed first-hand the grotesque results of his experiments. The thought that he might still be out there somewhere, broken but alive, was a constant cause of anxiety. She felt her mechanical heart flutter with the uptick of her blood pressure and tried to tear her thoughts away from the past, to focus on the present danger.

Gunfire sounded above, followed by thundering footsteps on the floor overhead. Veronica grabbed the bags and slid behind one of the tall glass tanks, just in case things hadn't gone as planned and one of Warlow's monsters was first down the stairs. To her left, the yawning mouth of the sewer tunnel was an ominous reminder that some of the people—just like the ones in the tanks—had survived, and were living wild in those same tunnels, keeping a watchful eye on any comings and goings through this abandoned laboratory. She cast around for anything she might use as a weapon, but there was nothing but fragments of a shattered tank scattered upon the tiles within reach.

A figure came charging down the stairs.

Newbury.

He took the steps two at a time, leaping down the last few to land on the tiled floor, wheeling his arms to maintain his balance. He searched the room until his eyes met Veronica's, and then backed up, taking up a similar position to her on the opposite side of the room, crouching behind an occupied tank. She noticed he'd discarded the pistol—presumably having used up the last of the ammunition.

Moments later, Warlow, flanked on all sides by boltheads, followed cautiously down the stairs. It seemed as if he were somehow contained in an orb of flickering blue light, picked out in the gloom, as crackling strands of lightning danced across the heads and along the arms of the boltheads.

"Newbury?" Warlow was casting about for them, but the light appeared to be working against him, limiting his field of vision. "We can make this a lot easier on you both. There's no point fighting or running. You already know that it's over. The Albion Initiative has failed. There will be no King Edward. Your friends have either betrayed you or are dead. Give it up now and be at peace. I promise I'll make it quick."

Warlow had reached the base of the stairs now, and Veronica cursed that they hadn't stopped to collect more ammunition or weapons before fleeing Newbury's house. She might have had a clear shot. As it was, she risked electrocution if she even attempted to get near to Warlow or tackle one of the boltheads.

She glanced over at Newbury to see that he had crept around the base of the glass tank he'd been hiding behind, working his way over to where a steel tray of surgical tools had been spilled upon the ground. As she watched, he selected a scalpel from amongst them, gripping it firmly in his fist.

Surely, he wasn't about to try to ambush Warlow with a blade like that?

He crouched, pulling back his arm, clutching the scalpel like a dagger. Warlow was moving down the central aisle of tanks, his expression a mix of revulsion and awe as he studied the victims inside.

One step closer, two . . .

Veronica wanted to scream at Newbury not to do it. He had no chance of making it. Had Warlow's words clouded his judgement? Was he so angry about Angelchrist and Charles that he would risk something so desperate?

He stood, making ready. Veronica tensed, ready to do what she could to help. And then Newbury swung his arm and tossed the scalpel as far and as hard as he could into the mouth of the sewer tunnel.

He dropped back into a crouch, edging away around the glass tank. Veronica exhaled. The scalpel struck the wall inside the tunnel with a dull clang.

Warlow's head snapped towards the sound. "In there," he said, gesturing to the boltheads. As one they turned, almost mechanical in their movements, and crossed to the tunnel mouth. Then, with Warlow following behind, they pushed on through into the enveloping gloom.

Veronica watched until their sparking electrics had shrunk to just a tiny pinprick in the depths of the tunnel before stepping out from her hiding place. She tossed Newbury one of the bags. "For a moment there I thought you were going after him with that scalpel."

"I considered it," said Newbury, his voice low.

"Well, I'm glad you didn't," she said. "The others are relying on us." She started for the steps back up to the house, then glanced back at Newbury, who was still staring after Warlow down the tunnel. "That should keep him busy for a while. Especially if our old friends are still lurking down there."

Newbury nodded. "We can't count on it, though. Nor can we put off the inevitable. Not with Charles and Amelia already at risk." He hoisted the bag over his shoulder and met her eye. "To the palace?"

Veronica nodded, and then hurried up the steps.

CHAPTER 27

Newbury stood on the dewy lawn of the palace gardens. Ribbons of thin mist still clung to the ground, not yet burned away by the rising sun, which was peeking above the roof of the palace, no more than fifty yards ahead of him. It was early morning, just after dawn. The people inside the palace would be stirring.

Their flight from Ladbroke Grove had been swift and purposeful. With Warlow and his boltheads diverted in the sewers, they'd been able to take a hansom directly across town. Newbury had instructed the driver to deposit them on the edge of Green Park, and from there, under cover of darkness, they had crept through the trees until they were almost abutting the palace grounds.

After stashing their bags in a small thicket, they'd hurried across Constitution Hill and up over the wall into the palace gardens. Thankfully, Newbury knew the movements of the patrolling guards and, even though the watch had clearly been doubled in light of recent events, they were able to slip amongst the trees and manicured hedgerows without being seen.

"It looks somehow different," said Veronica, quietly, from beside him. She was staring up at the towering edifice of the palace, as if seeing it with new eyes. "As if it doesn't represent what it used to."

"I know," said Newbury. "It's nothing but the seat of a rotten monarch at the heart of a broken empire."

The Queen's betrayal had hit them all hard, but it had not been entirely unexpected, not after all these years of watching her machinations and hearing her spit venom at the very people she was supposed to serve. Foulkes on the other hand–Newbury still found it near-impossible to believe that the inspector would side against them in all of this. After all, the man knew the truth of what the Queen had been doing, all her murderous schemes. How could he have chosen *that* over his friends?

Newbury started forward. "We don't have long. We need to keep moving." The Queen, he knew, wouldn't tolerate any of them, Bainbridge and Amelia included, to live for very much longer. It was now or never. "Time to end this, Veronica."

"Maurice?" He felt her catch his sleeve, and turned back. "Yes?"

She reached for him, pulling him close, so that her warm breath brushed his throat as she leaned into him. Her lips touched his, parted. Newbury sank into the embrace.

And then it was over, and she was pushing him away, both hands against his chest. Their eyes met. Veronica smiled, and it was a smile he knew he would lose himself in again and again if they ever made it out of there alive.

"Well, there's no use standing here until we're spotted," said Veronica, straightening her shoulders. She pointed towards the building. "We can go in through that servants' door over there, beside the parked carriage."

And with that, she set off across the lawn with a determined stride.

Newbury grinned. "After you, then, Miss Hobbes."

Quint woke with a start.

Someone was banging. Loudly. And shouting.

"Oi!"

Quint blinked gummy sleep from his eyes. He was cold and wrapped in a heavy woollen overcoat that wasn't his.

Where . . . ?

And then he remembered.

Ah.

He glanced down at the angry man who was pounding on the side of the carriage. A palace servant of some kind. Maybe a valet?

"What the hell do you think you're doing?" the man bellowed. "You should have been gone hours ago!"

"I . . . umm . . . hold on," said Quint. "Let me come down there and explain." He stretched, the muscles of his back and shoulders protesting wickedly. He must have been there all night. Now the sun was coming up, and he had no idea what to say to the man.

"*I'm here to help the government bring down the murderous Queen of England*" didn't sound like what the man wanted to hear.

Nevertheless, it was the least he could do, after the way Angelchrist had tackled Herod back at the funeral parlour. The way he snuck up on the shotgun-wielding lunatic and whacked him across the back of the neck with his shoe was positively masterful. Quint had no doubt it had saved his life—Herod didn't seem the type to listen to reason.

They'd left the funeral director bound and restrained in the very same room he'd held his victims. Angelchrist had promised to deal with him properly later, just as soon as the professor had secured the tomb at Highgate and taken the evidence to his superiors at Whitehall. Meanwhile, Quint had agreed to drive one of the carriages back here to the palace, containing Amelia Hobbes, who, insistent as she was about getting back inside to free Sir Charles Bainbridge, had posed as one of Herod's victims, sent over by late delivery. It had worked, too, and Quint had remained outside with the vehicle, ready to assist in a quick getaway, should Amelia prove successful before Angelchrist arrived with the government men to take control of the situation.

Only, Angelchrist wasn't yet here, and Amelia was still to emerge. And now a burly man in a suit was bellowing at him, risking drawing the attention of the entire household.

"Well, come on, then!"

Quint clambered down from his perch on the dickey box. "Is that the time?"

"Is *what* the time?"

Quint shrugged. "Well, I don't know. I was hoping you could tell me. I have been asleep, after all."

The valet grunted something under his breath and pulled a watch out from the pocket of his waistcoat. "It's a quarter to–"

He didn't see Quint's fist coming as it caught him squarely in the jaw. He went down like a sack of potatoes, splayed in the damp gravel, and Quint fought back a howl, shaking his hand as the smarting pain spread from his fingers, through the back of his hand, and up into his wrist.

Just at the same moment, two newcomers strode by, making a clear beeline for the side door into the palace, from which the valet had presumably emerged.

As they passed, the woman turned to glance in his direction, and he almost let out a little yelp in startled recognition.

"Miss Hobbes!" he called, for the second time in just a handful of hours. "Miss Hobbes!"

Newbury turned to glare at the buffoon calling Veronica's name. They didn't have time for this, nor, in Newbury's case, the patience.

The man–who was wrapped in a thick woollen overcoat and looked somewhat bedraggled–was clearly the driver of the parked carriage. He was shaking his hand, wincing, and standing over the unconscious form of one of the palace valets. He looked, wide-eyed, from Newbury to Veronica and back again. Something about him seemed vaguely familiar.

Veronica had stopped in her tracks and was peering at the

strange man as though struggling to place him. "Sergeant . . . ?" she ventured.

"Quint," completed the man. "Sergeant Quint. We worked together, briefly–"

"–at the site of *The Lady Armitage* crash. I remember," said Veronica. She started to turn away. "But I'm sorry, I don't have time–"

"I'm here with your sister," blurted Quint. "Professor Angelchrist sent us."

Newbury took a step towards the man. "You *what*? Say that again."

"Professor Angelchrist. He works for the government. He sent us here, last night–"

"Last night!"

Veronica interposed herself, putting a hand on Newbury's chest, pushing him gently back. "Yes, all right, Maurice–let the man speak."

"It started at the hanging," said Quint.

"The hanging?"

"Of the prisoner, Matthew Parker. That's where all of this began."

"We don't have time for a fireside tale, Sergeant," said Newbury. "Please, the summary will have to do."

Quint frowned. "Very well. The Queen has been involved in faking the deaths of prisoners and other unfortunates, but secretly having them brought here to the palace, where they are murdered for some unknown reason. The desiccated bodies are then shipped out *en masse* to Highgate Cemetery, where they are hidden. Your sister, Miss Hobbes, uncovered much of this, and last night, following a similar trail, we encountered one another at a funeral parlour used as a staging house by the perpetrators. There we met Professor Angelchrist, who–after saving my life– hurried off to Whitehall with the evidence needed to storm the palace later this morning."

"Good Lord," said Veronica.

"He's alive," said Newbury. "Then that body . . . it must have been someone else."

Veronica frowned at Quint. "Where's Amelia now?"

Quint swallowed, visibly uncomfortable. "She's inside."

"The carriage?"

"The palace," confirmed Quint.

"Why on Earth did you let her go back in there alone?" said Newbury. Elated as he was at the news of Angelchrist's survival, as well as the blossoming hope that their plan might not be entirely in tatters, his concern for both Amelia and Bainbridge greatly outweighed any sense of celebration. Not to mention the disturbing news about the bodies.

"We agreed she'd have a better chance of remaining undetected if she went alone," said Quint, "posing as one of the unfortunates shipped in from the funeral parlour. She insisted on going back for Sir Charles. She was worried Angelchrist would be too long mustering the folks at Whitehall to launch their investigation. I was to wait out here with the carriage, ready for a quick getaway."

"I see," said Veronica. "It certainly sounds like Amelia."

"Well," said Newbury, glancing at the unconscious form of the valet on the ground between them, "you seem handy enough in a tight spot, and I'm afraid there's unlikely to be any quick getaways this morning. I think it's best you came with us."

"Came with you where?"

"In there," said Newbury, indicating the door. "It seems we still have two people to rescue. Not to mention the Prince of Wales."

"The Prince of Wales?" echoed Quint.

Newbury sighed. "It's a long story. Come on."

CHAPTER 28

It was a thing to behold, Quint knew, seeing Sir Maurice Newbury and Miss Veronica Hobbes in action. He'd glimpsed it only once or twice before, and then only from the sidelines, but their reputation amongst the men at the Yard was something akin to legendary. It was also, he could now testify, very well earned indeed.

He watched with wonder as they strode through the corridors of the palace–*Buckingham Palace!*–side by side, unwavering, determined, focused. Every person they met, be they butler, maid, groom, or guard, was greeted with an apology, before they were neatly and efficiently laid out cold. Both Newbury and Veronica struck their blows with a surgical precision that dropped said member of the household to the ground. They were rendered unconscious with the minimum of injury or fuss.

Quint walked behind them in something of a daze, still wondering what the hell he had got himself mixed up in. There was every chance he'd hang for his part in all this, or at the very least spend his remaining years rotting in a dank cell. Worse, he hadn't even seen the evidence against the Queen himself. He'd long ago learned to trust his gut, however, and everything about both the younger Miss Hobbes and Professor Angelchrist had rung true. Not to mention the evidence they'd uncovered of Herod's part in things and the people they'd rescued from those terrible conditions at the funeral parlour. And now, to have Sir Maurice Newbury and Veronica Hobbes confirm the worst. Well, there was very little reason left to doubt. Quint had never been one to sit on his laurels while injustice went unchallenged . . . and so now he was here, delving into the bowels of Buckingham Palace, on a mission to rescue the chief inspector of police.

If nothing else, it would make for a good penny dreadful.

Two more thuds, two more guards hitting the ground. There were raised voices now, coming from somewhere behind them. Someone had evidently happened upon their trail and raised the alarm. Not that it seemed to unduly worry either of the two agents ahead of him. They seemed to know exactly where they were going—through a door in the servants' quarters, along a maze of increasingly bare, unfurnished corridors, down a flight of spiralling stone steps, and along a bare stone passageway.

It was dank down here, the walls slick with moisture and rank, slimy mould. Their footsteps rang out, echoing loudly off the bare stone. The air was thick and stale, and Quint was forced to take deep, steady breaths, gulping it down into his lungs. He had no idea how far underground they were but judging by the sloping tunnels and stairwells they'd marched through, he guessed at least several storeys, perhaps more.

Quint wasn't entirely sure why Newbury had insisted he come along with them. They'd hardly needed any assistance from him as they'd cut a swathe of unconsciousness through the palace staff. He supposed it was a case of keeping your friends close . . .

Newbury glanced back at him as they approached the point where the passageway opened out into a small underground room lined with barred cells. His expression was unreadable. They slowed their pace, and Quint could see the tension in Newbury's stance, the little vein throbbing in Veronica's temple. They were expecting more guards to come charging out at them at any moment. Their approach had hardly been subtle, and here, by these cells—Quint had been surprised to learn that

Buckingham Palace even *had* cells–it was likely they'd meet the most resistance in their efforts to free Sir Charles. He wondered for a moment what had become of Amelia, and why he hadn't yet seen evidence of her passing down here, too.

"Come on out then," said Newbury, his voice booming in the confines of the narrow passage, "let's get this over and done with."

There was a scrabbling sound from somewhere inside the room. Then silence, followed eventually by shuffling footsteps.

When a figure did finally emerge from the shadowy opening, Quint was amazed to find that he recognised them, despite their somewhat weary appearance. "Inspector Foulkes! What are you doing down here?"

"Foulkes!"

Newbury saw only red. Here was the man who'd betrayed them, whose traitorous act had allowed Bainbridge and the Prince to be captured and for Warlow to be set on Newbury and Veronica's trail. Here was the man who had brought an end to the Albion Initiative and Newbury's hopes for a better future. Here was a man who had once claimed to be his friend.

All sense of Newbury's self control dissolved. He flung himself at the man, striking him once, twice, three times, until the big bear of a man staggered back, falling to one side, grasping for the iron bars of a nearby cell to keep himself upright.

"Maurice!" Veronica was calling his name, but he paid her no heed. He could not tear his attention away from the man before him.

"You traitorous bastard!" bellowed Newbury, punching Foulkes again, hard, in the gut. Foulkes spluttered, coughing up stringy blood. With a gasp Foulkes dropped to one knee.

He had not tried to defend himself. He had not thrown a single punch in anger.

Newbury hovered over him, his bloodied fist drawn back. "Why, Foulkes? How could you?"

Foulkes looked up at him, the anguish so genuine in his bloodied, broken-lipped aspect that Newbury's resolve wavered for a moment. His fist dipped but did not drop. "She has my children," said Foulkes. Tears were welling in the man's eyes. "My *children,* Newbury. I'm sorry, I'm so, so sorry."

Newbury felt suddenly hollow. He staggered back, as if the world had just tilted beneath him. His children. The Queen had taken the man's children and used them as leverage to get what she wanted.

It all made sense. Why else would Foulkes stand against them, after all this time. She'd left him with no choice.

The man was weeping now, wiping blood and tears from his face with his sleeve.

"Maurice . . ." Veronica was by his side. "Look. The guards."

Newbury glanced around. Just inside the door, four guards lay unconscious and bound."

"I was coming for Charles," said Foulkes. "I couldn't stand it any longer. What they were doing to him. What she . . ." He broke off again, then raised his head, meeting Newbury's eye. "If she's harmed them, Newbury, then God help me . . ."

"We'll get them back. I promise." Newbury crossed to where Foulkes was still on his knees. He reached out a hand. Foulkes regarded it for a moment, and then, his shoulders sagging, he reached out and took it, allowing Newbury to pull him back to his feet. "I'm sorry, Foulkes. I didn't know. I should have trusted—"

"No," cut in Foulkes. "I'm the one who's sorry, Newbury. You weren't to know. And I shouldn't have . . . I could never . . ." He drew a deep breath. "The things she's done to Charles, Newbury. If I'd known . . ."

Newbury's mouth was dry. "Where is he?"

"Over here," said Quint, from outside one of the cells.

"The keys," said Foulkes, pulling a clanking ring from the pocket of his overcoat. Newbury took them and, heart thudding, approached the cell where Quint stood.

The cell itself was small—just a hollow carved out of the bedrock, with a heap of straw for a bed and an old, chipped chamber pot in one corner. Bainbridge was laying on the bed with his back to them, curled in a foetal position. He was dressed in his shirtsleeves and trousers, with no boots, and his clothes were badly torn, revealing red welts in the flesh of his torso, arms, and thighs. What remained of the shirt was bloodstained and grimy.

"Charles?" said Newbury, softly. "Charles, it's Newbury. We're going to get you out of here."

No response.

"Charles?"

Newbury tried one of the keys in the lock. Then another, and another, until one of them finally engaged and the mechanism clicked over. He yanked the door open and stepped inside. The stink was horrific. He could see Bainbridge's chest rising and falling with deep, even breaths.

"Charles, it's me."

He crossed to his old friend, worried now more than ever by the lack of response. Couldn't he hear? What was wrong?

"Charles." He put a gentle hand on Bainbridge's shoulder, watched appalled as the other man flinched away.

"*Charles!*" Newbury grabbed him with both hands, turning him over onto his back. "It's me, Charles. It's—"

The ruin of his friend's face stared up at him without recognition. Bainbridge emitted a long, low wail and tried to draw himself back into a ball. His left eye was a bloody mess, blinded, milky, and burst. Several burns were red and livid down his cheeks, and when he flailed, evidently thinking Newbury was one of his tormentors, Newbury saw that two digits on his right hand had been shorn off at the knuckles, then badly cauterised. He looked wild, mindless, a wreck of the controlled, precise man he had been.

"Charles," he said softly. "It's Maurice. I'm here with Veronica. It's going to be all right. We're going to get you out of here."

Bainbridge's remaining eye flickered, searching Newbury's face. His brows creased. "Newbury?" he said, as if shocked by the sudden realisation. "Newbury?"

"Yes. It's me." Newbury was fighting back tears. "I'm here."

"I didn't tell her anything, Newbury. Nothing at all. I promise."

"I know you didn't, Charles." He patted his friend's chest. "I know."

He stood, turning away, to see Veronica by the door to the cell, wiping her eyes.

"He'll be all right," he said, as much to convince himself as her. "He'll be all right, once we get him to a doctor."

Veronica nodded. The set of her face had changed. "She's going to pay for this."

Newbury gave a single nod in affirmation. "Quint," he called.

"Yes, here," replied Quint from just outside the cell, where he'd evidently been in deep conversation with Foulkes.

"The other cells," said Newbury, his voice cracking. "Amelia? The Prince of Wales?"

Quint came to the cell door, standing beside Veronica. "No, they're empty."

The look of relief on Veronica's face was palpable.

"All right, here's what's going to happen," said Newbury. "You and Foulkes are going to get him out of here. Take him back the way we came, put him in that carriage you brought with you and get him to a hospital. Can you manage that?"

"But what abou–"

"Yes," said Foulkes, his voice level. "We can manage that."

"What about you?" said Quint. "You're going to look for Amelia?"

Newbury rolled his neck and unclenched his jaw. The ball of anger in his chest was like a well of white-hot rage, threatening to overflow. "Yes," he said. "But first, we're going to pay our respects to the Queen."

CHAPTER 29

Newbury kicked open the door to the audience chamber with a display of violence that shocked even Veronica. It rocked back and forth on a single bent hinge.

Newbury stalked through into the darkness, his jacket long abandoned, his breathing ragged as a result of several fistfights they'd been forced to engage in to clear a path through the palace guards. Her own dress was torn in several places and she had a fiery scratch on her right cheek—the result of a jagged fingernail clawing unsuccessfully for her eye. The man responsible, a footman, had paid for the wound with a square blow to the jaw. He was probably still unconscious now, slumped against a wall somewhere in the servants' quarters, along with several of his colleagues.

She hurried after Newbury into the enveloping gloom. The only sounds were the brisk scuffing of Newbury's footsteps and the wheezing hiss of the monarch's bellows, rattling and hissing like some hideous, relentless engine.

"Show yourself," bellowed Newbury, his voice dripping with ire. "You coward. You can't hide in here forever."

The Queen's familiar, watery cackle erupted from the shadows. The very sound of it caused Veronica's hackles to rise, her jaw to clench.

This is it, she thought. *This feels like the end. One way or another, something is going to give. The only question is what . . . or who.*

"Hide?" said the Queen. Her voice seemed disembodied, as if the darkness itself had somehow come to speak on behalf of the ancient woman in her life-preserving chair, amplifying her every utterance, granting her some obscene omnipotence, some semblance of the godhood she clearly craved. "How rich, coming from two dissident traitors. Two runaways, with no homes left to go to."

A vesta flared, and the lantern on the woman's lap bloomed with light. It seemed to unfold like an expanding star until it encapsulated the woman in its flickering bubble, deepening the shadows all around her. To Veronica's eye, Victoria looked to be in worse health than she'd ever been. Her skin, so long in the dark, had taken on a pellucid quality, so that the blood that pulsed beneath it was grotesquely visible, coursing through her poisoned veins. Her lips were cracked and bloody, and yet saliva ran from the corner of her mouth, slack with apparent disinterest. The whites of her eyes had turned a sickly yellow, and her bound, useless feet had begun to fester, mouldering through disuse and improper care. She had the appearance of some ancient horror, reanimated from beyond the grave and maintained through chemical compounds and wicked sorcery alone.

Queen Victoria shifted in her seat, and then held her lantern aloft in her claw-like left hand, so that she might look upon her visitors with its weak, yellow glow. She emitted another ugly laugh as she peered at them. "Such disappointments. Such failures."

Veronica saw Newbury flinch, as if the words had stung deeply, just as the Queen had intended. "Ignore her, Maurice," she said, her voice low. Newbury glanced at her, but his thoughts were clearly elsewhere.

"You have amounted to nothing, Newbury. Just like your friend the *policeman.*"

At the mention of Bainbridge, Newbury finally lost any sense of composure that remained. He stalked forward, a look of grim determination on his face. He meant to kill her.

Veronica hurried after him, catching his arm, holding him back. "Don't, Maurice. Don't let her goad you into doing something you'll regret. She knows it's over—she's trying to implicate you; a final, damning command. A last trap."

Newbury paused, but Veronica could feel the bunched muscles of his arm. She knew it wouldn't take much more for him to snap. If she let him do this now, she would lose him forever. Angelchrist could never let it stand, irrespective of the intent behind it. Besides, she doubted Newbury would be able to live with the guilt. It would eat him up. Destroy him.

"Yes, that's right," laughed Victoria. "He always did enjoy having a woman tell him what to do. Always a follower, Newbury."

"There's no shame in following," said Newbury, "so long as the cause is worthy of being followed. You, *Your Majesty*, have not been worthy for some time."

The Queen waved a hand, nonchalant. "We do not care for or require your approval, Newbury. Only your obedience. And in that you have failed once again."

"No," said Newbury. "I've finally seen you for what you are. It's time to step aside. To allow your son to rule in your place."

"Bertie?" The Queen sounded incredulous as she spat the word. She leaned forward in her chair, the rubber feeding tubes straining with the motion. "Oh, I don't think so. That's simply impossible. Besides, Bertie has confessed his sins and pledged himself to my cause."

That didn't sound like the Prince of Wales that Veronica had come to know. Judging by the expression on Newbury's face, he evidently felt the same.

"We are not alone in this. The government sees it, too. They understand what must be done. They'll be here soon. They're coming for you, Victoria. To put an end to all of this."

"Oh," said the Queen, with a wicked smile. "So, they seek to force me out. On what possible grounds?"

A mechanical *clunk* sounded from somewhere behind them.

Veronica, sensing a threat, turned on the spot, eyes searching the gloom. After a moment, three small lights began to glow, swimming out of the darkness, nothing but pinpricks at first, but glowing larger with every passing second, accompanied by a deep, bass hum that seemed to rumble through the chamber floor, vibrating through the soles of Veronica's boots. She watched, entranced, as the lights—which she now understood to be massive electrical bulbs—swelled with light and power, until, after just a few seconds, the entire audience chamber was filled with a bright, actinic glow, stinging Veronica's eyes with their powerful glare.

Standing behind the bank of brilliant lights, right in the centre of the chamber, was a single figure. A tall, slender figure dressed in a dirty blouse and a pair of familiar culottes. Veronica's heart sang.

Amelia.

She smiled at Veronica, and then gestured expansively. The bright light had revealed scores of previously hidden alcoves set around the edges of the vast room. Appalled, Veronica realised that each of them contained the withered remnants of a person, shackled to the walls, tubes erupting from roughly hacked holes in their chests. This obscene tubing snaked across the marble floor, coming together to merge in a single knot, feeding a burbling tank, which in turn was fed by a pump to a socket in the rear of the Queen's chair.

Some of the people were still twitching with the last vestiges of life. Others were still and dead.

"On the grounds that you have wilfully sacrificed the lives of thousands of your own people to preserve your own bleak existence," said Amelia. "On the grounds that you have so much blood on your hands you will never be free of it, in this life or the next."

"No!" screamed the Queen, hissing and spitting as she covered her eyes in the crook of her arm. "Turn it off! Turn it off!"

In all the many times she had visited this chamber, had faced this horrible apparition of a woman, Veronica had never imagined that such horrors lurked within mere feet of her. Every time one of her conversations with the Queen had played out in here, people had been dying all around them.

Dying to sustain a woman who should have died long ago, whose desire to hold onto her Empire was so profound that it had led her to feed on her own people to do it. If it hadn't been so appalling, so heinous, she would have almost felt sorry for the woman.

Veronica ran to her sister, gathering her up in a tight hug. "I was so worried," she said.

"We've got her," said Amelia. "We've finally got her. This is it, Veronica. Angelchrist has all the evidence he needs. He knows where the bodies are buried. We've done it."

Newbury, silent, had crossed to one of the nearest alcoves, where a figure dressed in the remnants of a smart black suit hung limp and dead from its shackles.

"The Prince?" said Newbury. He glanced at the Queen, who had discarded her lantern and was shielding her eyes from the glare of the lights. "Your own son!"

Veronica joined him. He was right—the man in the alcove had once been the Prince of Wales, but his former plump flesh and rotund aspect were now gone, his skin desiccated and paper thin, his cheeks gaunt and frail. His eyes had rolled back in their sockets, but his long grey beard was still full and bushy, and unmistakable. She felt sick. "What have you done?"

"Whatever we had to!" spat the Queen. "We survived. We took what we needed from the Empire and gave it back tenfold! The colonies paid their tithe, and so did London."

"A tithe of blood," said Amelia.

"And Bertie?" said Veronica. "What tithe did *he* pay? The cost of being your son?"

"Traitors get what they deserve," hissed Victoria. She twisted in her chair, straining towards a door in the rear wall of the chamber. Her eyes were streaming with the pain of the light. She looked pathetic, a tiny, swollen figure at the heart of an immense machine that's only purpose was the preservation of her life, at all costs. A corpse queen, squatting on the rotten throne of England. "Warlow! *Warlow!*"

The door flew open. Figures began to file in. Figures that spat and crackled with blue electrical light.

"Warlow," said Newbury, as the man emerged from amongst his terrible wards, still rank with the foetid stink of the sewers.

Warlow offered them a crooked grin, yet Veronica could see the uncertainty writ large in his expression. He, too, was seeing what the lights had revealed, the true horror behind the woman who claimed to be the embodiment of their great nation.

A murderer. A charlatan.

A disease.

Yet there was resignation there, too. An acknowledgement that he had already gone too far, had followed this path for too long without question. An acceptance that he, too, was a part of the problem, a lodestone of the corruption on show. He intended to see it through.

As his boltheads began to file past him, Warlow reached for a pistol. He levelled it at Newbury. "This would have been far easier if you'd just accepted what was coming. You had to go and make a meal of it."

Warlow squeezed the trigger.

Newbury shifted to the right. The bullet hummed past him, ricocheting loudly off one of the alcove walls and skittering away across the marble floor. Warlow growled in frustration and took a second shot. Again, Newbury moved, and the bullet sailed harmlessly past.

Keeping the gun raised before him, his arm outstretched, Warlow strode forward, attempting to narrow the gap between them. Newbury, seeing his opportunity, charged, rushing the man, colliding with him heavily and sending them both sprawling to the floor.

Meanwhile, the veritable army of boltheads—Veronica had counted seven—were closing in on her and Amelia, who were now standing back-to-back, their fists raised in what Veronica knew would be paltry defence against such monstrous things. Lightning hissed and spat, arcing between the metal studs in their skulls, describing traceries across their forearms and fingers, like tiny rivers adjusting their flow across landscapes of pale flesh.

Three of them, Veronica noted, were women. Or had been, once, before they'd been *manufactured,* turned into these mindless slaves. Presumably, once again, on the orders of the Queen, who sat watching over proceedings from the safety of her chair, her lips twisted in a feral grin.

The circle was tightening. Veronica searched for something they could use as a weapon, but there was nothing but the shells of the dead and dying, propped up and wired into their alcoves like the ancient mummies on display in the British Museum.

She caught only glimpses of the battle raging between Newbury and Warlow, who had now edged into the centre of the chamber, close to the three massive electrical floor lamps. They were trading vicious blows, and both were bleeding profusely from burst lips or, in Newbury's case, a gash to the forehead where Warlow had evidently struck him with the heel of his gun.

"What *are* these things?" said Amelia, from beside her.

"Monsters," replied Veronica.

"Well, you know what we do to monsters," said Amelia. She drew back her fist.

"Amelia—no!"

But it was too late. Amelia had already launched herself at the bolthead closest to her. It was a bulky-looking man dressed in rags, with wide, fixed eyes and teeth that chattered constantly with the buzzing electrical charge passing through his body.

Veronica swept her arms out, trying to catch Amelia, to pull her back, but her sister was out of reach, and as Veronica watched in horror, Amelia's fist collided with the side of the bolthead's face.

The blow seemed to jar the man, causing him to stagger back, dropping to one knee unsteadily, but the effect on Amelia was immediate and shocking—literally. Lightning erupted like a violent strike at the site of the impact, blossoming into a flower of startling, blue-tinged light. The jolt was sufficient to lift Amelia from her feet, throwing her back, violently, so that she landed in a crumpled, steaming heap on the floor several feet away.

"Amelia!"

Veronica ran to her sister's side, turning her over, slowly. She was unconscious, but still breathing. Her hair was wild, a prickly halo around her head, and her forearm was scorched and black. Veronica laid her carefully upon the ground.

From behind the semicircle of boltheads, still closing in on her, she could hear the Queen was laughing, a hideous, burbling cackle of glee. The boltheads, too, were grinning inanely, their expressions almost innocent, child-like.

Veronica stood before Amelia's unconscious form, turning on the spot. "I won't let you near her," she said. "I won't."

Amelia had suffered enough for a lifetime.

One of the boltheads lurched, grabbing for Veronica's wrist. She ducked it, swung out of the way, held her position. But the net was closing. Another came in, and this time she wasn't so lucky, its hand brushing her shoulder.

The jolt ran through her like fire, like a hot poker skewering her very soul, and she screamed, part in rage and part in pain, as her muscles spasmed and her body seemed to rebel against her every thought.

Her heart, however—now replaced by Faberge's delicate clockwork mechanisms—did not even stutter. She gasped for breath, her mind on fire, her vision swimming. A shadow loomed over her. Without thinking, she whirled, her fist coming up beneath the bolthead's chin, snapping its head back and sending it tumbling over onto the marble floor. The other boltheads hesitated for a moment, as if shocked by this sudden new development.

She looked up, just in time to see Warlow wrestling Newbury to his knees. The pistol in his hand went off, the shot ringing out in the immense space of the chamber. Newbury bucked, blood spraying from his shoulder as the bullet ripped through flesh, tendon, muscle. He groaned in pain and sagged back, releasing his grip on Warlow, who stood, pushing Newbury away, a wan smile on his lips.

"No!" screamed Veronica, over the Queen's insistent laughter. *"No!"*

Warlow levelled the pistol at Newbury's head. "And so, it ends."

"Like hell it does," roared Newbury, launching himself up at Warlow with a howl of agony and rage. He grabbed the man about the waist even as he twisted, propelling himself forward, lifting Warlow off his feet and tossing the man bodily into the huge central bulb on the ground beside them.

Warlow, arms flailing, crashed through the thin glass dome, unable to stop himself from going over. There was a wet, sickening crunch as the twin spokes of the bulb's central structure skewered him through the back, erupting from his gut in a violent, bloody spray. Electricity coursed through his body as he bucked and fought, blood gushing from his parted lips, the air filling with the scent of charred meat. Lightning crawled over his flesh, searing his face, hands, torso, causing his eyes to bubble and blister, his lungs to burst. His clothes took hungrily to the flame, and within moments he was still—the smoking, blackened ruin of a man.

Around Veronica the boltheads began to screech, tilting their heads back and wailing, clutching at their own faces, scratching long gouges in their cheeks. They staggered back, away from her, all semblance of direction lost.

The sound of their screams was horrific, like the wail of an Elder God from some nightmarish tale. Like children who had just watched their father burn.

She thought for a moment that they were about to turn on Newbury, to seek vengeance for what he had done, but instead they turned and ran at the boarded up windows, throwing themselves against the wooden planks until their limbs shattered, their ribs cracked, and they either dropped, twitching, to the ground, or the planks finally gave, and they lurched on through, shattering glass, escaping into the misty morning beyond the palace walls.

Behind Veronica, Amelia was stirring. She lifted her head, met Veronica's eye, nodded that she was all right.

Veronica ran to Newbury's side. He was slumped on the ground before the lighting array, blood flowing freely from the pulsing wound in his shoulder. He was sweating, and barely holding onto consciousness. She dropped to her knees amongst the broken glass, tearing the sleeve from her dress. She pressed it against the wound, then took his hand, holding it there against his shoulder. "Hold it there. Press as firmly as you can. We'll get you help, soon. I promise. You're going to be fine."

Across the chamber, the Queen emitted a wet splutter. "And here it ends. The so-called hero has proved his uselessness, downed by a simple bullet. The sister—once so very useful to us—now broken and discarded. And you, Miss Hobbes, are all alone. We once thought you were destined for great things, but now . . . well, you fell in *love,* and that was the beginning of your pitiful downfall."

Veronica stood, broken glass crunching beneath her boots. She crossed the chamber to stand before the Queen, tired, bedraggled, but defiant. "Love is not a failure."

"It is an illness. A disease. A malfunction of the mind. Love corrupts. It destroys, it turns our heads and whispers lies into our ears. It is the ruin of humankind. The only true love is the love of a people for their ruler."

Veronica stared at the woman. "If Albert could hear you now . . ."

"Albert is dead," snapped Victoria. "Albert abandoned us, and in doing so, he proved the fallibility of love. That, Miss Hobbes, was his parting gift—to teach us the truth of love."

"You're wrong." Veronica glanced at Newbury, propped against the lighting rig, clutching his wounded shoulder. She looked to Amelia, who was unsteadily getting to her feet, her hair wild from the shock, her burned hand clutched across her chest. "Love reminds us why we fight, why we live. It gives us purpose, teaches us compassion. Without it, we're mere husks."

The Queen laughed. "We see that you are well and truly caught in its spell. But it is a transitory thing, a fleeting whim, and brings only pain."

"All this time, all those people who've died to sustain you—and you did it out of a lack of love."

"No!" bellowed the Queen, before descending into a wet, racking cough. When she had finally finished spluttering, Veronica saw that there was bright blood on her lips. Despite everything, she could feel only sadness for this wreck of a woman. This thing had once known happiness, but now sought to replace that happiness with power, and rage, and sheer persistence. "I did it because I *deserve* it. These petty creatures," she gestured to the alcoves and their unfortunate dead, "what are they to us? Subjects to be ruled. The poor and the hungry, draining the coffers of the Empire. Upstart colonists who would shirk off our gifts. Don't you see? We have made their sorry lives worthwhile. We have given them purpose. They should be honoured to have served us as their Queen, their Empress! It is the truest demonstration of their love. The only love that matters."

Veronica shook her head. "This is no love. This is murder. It's grotesque. And it must be stopped."

"And who are you to judge *me*!" roared Victoria, rocking forward in her chair, her slimy tongue sliding across the blackened stumps of her teeth. "You are nothing but an inconvenience! Just like your sister, or the policeman, or that ridiculous man on the floor. I am the Queen of England! The Empress of India! And I shall take my tithe and live!"

Veronica's mind was reeling. The woman was utterly insane. "This is madness! Can't you see that? Those people—they don't exist simply at your pleasure. Their lives are not yours to give or take. They're not lesser than you by virtue of their birth or their beliefs!"

Victoria scoffed. "How small-minded you prove to be, Miss Hobbes."

"Professor Angelchrist is coming. With proof of what's been happening here. The government will stop it. They'll stop *you*."

Victoria laughed again, and it was a caustic, knowing laugh. "Oh, we don't believe they will. After all, we're just a defenceless old woman, confined to her chair and kept in the dark. How could we have known the truth of the horrors our doctors have perpetrated in our name? We are but a victim in this terrible tragedy."

"They'll never believe you."

"They won't have a choice."

"You're inhuman!"

Victoria chuckled.

Behind Veronica, Amelia had shuffled over to sit beside Newbury, helping to stem the tide of blood still flowing freely from his wound. He was still somewhat delirious, sweating and breathing heavily through the pain. Amelia looked up, met Veronica's gaze. "Do it, Veronica. End it now, while we can. It's only the machines that are keeping her alive. She's only breathing because of the people she's murdered. Is *still* murdering, right now. And she won't stop. She won't ever stop."

Veronica took a step closer to the Queen and her life-preserving chair. Then hesitated.

Could she really do it? Just switch it off. End it now. Perhaps even save the lives of those few poor people still suffering in the alcoves. Wasn't that her *duty*? To protect the people of the Empire from those who would see them harmed. Wasn't that real love? Real compassion?

"She hasn't the guts," spat Victoria. "She's never been able to do what was necessary."

Veronica looked the woman in the eye. "I pity you," she said. "And I'm sorry that you've lived like this for so long. That you've been allowed to sink so far into your misery that you've lost sight of what it is to be human. I want you to understand something." She circled around behind the Queen's chair. Her palms were slick. She could hear the blood roaring in her ears like waves, crashing against a rocky shore.

"What?" said Victoria, spluttering on more regurgitated blood. "What would you have us *understand*?"

"That I do not do this out of hate or revenge. I do not do it to secure my own survival, or for political gain. I do it out of compassion. Because I still know what love is. Because I see you for the woman you were and know that woman is long dead. Because I do not believe that a single life is worth more than many, and there are people here who deserve to be saved. You are one of them."

"What are you blathering on about, woman? Come back around here, back where we can see you!"

Hands trembling, Veronica reached for the burring pump that was still circulating fluid—she could not fathom what, exactly—through the pipe in the back of the Queen's chair.

And then she twisted the handle and turned it off. It creaked mechanically, a sound like the clinking of chains.

At first, nothing happened.

Victoria was attempting to twist around in her seat to see what Veronica was doing. "Get back here! Get back where we can see you!"

Veronica felt a sense of calm wash over her. Her clockwork heart measured the seconds in steady, even strokes.

It's done. We've reached the end. From here, there are only consequences.

She walked around to face the woman who had once been her Queen.

"We knew you didn't have it in you. We knew yo–" Victoria hunched forward suddenly, creasing into a violent coughing fit. Blood oozed from her lips. She sat back, and for a moment it seemed to pass. She regarded Veronica with humourless yellow eyes. And then those eyes widened in sudden realisation. She lifted her arm, started to say something–and then, suddenly, was still.

Veronica realised she'd been holding her breath. She let it out. Victoria's chest was still rising and falling harshly with the wheezing of the bellows, but the life had gone from her eyes, and her expression was slack, the harsh lines now soft, the frown now relaxed into an open, welcoming expression. For the first time since Veronica had known her, she looked at peace.

Veronica turned away, staggered over to where Amelia still hunched over Newbury, and collapsed onto her knees. The tears came then, rolling freely down her cheeks, coming in great, gasping sobs.

Newbury, grimacing, put his arm around her shoulders, drawing her close. "I love you," he said. The noise of shouting and running footsteps sounded in the hall.

CHAPTER 30

It was turning out to be a pleasant day. The mist had lifted, burned away by the awakening sun, and the sky was a canopy of the clearest blue shot through with only a handful of pale, fluffy clouds.

An auspicious sign, thought Newbury. *The dawning of a new day over an Empire that will be forever changed.*

He was sitting on a flight of stone steps at the rear of the palace, his back to the tall, broken windows of the audience chamber. He was smoking a cigarette, enjoying the lightheaded rush of the opium that was working to dull the pain of the gunshot wound in his shoulder, which had now been cleaned and dressed, and would be looked at by a surgeon just as soon as matters had been dealt with here.

Inside, Angelchrist and the government men were swarming over the palace, picking over the wreckage, gathering evidence and otherwise drawing what conclusions they could regarding the Queen's nefarious activities and her plot to murder thousands of her own subjects.

Six survivors had been rescued from the alcoves, although it was unlikely any of them would survive the trip to hospital and the ensuing treatment—whatever it was that had been extracted from them, their organs were likely all in terminal failure. A report had reached him, too, that Foulkes and Quint had delivered

Bainbridge safely to a hospital, and his injuries were now being treated. His scars would not heal swiftly, but he would live.

He watched Veronica, just a few yards away, deep in conversation with Amelia, who kept looking his way and smiling in a most disconcerting fashion. Probably planning some sort of grand wedding, he decided, and was surprised that the thought made him smile, where once it might have made him cringe.

Yes. It's time. I'm ready for this. We both are.

The two women embraced, and then Veronica came to join him, sitting beside him on the cold step. She nudged him with her shoulder. Her smile was the most glorious thing he'd seen all day. She looked free, for the first time.

A commotion across the yard caused both Newbury and Veronica to look around. A man in a black suit was marching across the flagstones towards Amelia, wagging his finger as if in severe admonishment of a child. "Constance Markham! Where have you been, girl? Don't you know that I've been looking for you? There are serious questions that require answers." He stopped before her, reaching out to take her arm. "You'll come with me no—"

"Oh, bugger off, Trimbey," said Amelia before ducking his grabbing hand and delivering what—to Newbury's mind— appeared to be a perfect right hook.

The man staggered back, looked at Amelia with appalled astonishment, and then toppled over on the flagstones. Amelia rolled her eyes and walked away.

Newbury hooted with laughter. "She really is quite impressive, you know."

"I know," said Veronica, smiling. "She had a good role model."

"Well, as big sisters go—"

"I'm talking about you, you fool," said Veronica, laughing. "You've made more of an impression on her than you could possibly know. On both of us."

Newbury sighed. "Now I know you're out of your mind."

Veronica's expression darkened. He noticed she was wringing her hands, chewing her bottom lip.

"You did the right thing," he said.

"How can you be sure? I . . . I killed her in cold blood. I just turned the machine off and walked away."

"*No*," said Newbury. "You saved the lives of six people. And countless others, if she'd had her way. That wasn't a life. She died a long time ago. That was some kind of self-styled purgatory, and in her grief, she'd fed off those less fortunate than her. It was time. You said it yourself: what you did was a kindness, a release."

"You heard that?"

"I heard *everything*. And I love you more for it with every passing moment."

She took his hand. "Thank you."

Newbury glanced behind him at the sound of approaching footsteps. "Archibald!" He scrambled to his feet, embracing his old friend, and then wincing at the sharp pain it elicited in his shoulder.

"It's good to see you both," said Angelchrist. He looked tired, with dark bruises beneath his eyes. He seemed to have gained several lines around them, too. "How's the shoulder?"

"Sore," said Newbury, "but I'll live. I . . ." He shrugged. "We thought you were dead."

"I know. I'm sorry. It was the only way. Once Warlow killed poor George Foster, my supposed doppelgänger, I had no choice. I had to lie low and gather the evidence I needed."

Newbury nodded.

"And Charles," said Angelchrist. "How is he?"

"In a bad way," said Newbury. "I fear it's going to take some time. She took his eye, some of his fingers. But he kept his promise. He didn't give anything away."

Angelchrist nodded, his lips thin and pursed. "He will, of course, have all of our support. I'll do whatever I can."

They lapsed into silence for a moment, until Angelchrist seemed unable to stand it any longer. "What happened in there,

Newbury? It's a godforsaken mess. And the Queen, like that in her chair. I'm going to have to give them something, you know. An explanation. Will you talk to me?"

"It was me," said Veronica, her voice wavering. "I was th–"

"The truth is," said Newbury, cutting her off, "that we're not entirely sure. It was chaos in there, Archibald. Warlow and his boltheads, coming at us from all sides. None of us were paying any attention to the Queen. She must have got spooked, tried to pull herself out of her chair to get away, and inadvertently unhooked herself from one of those damnable machines. Or the stress of it stopped her heart. She was well past her prime, as you know. A shock like that . . . Well, you know what it can do. By the time I'd dealt with Warlow and the boltheads had fled, she was already dead."

Angelchrist narrowed his eyes. "And that's the truth of it?" he said. He glanced at Veronica.

"Yes," she said, "just as Newbury described. Perhaps it was just her time."

Angelchrist sighed. "I think you and I both know, Miss Hobbes, that her time was well past. Whatever happened, a great service has been done for our nation. If I could look the person in the eye who turned off that valve . . . well, I would offer them my heartfelt thanks."

"Valve?" said Newbury.

"I'm not sure what you mean," said Veronica.

Angelchrist nodded. "Very well, I'll see to it that your version of events gets reported here today." He patted Newbury on the arm. "I suggest the two of you get off home. You look like you could do with the rest."

"And a surgeon," said Newbury. "Not to mention a cleaner."

"A cleaner?"

"Warlow's men paid a visit to my house," said Newbury, by way of explanation. He cringed at the thought of all the mess– and Scarbright, too. The man would be desperately worried.

"Ah, I see. Well, I won't keep you. We'll speak soon, yes? Both of you. There are things to be discussed."

"Yes, of course," said Veronica, "but Professor—what'll happen now?"

"Now? We'll probably spend the next year rounding up and prosecuting everyone involved in this dreadful scheme and trying to get justice for those who died at her hands. It's going to take months, if not years, to identify the bodies your sister uncovered at Highgate. Our first priority is her doctor, Warrender. Seems he's already upped sticks and made a run for it."

Veronica nodded. "I'm sorry, Professor, I meant about the throne. With Prince Edward already dead . . . ?"

"Ah," said Angelchrist. "*That.*" He grinned. "Well, suffice it to say, Miss Hobbes, that I always ensure there's a 'plan b.'" He nodded, satisfied, then turned and walked away.

Newbury and Veronica watched him go. Then, sliding her arm around his back, Veronica steered Newbury in the other direction. "Come on," she said. "Let's get that shoulder seen to."

The child sat alone on the edge of her bed, plucking fur from the arms of her teddy bear and letting it fall in a little heap onto the floorboards. This was the third toy she'd destroyed this way in a week, and the satisfaction she'd once derived from the act was diminishing rapidly. Soon, she'd have to search for some other form of amusement.

She heard footsteps approaching the door, followed by the scraping of a key in the lock. She dropped the bear on the floor and stood, folding her hands behind her back as she'd been taught.

The door opened and a familiar face appeared. He was smiling, but she could see it was forced—he was worried about something and was trying to hide it.

"Doctor Warrender. Is it time to go and see Mother?"

Warrender shook his head and dropped into a crouch to look her in the eye. "I'm afraid not, Alberta. Your mother is . . . well, she's indisposed. She's going to be busy for some time, I'm afraid, and so she's asked me to take you away for a holiday."

"A holiday!" Alberta's mind whirled. She'd never been on a holiday before. She'd never even left the city. "Where are we going?"

"To France," said Warrender. "You'll like it across the Channel. There are people who can't wait to meet you."

"Really?"

"Really."

"All right, then. Will Nurse be coming with us?"

Warrender nodded. "Yes, Nurse will be coming, too."

Alberta smiled. She wouldn't know what to do if she wasn't able to torment her nurse anymore. "When do we leave?"

"Right away," said Warrender. He held out his hand for her.

"But what about my things?"

"Leave them. We'll have them sent on. And we'll buy new things in France. You'll see."

Hesitantly, Alberta took his hand and allowed him to lead her out into the dark passageway. "Is everything all right, Doctor?" she said, after a while. "Is Mother quite well?"

Warrender glanced down at her. That forced smile again. "Yes, Alberta," he said, in a tone that made her feel just the opposite. "Everything's going to be just fine."

♛

EPILOGUE

The people lining the Mall seemed full of celebratory joy, despite the inclement weather.

Newbury and Veronica stood at the front of the press, close to Buckingham Palace, holding hands and sheltering beneath a broad umbrella. Soon, the coronation procession would pass by, and the entire crowd would go wild. A young man in a gold carriage would wave at them, still somewhat bewildered and unsure whether his newfound fortune was a blessing or a curse.

Newbury wasn't entirely certain, either.

"So," said Veronica. "The professor really did have a 'plan b.' Arthur must have been on the boat back from Canada before any of this even began."

Newbury nodded. "The wily old devil. The annals of his mind are like a labyrinth to me. I don't know how he does it, juggling all of these plots-within-plots, considering all of these different permutations. I mean—who would have thought that we'd be standing here, about to herald the onset of a new Arthurian age?"

Veronica laughed. "You're not so unalike, you know. Sometimes it's difficult to fathom what you're thinking, too."

Newbury smiled.

"I just hope he knows what he's doing. Arthur's been away for some time."

"Which means he's largely free from his late mother's influence," said Newbury, "and ready for a fresh start. I believe it bodes well. I understand he's picked up a lot of ideas in the New World. I sense a period of change ahead. That can only be a good thing, don't you agree?"

Veronica shrugged. "Time will tell."

A roar went up from the crowd as the palace gates hinged open and, with great fanfare, the golden carriage rolled out onto the Mall, pulled by a procession of gleaming white horses.

"Look," said Newbury, pointing to a knot of people across the street, where a burly-looking man with a beard was hoisting his children into the air for a better view, one hooked under each arm. He was laughing heartily as the two boys wriggled and fought to get free. "There's Foulkes."

"It looks as if retirement suits him," said Veronica, laughing. "I know he's grateful for what you did, recovering his children."

"I made the man a promise," said Newbury.

In truth, he hadn't yet fully forgiven Foulkes for the part he had played in Bainbridge's torture and Prince Edward's death. He understood the man's reasons, of course—he just wished that Foulkes had come to him in the first instance. Perhaps then, things might have been different. But, as Veronica kept on telling him, there was no use looking back. A brand-new future lay ahead of them now.

"Speaking of retirement . . . ," said Veronica.

"Yes," said Newbury. He'd been dreading this moment. "I've been meaning to talk to you about that . . ."

"Really? Me too. It's just—"

A hand clapped Newbury on the shoulder.

"Now here's a sight for sore eyes. Or should I say, a sore *eye!*"

Newbury turned to see Bainbridge standing behind him. The man looked well—or at least, far better than he had in some weeks. His left eye was cloudy and unseeing, and he was thin and drawn, but his colour had returned, and with it, his crotchety demeanour and general rambunctious self.

Newbury looked the man up and down for a minute, and then pulled him into a firm embrace.

"Good Lord! What the devil's gotten into you, man!"

Newbury wiped an errant tear from his eye. "It's good to see you, Charles."

"Yes, yes. Indeed." He turned to Veronica and winked. "No need to make a fuss."

"No, of course not," said Newbury. "My apologies."

Behind him, the golden carriage was now halfway up the Mall, and the newly crowned King Arthur was dutifully waving to the gathered throng, eliciting cheers of support and encouragement.

"I think he'll do all right, you know," said Bainbridge. "With a little bit of help."

"I do believe you're right," agreed Newbury.

"Well, that's enough standing around taking in the occasion," said Bainbridge. He fixed Newbury with his good eye. "Angelchrist has sent for us. Something to do with a ruddy ghost ship on the Thames, or something. We're needed."

Newbury coughed. "Ah, yes, well . . . I was just about to explain to Miss Hobbes here, that my services might be required."

Veronica raised her eyebrows. "Oh, they will, will they?"

"I fear so. I'd ask that you forgive me, my dear, if I leave you here to enjoy the celebrations while I cut and run."

"No."

"No?"

"You'll do no such thing, Sir Maurice Newbury! I don't want you thinking this is how it's going to be from now on."

"But . . . ," Newbury mumbled. "You heard the man. I'm needed."

"I believe you'll find that Sir Charles's precise words were: '*we're* needed.' I'm coming, too."

"You are?"

"Quite so," said Bainbridge, with a broad grin. "Miss Hobbes is quite essential to our plan."

"Oh, right," said Newbury. "Very good, then." He held his arm out to Veronica, who accepted it with a gleeful smile. "Shall we?"

"Let's," she said, and together, they strode off in search of adventure.

ACKNOWLEDGEMENTS

An extra special thanks this time to my editors, Diana Pho and Molly McGhee, for their wonderful support during the writing of this novel. Thanks also to Tor Books and to Liz Gorinsky, for backing the series from the very start, way back when Newbury and Veronica first appeared in *The Affinity Bridge*.

Thanks are also due to my agent, Charlotte Robertson, and to Cav Scott–my brother from another mother.

As ever, my family have been tremendous in their support and encouragement.

The soundtrack for this one was provided by PJ Harvey, Laura Marling, Johnny Flynn, Nothing But Thieves, and the estimable Brad Hoyt, whose wonderful Newbury & Hobbes soundtracks have truly helped to bring the characters and their world to life.

ABOUT THE AUTHOR

George Mann is a *Sunday Times* bestselling novelist, comics writer, and screenwriter. He's the creator of the *Newbury & Hobbes*, *Wychwood* and *Tales of The Ghost* novel series, two of which are in development as television shows. He's written comics, novels and audio dramas for properties such as *Star Wars*, *Doctor Who*, *Sherlock Holmes*, *Judge Dredd*, *Teenage Mutant Ninja Turtles* and *Carnival Row*. He's currently lead writer on a genre television show and is the Creative Director and Joint-CEO of Strange Matter Media.

George lives near Grantham, UK, with his wife, children and two noisy dogs. He loves mythology and folklore, Kate Bush and chocolate. He is constantly surrounded by tottering piles of books.

For more fantastic fiction, author events,
exclusive excerpts, competitions, limited editions and more

VISIT OUR WEBSITE
titanbooks.com

LIKE US ON FACEBOOK
facebook.com/titanbooks

FOLLOW US ON TWITTER AND INSTAGRAM
@TitanBooks

EMAIL US
readerfeedback@titanemail.com